THE
THORN CROWN
MURDER

Volume 14: Zen and the Art of Investigation

ANTHONY WOLFF

authorHOUSE®

AuthorHouse™ LLC
1663 Liberty Drive
Bloomington, IN 47403
www.authorhouse.com
Phone: 1-800-839-8640

This is a work of fiction. All of the characters, names, incidents, organizations, and dialogue in this novel are either the products of the author's imagination or are used fictitiously.

Published by AuthorHouse 9/22/2014

ISBN: 978-1-4969-3977-7 (sc)
ISBN: 978-1-4969-3976-0 (e)

For Lise, who can finally get some sleep.

PREFACE

WHO ARE THESE DETECTIVES ANYWAY?

"The eye cannot see itself" an old Zen adage informs us. The Private I's in these case files count on the truth of that statement. People may be self-concerned, but they are rarely self-aware.

In courts of law, guilt or innocence often depends upon its presentation. Juries do not - indeed, they may not - investigate any evidence in order to test its veracity. No, they are obliged to evaluate only what they are shown. Private Investigators, on the other hand, are obliged to look beneath surfaces and to prove to their satisfaction - not the court's - whether or not what appears to be true is actually true. The Private I must have a penetrating eye.

Intuition is a spiritual gift and this, no doubt, is why *Wagner & Tilson, Private Investigators* does its work so well.

At first glance the little group of P.I.s who solve these often baffling cases seem different from what we (having become familiar with video Dicks) consider "sleuths." They have no oddball sidekicks. They are not alcoholics. They get along well with cops.

George Wagner is the only one who was trained for the job. He obtained a degree in criminology from Temple University in Philadelphia and did exemplary work as an investigator with the Philadelphia Police. These were his golden years. He skied; he danced; he played tennis; he had a Porsche, a Labrador retriever, and a small sailboat. He got married and had a wife, two toddlers, and a house. He was handsome and well built, and he had great hair.

And then one night, in 1999, he and his partner walked into an ambush. His partner was killed and George was shot in the left knee and in his right shoulder's brachial plexus. The pain resulting from his injuries and the twenty-two surgeries he endured throughout the year that followed, left him addicted to a nearly constant morphine drip. By the time he was admitted to a rehab center in Southern California for treatment of his morphine addiction and for physical therapy, he had lost everything previously mentioned except his house, his handsome face, and his great hair.

His wife, tired of visiting a semi-conscious man, divorced him and married a man who had more than enough money to make child support payments unnecessary and, since he was the jealous type, undesirable. They moved far away, and despite the calls George placed and the money and gifts he sent, they soon tended to regard him as non-existent. His wife did have an orchid collection which she boarded with a plant nursery, paying for the plants' care until he was able to accept them. He gave his brother his car, his tennis racquets, his skis, and his sailboat.

At the age of thirty-four he was officially disabled, his right arm and hand had begun to wither slightly from limited use, a frequent result of a severe injury to that nerve center. His knee, too, was troublesome. He could not hold it in a bent position for an extended period of time; and when the weather was bad or he had been standing for too long, he limped a little.

George gave considerable thought to the "disease" of romantic love and decided that he had acquired an immunity to it. He would never again be vulnerable to its delirium. He did not realize that the gods of love regard such pronouncements as hubris of the worst kind and, as such, never allow it to go unpunished. George learned this lesson while working on the case, *The Monja Blanca*. A sweet girl, half his age and nearly half his weight, would fell him, as he put it, "as young David slew the big dumb Goliath." He understood that while he had no future with her, his future would be filled with her for as long as he had a mind that could think. She had been the victim of the most vicious swindlers he had ever encountered. They had successfully fled the country, but not the range of George's determination to apprehend them. These were master criminals, four of them, and he secretly vowed that he would make them fall, one by one. This was a serious quest. There was nothing quixotic about George Roberts Wagner.

While he was in the hospital receiving treatment for those fateful gunshot wounds, he met Beryl Tilson.

Beryl, a widow whose son Jack was then eleven years old, was working her way through college as a nurse's aid when she tended George. She had met him previously when he delivered a lecture on the curious differences between aggravated assault and attempted murder, a not uninteresting topic. During the year she tended him, they became friendly enough for him to communicate with her during the year he was in rehab. When he returned to Philadelphia, she picked him up at the airport, drove him home - to a house he had not been inside for two years - and helped him to get settled into a routine with the house and the botanical spoils of his divorce.

After receiving her degree in the Liberal Arts, Beryl tried to find a job with hours that would permit her to be home when her son came home from school each day. Her quest was daunting. Not only was a degree in Liberal Arts regarded as a 'negative' when considering an applicant's qualifications, (the choice of study having demonstrated a lack of foresight for eventual entry into the commercial job market) but by stipulating that she needed to be home no later than 3:30 p.m. each day, she further discouraged personnel managers from putting out their company's welcome mat. The supply of available jobs was somewhat limited.

Beryl, a Zen Buddhist and karate practitioner, was still doing part-time work when George proposed that they open a private investigation agency. Originally he had thought she would function as a "girl Friday" office manager; but when he witnessed her abilities in the martial arts, which, at that time, far exceeded his, he agreed that she should function as a 50-50 partner in the agency, and he helped her through the licensing procedure. She quickly became an excellent marksman on the gun range.

As a Christmas gift he gave her a Beretta to use alternately with her Colt semi-automatic.

The Zen temple she attended was located on Germantown Avenue in a two storey, storefront row of small businesses. Wagner & Tilson, Private Investigators needed a home. Beryl noticed that a building in the same row was advertised for sale. She told George who liked it, bought it, and let Beryl and her son move into the second floor as their residence. Problem solved.

While George considered himself a man's man, Beryl did not see herself as a woman's woman. She had no female friends her own age. None. Acquaintances, yes. She enjoyed warm relationships with a few older women. But Beryl, it surprised her to realize, was a man's woman. She liked men, their freedom to move, to create, to discover, and that inexplicable wildness that came with their physical presence and strength. All of her senses found them agreeable; but she had no desire to domesticate one. Going to sleep with one was nice. But waking up with one of them in her bed? No. No. No. Dawn had an alchemical effect on her sensibilities. "Colors seen by candlelight do not look the same by day," said Elizabeth Barrett Browning, to which Beryl replied, "Amen."

She would find no occasion to alter her orisons until, in the course of solving a missing person's case that involved sexual slavery in a South American rainforest, a case called *Skyspirit*, she met the Surinamese Southern District's chief criminal investigator. Dawn became conducive to romance. But, as we all know, the odds are always against the success of long distance love affairs. To be stuck in one continent and love a man who is stuck in another holds as much promise for high romance as falling in love with Dorian Gray. In her professional life, she was tough but fair. In matters of lethality, she preferred *dim mak* points to bullets, the latter being awfully messy.

Perhaps the most unusual of the three detectives is Sensei Percy Wong. The reader may find it useful to know a bit more about his background.

Sensei, Beryl's karate master, left his dojo to go to Taiwan to become a fully ordained Zen Buddhist priest in the Ummon or Yun Men lineage in which he was given the Dharma name Shi Yao Feng. After studying advanced martial arts in both Taiwan and China, he returned to the U.S. to teach karate again and to open a small Zen Buddhist temple - the temple that was down the street from the office *Wagner & Tilson* would eventually open.

Sensei was quickly considered a great martial arts' master not because, as he explains, "I am good at karate, but because I am better at advertising it." He was of Chinese descent and had been ordained in China, and since China's Chan Buddhism and Gung Fu stand in polite rivalry to Japan's Zen Buddhism and Karate, it was most peculiar to find a priest in China's Yun Men lineage who followed the Japanese Zen liturgy and the martial arts discipline of Karate.

It was only natural that Sensei Percy Wong's Japanese associates proclaimed that his preferences were based on merit, and in fairness to them, he did not care to disabuse them of this notion. In truth, it was Sensei's childhood rebellion against his tyrannical faux-Confucian father that caused him to gravitate to the Japanese forms. Though both of his parents had emigrated from China, his father decried western civilization even as he grew rich exploiting its freedoms and commercial opportunities. With draconian finesse he imposed upon his family the cultural values of the country from which he had fled for his life. He seriously believed that while the rest of the world's population might have come out of Africa, Chinese men came out of heaven. He did not know or care where Chinese women originated so long as they kept their proper place as slaves.

His mother, however, marveled at American diversity and refused to speak Chinese to her children, believing, as she did, in the old fashioned idea that it is wise to speak the language of the country in which one claims citizenship.

At every turn the dear lady outsmarted her obsessively sinophilic husband. Forced to serve rice at every meal along with other mysterious creatures obtained in Cantonese Chinatown, she purchased two Shar Peis that, being from Macau, were given free rein of the dining room. These dogs, despite their pre-Qin dynasty lineage, lacked a discerning palate and proved to be gluttons for bowls of fluffy white stuff. When her husband retreated to his rooms, she served omelettes and Cheerios, milk instead of tea, and at dinner, when he was not there at all, spaghetti instead of chow mein. The family home was crammed with gaudy enameled furniture and torturously carved teak; but on top of the lion-head-ball-claw-legged coffee table, she always placed a book which illustrated the elegant simplicity of such furniture designers as Marcel Breuer; Eileen Gray; Charles Eames; and American Shakers. Sensei adored her; and loved to hear her relate how, when his father ordered her to give their firstborn son a Chinese name; she secretly asked the clerk to record indelibly the name "Percy" which she mistakenly thought was a very American name. To Sensei, if she had named him Abraham Lincoln Wong, she could not have given him a more Yankee handle.

Preferring the cuisines of Italy and Mexico, Sensei avoided Chinese food and prided himself on not knowing a word of Chinese. He balanced this ignorance by an inability to understand Japanese and, because of its inaccessibility, he did not eat Japanese food.

The Man of Zen who practices Karate obviously is the adventurous type; and Sensei, staying true to type, enjoyed participating in Beryl's and George's investigations. It required little time for him to become a one-third partner of the team. He called himself, "the ampersand in *Wagner & Tilson.*"

Sensei Wong may have been better at advertising karate than at performing it, but this merely says that he was a superb huckster for the discipline. In college he had studied civil engineering; but he also was on the fencing team and he regularly practiced gymnastics. He had learned yoga and ancient forms of meditation from his mother. He attained Zen's vaunted transcendental states; which he could access 'on the mat.' It was not surprising that when he began to learn karate he was already half-accomplished. After he won a few minor championships he attracted the attention of several martial arts publications that found his "unprecedented" switchings newsworthy. They imparted to him a "great master" cachet, and perpetuated it to the delight of dojo owners and martial arts shopkeepers. He did win many championships and, through unpaid endorsements and political propaganda, inspired the sale of Japanese weapons, including nunchaku and shuriken which he did not actually use.

Although his Order was strongly given to celibacy, enough wiggle room remained for the priest who found it expedient to marry or dally. Yet, having reached his mid-forties unattached, he regarded it as 'unlikely' that he would ever be romantically welded to a female, and as 'impossible' that he would be bonded to a citizen and custom's agent of the People's Republic of China - whose Gung Fu abilities challenged him and who would strike terror in his heart especially when she wore Manolo Blahnik red spike heels. Such combat, he insisted, was patently unfair, but he prayed that Providence would not level the playing field. He met his femme fatale while working on *A Case of Virga*.

Later in their association Sensei would take under his spiritual wing a young Thai monk who had a degree in computer science and a flair for acting. Akara Chatree, to whom Sensei's master in Taiwan would give the name Shi Yao Xin, loved Shakespeare; but his father - who came from one of Thailand's many noble families - regarded his son's desire to become an actor as we would regard our son's desire to become a hit man. Akara's brothers were all businessmen and professionals; and as the old patriarch lay dying, he exacted a promise from his tall 'matinee-idol' son that he would never tread upon the flooring of a stage. The old man had asked for nothing else, and since he bequeathed a rather large sum of money to his young son, Akara had to content himself with critiquing the performances of actors who were less filially constrained than he. As far as romance is concerned, he had not thought too much about it until he worked on *A Case of Industrial Espionage*. That case took him to Bermuda, and what can a young hero do when he is captivated by a pretty girl who can recite Portia's lines with crystalline insight while lying beside him on a white beach near a blue ocean?

But his story will keep...

Who is Akara Chatree (Shi Qian Fa)?

It could be argued, and frequently was, that Akara Chatree's solitary personality had been occasioned by his having inherited a considerable amount of money, so much so that less affluent persons - which included all of his associates at the time that he was financially blessed - pestered him so relentlessly to lend them money or to invest in their business ventures, that for the sake of his sanity he was driven to eschew all "friendships." But this would not be true.

It was also suspected that when he realized that the degree of difference between his intelligence and the common man's was many times greater than the difference between the common man's and the ape's, he was forced into a peculiar taxonomic niche, one in which he could "interbreed" socially and sexually with only those individuals who were similarly endowed. This was a ludicrous surmise.

And then it was supposed that he had "taken up the cloth" because he had spiritual ambitions which only the hermit's life could accommodate. Yet, he chose to be a priest rather than a monk, a choice which belied a preference for isolation.

Akara Chatree had simply been purged of the human tendency to assign values to groups of people. He was convinced that beyond saying some five or six billion individuals occupied the earth, no further qualitative descriptions of the psychological sort could be applied. He therefore limited his interactions to specific persons, persons that he could trust and appreciate for their integrity and kindness. He avoided parties, assemblies, and gatherings of any kind that would subject him to the vagaries of strangers.

Bold assertions such as these are not made in the glacial tempo of evolution. They are the stuff of a revolutionary *coup*. All of a man's channels of opinion must be diverted and directed to engage the turbines of a new uber-view generator, a vantage point that encompasses all universals.

Akara Chatree's revolution occurred when he was fourteen years old. As a child he had casually accepted those class distinctions which served to maintain his family's social position. He was told that the members of his family were judicious and responsible because of their inherent sense of *Noblesse Oblige*. Money, he was assured, had nothing to do with it. Attending private schools in England did not dull the blade of class division.

And then when he was fourteen his "dominion" class made a trip to India to attend a *puja* in Bihar and to tour the state. Akara, the only child of his father's second marriage, expected to meet with four of his half-brothers, sons of his father's first and third marriages. All of Akara's relatives, with the exception of his mother, lived in Thailand, and Bihar was not considered a distant place.

Shortly after the class arrived in India, all three chaperones and half of the student group were stricken with an intestinal disturbance, leaving the hardy half of the young tourists, which included Akara and a school friend, without much in the way of supervision. His half-brothers, however, were chaperoned by a Draconian Theravadin Buddhist uncle.

Told that several pornographic films were going to be shown in a nearby town, Akara, his brothers and his school friend arranged to meet outside the theater. More than familial enjoyment was involved in the reunion. Akara's friend had borrowed money from him to pay a gambling debt which he had not taken seriously until he was beaten senseless by a debt collector. He had not wanted his parents to know the truth of his loss, and so he begged Akara not only to lend him the repayment money but to keep secret its purpose. Akara obliged and asked his older half-brothers if they would lend him five-thousand pounds so that he could pay a personal debt. Akara's friend had promised to give him a substantial part of the repayment when they met at the theater.

As they sneaked away to the town, a late and heavy rain was falling; and just as they assembled, a levee broke and the boys were separated in the ensuing muddy flood. Akara was carried by the current until finally he found himself buried waist-deep in mud from which he could not extricate himself. His school friend heard and acknowledged his cries for help and told his brothers where he was, and then he left. None of them came to help Akara or to direct any of the official rescue personnel to his location.

His brothers had run from the area because they did not want their uncle to learn where they had been and why they had been there. His friend, he realized, had seen a financial opportunity. With Akara dead - as he was sure he would be since so many others in the path of the flood had already perished - he would be relieved of having to repay the debt.

All night, Akara shivered and whimpered, distraught by his abandonment. Towards dawn, a man who cleaned out cesspools for a living began to use his tools to dig a circle around him. The man refused to look in Akara's face or even to speak to him. He simply dug until enough of the thick mud was removed. Then he pulled the exhausted boy out of the morass, put him on a kind of pontoon raft, and poled his way to firm land. He refused to accept money for his efforts, and only after Akara repeatedly asked him his name, did he finally mumble what sounded like "Kyamay Apkimadah."

As he lay Akara on the doorstep of a medical facility, a villager came and hit the man with a broom handle and told Akara to bathe carefully with Ganga River water since his body had made contact with an Untouchable.

It was on that night that Akara Chatree gained his world-view. He did not return to England but instead went directly to Sao Paulo where his mother met him at the airport and took him home to the building that housed her Zen Buddhist Center.

In a room that measured two meters by three meters, he had a bed, a closet, a desk, a lamp, and courtesy of the last man who occupied the room, six books: an English dictionary; the complete works of William Shakespeare; three mathematics books that took him through intermediate and advanced Calculus; and a first year University text in Physics. The bathroom was at the end of the hall. The kitchen was downstairs. Akara went nowhere else for nearly two years — and two hundred books later. When he did emerge from the Center, it was to matriculate at the University. He only agreed to go there because he wanted to master computer science and needed access to the equipment. (Shakespeare he knew and understood far better than any and all members of the English Department.) He had no friends or enemies and he neither carried a cellphone nor accepted visitors at his Zen Center residence. He was pleasant and cooperative, but he said nothing that did not need to be said.

He had one quirk. On the flyleaf of every book he bought from the date beginning with the mudslide, he wrote the name (as he remembered it) of the man who had helped him. Kyamay Apkimadah

Akara was twenty-three years old and working on his PhD in Computer Science before he learned from a Sanskrit professor that no doubt the words that had been spoken to him were not anyone's name, but simple Hindi for "I help you."

Kyā maiṁ āpakī madada. क् या मैं आपकी मदद.

That night, in 2007, Akara Chatree cried for several hours and then asked his mother to prepare him to take Holy Orders. He became the Zen Buddhist priest, Shi Qian Fa of the Yun Men (Ummon) lineage.

In China he mentioned to his master that he did not want to join the clerical staff of a large business-like temple. He was therefore directed to the little Zen temple on Germantown Avenue, in Philadelphia, and in 2012 he became an assistant to his master's old friend, Sensei Percy Wong (Shi Yao Feng). He moved into the second floor of the temple along with his sixteen server cluster of computer "stuff." He also rented a garage nearby so that he could park his new bright red Corvette inside it.

Eventually, he obtained his private investigator's license. The first case he worked on was The Case of the Insurance Fraud Sacrifices; The Thorn Crown Murder is the second case.

FRIDAY, MAY 10, 2013

The delivery truck of a high-end Philadelphia Main Line florist pulled up to the curb in front of the offices of Wagner & Tilson Private Investigators. Beryl Tilson sat at her desk and looked out of the storefront window, watching as the liveried driver hopped out, jogged to the back doors, opened them and extracted a meter-high "M" of pink carnations and a wooden stand to set the "M" on.

Beryl, knowing what was coming and why it was coming, began to laugh. She had called Groff Eckersley, one of the investigation agency's rich young clients, to remind him to send his grandmother flowers for Mother's Day; and he had called her son, Jack, to remind him to send *her* flowers. Jack, being short of funds as usual, would have said, "Uh, oh," and Groff would have said, "No problem. As long as I'm ordering for my grandmother, I'll order some for your mom in your name."

The delivery man brought the "M" into the office and set it up. He returned to the truck to pick up an "O," which he brought into the office and set it on its own stand. About four hundred carnations were now arranged to read "MO."

Beryl expected him to return to the truck for the final "M." Instead, he checked his delivery slip, moved the "O" to the other side of the "M" and handed her the gift card that read, *Namaste! Jack.*

It was silly. It was stupid. It was a complete waste of money; and naturally she was delighted by the gesture.

She took out her iPhone and photographed the OM greeting.

Francis "Frank" Goodrich, vice-president of his father-in-law's medical equipment company, stood at the bar of his hotel's supper-club and sipped his second scotch mist as he waited to be joined by a colleague who was already twenty minutes late. He noticed the pretty blonde sitting at the end of the bar who kept looking at her watch. She had a red lanyard and plastic I.D. holder around her neck which indicated that she, too, was an attendee of the convention taking place at a nearby arena. He had a dinner reservation for two and if his colleague didn't show up - and if her date didn't show up, either - he'd ask her to join him. After all, she clearly wasn't a hooker and "common business interests" would give him a valid reason for being in a strange woman's company.

His phone rang. His dinner partner was discussing business with a client and couldn't break away. Frank expressed regret and immediately approached the pretty blonde. "I couldn't help but notice that you keep looking at your watch," he said. "I've been stood-up by a colleague of mine. If you've been doomed to the same fate, maybe you'd like to have dinner with me. I've got two hard-to-get reservations. No one should ever decline an opportunity to eat at this place. The food is great."

She smiled. "So's the music. I can't comment on the food since I've never eaten here before; but I do like that band. They're really good."

"Then after dinner maybe we can do a little dancing. I'm Frank Goodrich." He extended his hand.

She put her hand in his and murmured, "Waverly Bryant." She shrugged her shoulders and put her hand on her purse. "Well, what can I say? I can't turn down such a sweet invitation to dine and dance."

He stood at the bar beside her and ordered another drink while they waited for the "table ready" pager to vibrate in his breast pocket. Keeping his priorities straight, he asked what business she was in. She answered, "No business... just research being done at the University of Wyoming. I work for a robotics engineer who, by rights, should have been here. You might say I'm carrying the flag in his absence. I'm also taking pictures and collecting brochures of the latest developments of medical equipment that interest him and the rest of the team. But please, after giving me your company's name, rank, and serial number, can we not talk about work." She pulled the lanyard over her head and put it in her purse.

He was pleased not to discuss business, and naturally, he gave her his business card and spoke about nothing else. "Let me give you some advice," he said in a joking manner. "Never work for your in-laws. It always leads to trouble." She promised to follow his advice and then asked him for details which he was primed to give. "My wife has two younger brothers who not only don't know anything about *this* business, they don't know anything about business, period. This qualifies them to be named vice-presidents - so now we have three vice-presidents. I'm senior vice-president, but Daddy wants one of them to succeed him as president."

"Ouch," Waverly said. "That must make for some interesting dinner-table conversation at your house."

"Yeah, ouch. I'm glad I don't have to draw you a map. Every day my mother-in-law calls my wife just to agitate the marital waters, stirring things up at home. Every day I'm reminded that her parents gave me my first job and that I work 'at their pleasure' - which means I have no contract." He sucked the scotch from the shaved ice as though it were a snow cone and signaled the bartender for a replacement. "But enough about my problems. What about yours? What happened to your date?"

"She wasn't my date. She was a nice gal who flew in with me from Cheyenne. She was afraid she wouldn't be invited to join some people for dinner and I told her that if it began to look that way, she should just say, 'Nice talking to you all, but I have a dinner appointment with the fabulous Waverly Bryant who is sitting at the bar waiting.'"

He nodded and grinned. "That was a really nice thing you did. It was considerate. I wish I knew more people like you... kind people. A couple of months ago some really nice people offered me a great job in Cleveland, but Gwen, my wife, refused to leave the Chicago area. Until her brothers came of age, my sixty hours of work a week were fine. Now nothing I do is good enough. It's one argument after the other. I'm beginning to read that '*Mene, Mene, Tekel*' on the wall."

"The end of your job or the end of your marriage?"

"Both."

"Don't fear the end of something. Welcome the freedom that allows you to begin a new life. I think Gwen would find you difficult to replace. You're handsome, smart, and very well put together, I might add. You can always get another job; and, assuming you're not head-over-heels in love with her - which I somehow suspect you are - you can always get another wife. What about her? Is there another man in her life?"

He talked about "Doug" the man his mother-in-law regarded as the man Gwen should have married. "But Dougie married somebody else so he was a dead letter until last year when Dougie's wife ran off with the pool boy and Dougie needed everyone's support to get him through 'the tragedy.' She left him with two of the brattiest kids you'll ever meet. Between him and his demon spawn my Sundays have been destroyed. We each have a boy and a girl. Teenagers in prep school. My kids used to come home on weekends. Before the games came on on Sundays, my boy and I would go to the park for a few hours and play ball. We'd come back with pizzas to watch TV. Even my daughter was a sports fan. Sundays made my week. No more. Dougie and his rotten kids are there. Yellin'. Knocking shit over. Constantly askin' stupid questions. They don't understand baseball. They don't understand football. Soccer... that's what they play. Doug phoned me, getting me out of the shower one Sunday before a *Bears* game, just to ask, 'What time is the *opening punt?*'

"My kids now stay at school on the weekends. I love my family but my wife has begun to treat me like I'm a stranger which is what I feel like trying to watch the *Cubs* with her and Dougie and the kids from Hell." He sighed. "And I can't complain. If my wife divorces me, I lose everything... job, kids, *her.* Even my car is in the company's name." The pager vibrated. A waiter led them to a table.

Frank Goodrich had by no means exhausted his repertoire of complaints; but Waverly had the magic touch that closed the lid of his container of woes. "I don't want to get religious on you," she confided, "but here is something that will work. Every time a thought about any of them rises into your mind, close your eyes and say, 'Lord Jesus Christ, have mercy on me.' You're not Jewish are you?"

Frank laughed. "I think you're supposed to ask that first. But no, I'm not." The laugh was cleansing. He took a deep breath. Suddenly she became a nostrum for whatever it was that ailed him. "Let's talk about you," he said as they ate their dinner. "You're not wearing any rings. Am I correct in assuming that you're not married?"

She replied that she was, in fact, married; but she didn't *feel* married. "My husband has his old friends, his school friends, his work friends, and his family. And I don't belong to any of those groups. So I keep my rings in my purse."

"In case you run into somebody?" he asked, laughing.

"You got it!" she concurred.

"You're adorable. Come on, let's dance."

"My bag is too big to carry onto the dance floor and I don't want to leave my rings unattended."

"So, put them on!"

She shrugged and opened her purse and unzipped a compartment. Frank Goodrich's eyes widened at the sight of her diamond rings - a marquise cut solitaire that was at least five carats and a V-cut wedding band, shaped to accommodate the marquise cut, that had two half-carat stones on either side of the solitaire. He told her that her rings were beautiful and led her onto the dance floor.

They laughed because they didn't know the latest steps. He clowned by doing the "mashed potato" and the "monkey" and she tried to follow. And then a slow dance played and by then Frank knew Waverly enough to hold her close to him. "Is a divorce in your future?" he whispered, ashamed for a moment that so much of their conversation had been about him and his problems.

"Yes, and I'm in pretty much the same boat as you. My in-laws let us live in a house they own. I don't make much as a secretary and I have no children. A divorce would put me right back where I was when we got married... except for my engagement and wedding rings. They're the only valuable thing I own. I'm glad I didn't meet you in Cheyenne. I wouldn't want it to get back to my husband that I was seen enjoying myself... really enjoying myself... with another man. I'd get the papers in the mail."

"So? Don't fear the end. The end of something is the beginning of something else."

"Sure," she laughed, and then soberly added, "but if I'm caught with another man, I'd lose my job, too. My husband's a professor at the university and there's a strict morals clause in my work contract. I'd lose my husband, my job, my home - not to mention my two dogs and three cats - and because so much of our lives are intertwined with university people, I wouldn't have a shoulder to cry on, either."

He pulled her closer to him and as they swayed to the music, he softly said, "Let's go someplace where we can be together."

"Oh, you *are* irresistible. I don't know... it's probably not the right thing for us to do."

"You'll have to define 'right.' I don't know what it is, anymore. Where are you staying?"

"Room 1217. Upstairs. There's a lot of convention traffic on the floor."

"Let's play it safe and leave this place. I know a place on Lakeshore Drive."

"It's a big convention. They'll probably have the 'no vacancy' sign up."

"My company maintains a cottage suite in one of them. I happen to know that as of yesterday, it's been vacant."

They returned to the table. "Are you sure we won't be seen?" she asked as she carefully removed her rings and put them back into her purse.

"Positive."

They left the hotel's supper club, got into Frank's company Mercedes and drove to a small and rustic enclave of suites - more condo than motel trade. "This is lovely," she said as he parked.

He unlocked the door and they entered. He did not turn on any lights but in the faint glow of the parking area's lighting, he put his arms around her and kissed her. He closed the window's drapes and tossed his jacket on a chair. She kicked off her shoes. He pulled his tie free of its knot. She pulled down her zipper.

In another minute they were naked in bed and he was kissing her breasts and telling her how good she smelled. And then a knock was heard. Someone was at the door.

"Is it some kind of room service?" she asked, frightened.

"Probably the management. I didn't check-in at the desk." He got up and went to the door, opening it only far enough to be able to stick his head around its edge. Before he had a chance to ask, "What is it?" the door was shoved back hard against him, sending him sprawling onto the floor. An intruder, wearing a business suit, dark wig, mouse mask, and surgical gloves, entered the room. A camera hung on a strap around his neck. Silhouetted against the outdoor lights, he pointed a gun at Frank, flicked on the lights, and shut the door behind him.

Waverly yelped, "Frank!"

Frank scooted backwards until his back was against the bed. "What the fuck do you want? If it's money, I've only got a few hundred on me. Take it. It's yours!" He reached up and took his wallet from the bedside table. "You want my watch? It's a Rolex."

"Both of you! Put your wallets and your phones at the end of the bed," the intruder said with a slight French accent, "and then get back into bed." They both obeyed the order. The intruder emptied Frank's wallet, put the cash into his pocket, and read Frank's name and address from his driver's license into a digital voice recorder in his breast pocket. He tossed the wallet onto the floor and picked up the iPhone, pressed "Home," swiped the locking bar to the right, touched the Settings' icon, accessed the Phone tab, and read Frank's phone number into his recorder.

Frank, momentarily fascinated to see the stranger do something to his phone that he did not know how to do, himself, sat dumbly on the bed watching until Waverly whined, "Frank! What's wrong with you?" He turned then to comfort her.

"Rolexes are registered," the stranger said. "Do you take me for an imbecile?" He recorded Waverly's name and address and then picked up her phone and recorded its number. "Where's her purse?" he asked Frank.

"My purse?" Waverly gasped. "Oh, my God! Is this some kind of set up! Is this why you didn't want to come to my room? You tricked me, you bastard!" she shouted at Frank.

As Frank tried to calm and quiet her, the intruder began to take pictures of them. As she struggled, her legs were splayed obscenely. She finally pushed him away and cried, "You bastards! You set me up!"

"Toss me the purse!" the intruder demanded.

Waverly reached for her purse on the bedside table and twisted open the clasp as she grabbed it. As she brought it forward she inserted her right hand into it and drew out a stun gun that crackled as she pushed it into Frank's abdomen. "Don't touch me again, you crook!" she cried, as he folded up in pain. "You set me up!" She zapped him again and then she leapt up and tried to stun the intruder, but he backhanded her and sent her thudding onto the bed.

"Stupid bitch," he said. "Toss the stun gun on the floor and put your purse on the edge of the bed, slowly." While continuing to point his gun at them, he began to screw a silencer onto its barrel. "I see you like to fight. Do as I say or I'll shoot you both."

Whimpering, Waverly tossed her weapon onto the floor and moved her purse to the corner of the bed. She did not speak as he opened it with one hand and turned it upside down. A few cosmetic items, keys, and the lanyard fell onto the bed. He tossed the purse back onto the bed. "You," he said to Waverly, "get on top of him and act like you're humping him - and look like you mean it!" He criticized Frank's performance. "Get into character! Smile as though you're enjoying it!" Frank faked a lascivious smile as the intruder moved around to get better shots of the action. He ordered them to assume various sexual positions and photographed them all. Then he said, "Everyone has to pay the piper. By next Friday, Francis better be prepared to pay $30,000 or the folks at home will see a photographic treat. And little *Gigi*? Let's make it $20K. You'll both be called and given further instructions. And all $50K will have to be paid. No partial payments." He turned and left.

Niles Portmann and five other men marched out of Lovelock Prison into freedom and a brilliant morning sun. Three of the men had family waiting for them and their reunions were joyous as they departed in private cars. Two of the men had been in prison so long that they had outlived everyone who could possibly have cared to meet them. They did not look around as they talked together and climbed into the prison bus. Niles' eyes scanned the area, but nobody was waiting for him. He, too, boarded the bus.

Niles had been imprisoned for only two and a half years of a six-year sentence. Several months earlier, he had volunteered to be tested as a possible tissue match for an Idaho legislator's son who had leukemia. He was an excellent match and willingly underwent painful surgery to donate bone marrow to the boy. He would have gotten early release for good behavior anyway, but with his humanitarian efforts, there was no parole board discussion. The boy's health immediately improved and the Governor "suggested" that Niles be released as soon as possible, a date that was later determined to be the tenth of May. Niles wrote to his wife Aleta stating his hope that she would drive up from Tonopah, Nevada to pick him up. They could spend a little vacation together at Lake Tahoe if she wanted. But she did not answer and she was not outside waiting for him.

He and the two other men rode the small bus into the town of Lovelock where they could get another bus that would take them to Reno. He hoped that Aleta had assumed that he intended that she should meet him in the town of Lovelock; and when he exited the bus, he looked around the terminal and even waited a few minutes in case she had gone into the ladies room. She was not there. Perhaps, he thought, she had gotten a late start and could make it only as far as Reno. He doubted that she would be there, but he knew that he would look for her anyway.

All the way to Reno the two men sat behind him and though, in the yard, they had been hard-assed cons, they chattered and squealed like excited children every time they noticed a new building or development where once only sagebrush existed. They had served out their time and were free to talk or to socialize with anyone. No conditions of parole applied and they reveled in their ability to communicate at will. They chattered incessantly, and when they approached Reno, one shouted, "The biggest little city in the West!" The other replied with an ear-damaging, "Yee Haw!"

Niles was not all that glad to see Reno. Aleta wasn't there, either. With no car ride, he'd have to take another bus down to Tonopah. And then what? His house was nearly ten miles outside of town. He didn't have enough cash on him for cab fare. He'd have to beg someone to give him a ride home. No. He wouldn't do that. He had good shoes on. They were prison shoes, but they fit him well. The people in Tonopah believed lies about him and found him guilty of a crime he had not committed. He wouldn't beg them for anything. He'd walk home. But then, maybe she would be at the bus terminal in Tonopah, waiting in their blue Buick to take him home.

In the two and a half years he was away, she had never come to the prison to visit him. Occasionally, she wrote to him in her "high school English" style; but the letters were requests for information about taxes or the management of their property. She had no cellphone. "Reception is so bad," she complained. They had satellite reception for their internet and TV. But she didn't know how to type and hated to use the laptop. He wouldn't have been able to exchange email with her, anyway, so what was the difference?

It was early in the afternoon when he arrived in Tonopah. Aleta was not there. A mining engineer he knew was putting gas in his pickup truck at a station near the terminal. "Yo, Niles! Is that you?" he called.

"Dave!" Niles answered, walking to the gas pump and happy to see one of the few people who believed in his innocence. "I just got out of the joint," he said, "and I could use a ride home. Any chance of ropin' you in?"

"Sure," Dave said, "hop in. Glad to see you back."

Dave continued to fill the tank. "I don't suppose it matters now, but that punk got drunk one night and told my brother that he really did hit you first. But he tells everybody else that you're the bully who got what he deserved. We heard you showed a lot of class with that kid from Idaho. It must have been tough servin' time for something you didn't do."

"Yeah," Niles agreed. "But you have to be philosophical about it. And if you protest your innocence, you join a chorus. I kept to myself and," he grinned, "caught up on my readin'." He looked back at the terminal. "You seen Aleta around? I was hoping she'd come to get me. It was short notice. I wrote to her a couple weeks ago and gave her the specifics."

"She's been away a lot... she got into religion. A real Evangelical. She passes through town, but aside from some shopping, she rarely comes in for anything. Spends a lot of time with her folks in Utah... or so my wife tells me." He got his receipt and as he opened the driver's side door, he said, "Maybe she didn't know you were coming home. She might not have picked up the mail at the post office. I'll wait here if you wanna go over to the post office and check."

Niles walked across the street and entered the post office. The clerk recognized him and went directly to Niles' bin. "Hey, Buddy... we're gonna start charging you a storage fee." He put a rubber band around a six-inch high stack of mail. Niles thanked him profusely. He had seen his letter's envelope in the stack.

He returned to Dave's truck, smiling broadly. "You were right. She didn't get my letter."

They drove to Niles' house in silence. When Dave parked at the gate, Niles invited him to come in; but Dave declined, saying that he had a few errands to run.

He walked to the garage and saw that the Buick wasn't there; but his old pickup truck was still parked where he left it and, he wad surprised to see, the registration tags were current. He went to the house and unlocked the front door. At first glance, nothing seemed to have changed. "Aleta?" he called, not expecting her to answer. "Aleta?"

The Portmann house had been constructed in stages, the first of which was an office and dwelling for Niles and his brother Trevor when they formed the Nitrev Company that developed and patented a silver mining claim on the site. Nitrev had also obtained a permit to appropriate the waters of the state which gave them exclusive use to a spring that flowed beside the mine site. They constructed a shoe-box building to use as a dwelling and office; and, as the operation thrived, they built an identical dwelling to house the miners. Water had enabled them to make concrete for the foundations and mortar for holding in place the stones that formed the walls. Since these two shoe-box shaped buildings paralleled each other at a distance of forty feet, Niles hoped that someday they could be joined to form one large building, with the two original structures forming the north and south wings.

When the original mineral resources were exhausted, the miners moved on, and Trevor married and moved to Texas; but the Nitrev Company was still a viable enterprise, and Niles had stayed on to exploit tungsten deposits that he had discovered. Eventually this mineral resource was exhausted, too, but since there were many tall pines available for use in constructing a more comprehensive building, Niles began the process of adding a second story to the wings and constructing the large two-storey high central room with its huge floor to ceiling fireplace and flue that now dominated the entrance room.

The house was finished when Niles was thirty-four.

At thirty-five Niles met and married Aleta Thurman of St. George, Utah. They intended that the building would house a large and extended family, but during the first five years of their marriage, Aleta had a series of miscarriages and they both accepted the fact that there would be no children in the home. Aleta did not realize that her grandparent's ranch, where she had spent all of her summers, was directly in the path of the nuclear test site's radioactive fallout. Eventually, one of her sisters died of leukemia. Her remaining sister and two brothers were to be as childless as she. Instead of being the residence of a family unit, the Portmann house developed a kind of split personality: one side was Niles' and the other was Aleta's.

Aleta also did not realize that the Portmann house was not included in the marital assets. It belonged to the Nitrev Company. Other properties that had been acquired during their marriage were, in fact, owned jointly by Niles and Aleta; but the house was separate and apart from their communal property.

Niles looked around and got an uneasy feeling. Something felt wrong. He closed the door behind him and tried to detect what it was.

He walked to the fireplace and saw ashes piled under and behind the grate. That was odd. Aleta always liked him to keep the fireplace free of old ashes that could blow into the room when the wind came down the chimney.

The large grizzly bear rug that was spread before the hearth had been moved closer to the center of the room.

The floors were natural slate and normally were waxed to a showroom luster, but now many feet seemed to have scratched the surface.

The leather furniture had backrest bibs and seat coverlets of heavy Indian cotton weave to prevent the discomfort of sticking to the leather. Some of the backrest bibs were now lying jumbled at the back of the seat cushions, a carelessness that Aleta never would have tolerated.

A half-dozen high quality native rugs of different Indian nations were on the walls, and beneath each stood a rustic styled chest or table on which were placed ceramic bowls from various tribes, brassware, fossils on stands, porcelain plates on stands, geodes of extraordinary beauty, and vases which, Niles now noticed, were filled with wilted and sere flowers and some residual muck at their bottoms. He had seen roses and other flowers blooming in the garden outside. Aleta must not have been home at all in the length of time it took for the flowers to desiccate and the water to evaporate.

Niles did not like to make decorative objects out of old articles that had once been used. There were no pedestals for old water buckets or antique Coleman lanterns and nowhere on the property were there any wagon wheels, spurs, or bridles to suggest that maybe horses were once stabled in the vestibule. "Resurrected trash," he called such things. He did not find romance in antiques of any kind. It was all too sentimental, the nonsensical admiration of the kind of people who would have regarded such objects with contempt if they had been forced to use them for their intended purpose. Niles owned many old lamps and candlesticks; but he used them every day. He noticed that the wicks in the oil lamps badly needed to be trimmed.

He opened a liquor cabinet and found that all of his single-malt bottles of scotch were gone. "And I see that Jim Beam and Jack Daniels are also missing," he said aloud. Aleta did not drink. Surprised, he added, "She used this room to entertain." He asked himself, "Who was here?" He checked his crystal glasses that had all been monogrammed with his initials... a wedding gift from his brother. They were all present and accounted for as were a couple of insulated ice buckets.

Wanting his house to be energy efficient, he had solar, wind, and, for times when these sources were not enough, a large back-up gasoline generator. Since the house faced west, it received afternoon sun all year long, an advantageous orientation since cold, being a function of altitude, kept his house chilled at its mile high elevation. Aleta could cook in four places... over the big fireplace's kitchen side, in a wood stove, on a Coleman stove, or outside with a charcoal grill.

On both sides of the large central room were stairways that led up to become a hallway for rooms on either side of the house. The hallway continued on behind the fireplace's floor-to-ceiling stone flue to form an unbroken U of connection. He decided to finish inspecting the downstairs. On his left was "his" side of the house.

The first room contained a large Steinway piano with its lid up. Still on the music rack where he had left it was Rachmaninoff's *Concerto #2 in C minor*. Niles had studied the piano early in life and at one point had intended to become a musician; but then his interests gravitated to geology and he earned his degree playing the piano in a whorehouse; accompanying singers for recitals and weddings; and playing with other musicians for an occasional concert. It was still light enough for him to see his pencil notations in the slightly worn paper margins of the score. A lamp on top of the piano was cleverly structured to conceal a four volt 10 amp sealed battery. He tried to turn the lamp on. No light came. The battery was dead.

The walls of the second room had built-in shelves filled with books that had actually been read - but by him, not Aleta. Two reclining chairs flanked a table in front of a bay window.

He sighed and went to the shelves to check the titles. "*The Alexandria Quartet*," he said aloud. "Lawrence Durrell. I ought to read that again. It was so long ago. All the classics are still here. Jane Austin. Shakespeare. Faulkner. Emily Dickinson. James Joyce. Charles Dickens. Dostoyevsky. D. T. Suzuki. *The Hagakure*! Jung. *Pedro Paramo*! I ought to re-read that, too."

The fireplace in the second room was filled with ashes that needed removing. Wind coming down the chimney had blown ashes onto the hearth. He recalled that he had neglected to clean it out during those dreary days of his trial. He had gotten into a barroom brawl. The fight had been about horses. It was in 2009, on a Wednesday evening. He was drinking alone, standing at the bar, when Joe Gregory, a young relative of one of the sheriff's deputies, came in and started bragging about the young horses he had run to death "dive bombing" them in a crop duster.

Niles always felt a special thrill watching the herds of mustangs run free in the mountains, and the Bureau of Land Management, using helicopters, was rounding them up, stampeding the horses so that the fillies and colts, unable to keep up, stumbled to their deaths. Joe Gregory's remarks antagonized Niles and he accused Joe of lobbying to lift the ban against slaughtering horses for the European market for horse meat. This was in fact true, and in 2011, while Niles was in prison, the ban was lifted, and people like Joe did make money selling horse meat. But in 2009, the charge embarrassed Joe; and the younger man, who had a "hair-trigger" temper, suddenly sucker punched Niles and sent him staggering back against the bar. Niles quickly regained his balance, took a step towards Joe who tried to defend himself by grabbing a beer bottle, intending to hit Niles with it. Niles pulled it up out of his hand, but in a split second that was caught by someone's camera phone, it appeared that Niles was wielding the bottle as a weapon to use against Joe. A witness at first gave a correct account of the sequence, but later was persuaded to change his story and Niles was tried and convicted of assault and battery. The bottle was considered a lethal weapon. He had been sentenced to six years in prison. When he added together all that the incident had cost him - the attorney's fees; the fees for filing an appeal; the civil suit brought against him for injuries incurred (Niles had broken Joe's jaw); for punitive damages; and the mismanagement of his business interests that occurred while he was gone - it had nearly bankrupted him. What was worse than the financial destruction was the torment of being convicted by his peers, and framed by an ignorant, useless wastrel like Joe Gregory. He had returned home, he knew, like a piece of meat that had marinated in battery acid for a couple of years. The one thing that could have cancelled out all the torment was Aleta's love. It rankled him to recall how sweetly she had written to tell him that she had transferred ownership of his dogs to her brother. He could not eat for two days after he received that letter.

Certain that he would be away for six years, she had sold off his mining equipment: his surveying instruments; his tunnel-measuring devices; laser distance meters; compasses and altimeters; GPS indicators; and his satellite phones. She even sold a portable generator and jack hammer. She wrote to say that she needed the money for living expenses and to give to the poor.

He looked into the room behind the library, a workshop of sorts that contained small tools, clamps, glues, and tapes of various kinds. Everything seemed to be as he had left it.

Under the staircases on either side of the central room were short hallways that led into the kitchen and to spiral staircases that led to the upstairs rear; but he decided to retrace his steps. "Let's see what's on Aleta's side of the house," he muttered to himself.

The twin to Niles' music room was Aleta's sitting or "morning room" as she called it. The sun entered her side of the house first.

The furniture, a couch and several chairs, had been upholstered in floral chintz fabric. A television and a DVD player along with a stack of Biblical DVDs sat opposite a Chippendale chair. Doilies and needlepoint-covered pillows that bore quotations from the Bible were everywhere a pillow could rest. He shook his head. None of the decorations had been there before. Cloying figurines of praying children and Biblical characters... Jesus and the poor widow giving her widow's mite... Jesus with a shepherd's crook saving the lost sheep... and Jesus as a boy debating in the temple, his finger pointing heavenward, were positioned on window sills and table tops.

Mass-produced pink and blue desert landscapes were framed and hung on the walls. "She must have bought these pictures at one of those 'Starving Artist' shows they hold in Death Valley," he said. "She always did have a soft heart for struggling artists." There were crosses and several gilt-edged Bibles and other religious books. A half-dozen photographs in decorative frames sat on the tables. He picked up one group photo and did not recognize any of the people.

He picked up another group photo, and this time he did recognize most of the people. Her parents and her brothers and sister were there, but there was an elderly lady on the right side of the group. Niles did not know who she was.

He opened one of the half dozen books that were between two bookends on a table. He fanned the pages and a photograph of a handsome clergyman of about thirty-five stopped the page run. Around his neck he wore a chain from which hung a large wooden pectoral cross. In one hand he held a Bible and in the other, pressed against his chest, he held what at first seemed to be a tambourine. Niles looked more closely at it. "Is this a 'Crown of Thorns'?" he asked himself. "Who is this guy?" He moved closer to the window and studied the picture.

"This isn't cactus," he said. "This is barbed wire!" The photograph was signed, "To Aleta, our Garden's most precious flower, from her admiring, Avery Christian, Pastor."

Niles looked through the remaining books in the group but found no other photographs or any inscriptions.

There were indentations in the pillows on the couch. Someone had recently sat there. He began to search the furniture to see if anything had fallen down between the upholstered parts and cushions into the frame box. He found nothing.

He returned to the books on the table. He checked each book's inside cover and found two self-published religious books that contained inscriptions on their end leaves. One entitled Personalizing Your Commitment to Christ read, "To Aleta, whose Grace is an inspiration to us all," was signed by the author, Dr. Lamont T. Marlowe. The second book, *Salvation As Sacrifice*, by the same author, was inscribed, "To Aleta,

The Embodiment of Christ's Joy," and was signed "Monty." There was a photograph of the author on the back of each book jacket. He was an elderly gentleman, distinguished in appearance; but he was not, and bore no resemblance to, Niles noticed, the younger man who carried the Crown of Thorns. He found a bookmark edged in black, like a Mass card. It commemorated the one year death of Pastor Lamont T. Marlowe of the *Church of Gethsemane Garden* who had died in 2011. Niles recognized the name. Aleta had written to him saying that she wanted to serve Christ as a Sister of the Gethsemane Garden.

Niles found nothing else inside the table drawers or furniture; and there were no additional papers or notable inscriptions inside the picture frames.

The far doorway led into the dining room which contained a long walnut table that sat twelve people on the velvet-covered seats of matching chairs. Against the walls stood a china and linen cabinet and a sideboard for serving. A large bay window let in the morning sun; but now, so late in the day, he could barely see the garden outside.

This room led into the kitchen with its working fireplace that used the same flue as the central room's fireplace. As expected, at the second-storey level, a steel and wooden walkway crossed in front of the flue to connect the two sides of the house.

He eagerly went into his favorite room: the rustically furnished kitchen with its copper pots and pans that hung on hooks in front of a tiled section of wall and its view, outside the window, of a pump-handled water faucet and, at the side of the flagstone patio, an old-fashioned windmill and a cistern's housing.

He opened the exterior kitchen door but did not go outside. He saw the charcoal grill he had bought before he went to prison. He did not have the chance to use it then, but, he noticed, it had been used since. He saw the patio furniture and the furled awning that protected it from the sun. Who had Aleta entertained? She would not have used the grill for herself or even for her family. None of them drank, and it was probably safe to assume that whoever did the drinking also ate at the grill.

He crossed the kitchen and, continuing to inspect the house, he climbed the spiral staircase that led to the rear of "his" side of the second storey.

The doors of the rooms were open. He glanced in the first room and saw that the bedroom now had a bunk bed in it. This shocked him. Why would Aleta have put bunk beds in a room that he had used to store rock specimens and some geology equipment? An empty bathroom led into another bedroom. This room, too, had bunk beds installed. At one side of the room stood a stack of disassembled baby furniture.

He walked ahead to look into a third large bedroom that had been used by him when Aleta was in one of her post-miscarriage depression phases. He recalled that when he went to court to hear the verdict, the bed had been freshly made. Now, clearly, it had been slept in. He examined the pillows and found a single long blonde hair. He lifted the lid of the clothes hamper. It was empty. In his bathroom he found his old toiletries.

He descended the staircase that led down to the first floor living room, crossed to the staircase on Aleta's side of the house, and ascended it.

The floor plan was the mirror-image of the other side. He looked into the front corner bedroom that was furnished with expensive furniture. Indentations in the pillows indicated that it had been used - and probably recently. He walked through the bathroom that connected to a smaller bedroom and noticed that it contained various soaps and lotions and appeared to be recently used. The smaller bedroom next to it contained no baby furniture. There was just a single bed and women's street clothes and shoes in the closet... and the usual toiletries on the vanity. This, obviously, was the room Aleta used. But who had used the other rooms? The religious group she had wanted to join? But then why was his liquor cabinet emptied? What kind of religion was it?

Her closet contained a normal array of garments and shoes. He opened a few drawers of a chest and found underwear neatly stacked.

He went into the hall and walked down to the next small bedroom which appeared to be used as a sewing room. There he found a couple of card-tables pushed together to act, he supposed, as a cutting table.

There were also a six-drawer vanity with a full-length mirror, a treadle sewing machine, and a dressmaker's manikin. On a shelf was a sewing basket with a variety of colored spools of thread. There were half a dozen empty hangers and two home-made gingham cotton dresses in the closet. Long dresses. They look like costumes from the old west, he thought. He wondered if they were uniforms of the religious group she belonged to.

He opened a drawer in the vanity and found a silk pouch on which had been embroidered, "Satan's Lure." He opened it and saw that it contained a shockingly sexy thong and bra in which the nipple tips had been removed. "What is *this?*" He began to tremble as he felt around in the drawer to discover what else was hidden there. He touched a small silk bag which contained make-up: kohl and eyebrow pencils; mascara; eye shadow; scarlet lipstick; false eyelashes and glue; rouge; and powder. Aleta never wore make-up of this bold sort. He returned the silk pouches to the drawer. His heart was beating faster and he felt definite fear. What had she gotten herself into?

He found the rear bedroom to be furnished in a guest bedroom's style. The room's closet and chest of drawers were empty.

At the end of the hallway, just before it curved to go behind the flue, another spiral staircase led down to the kitchen. He descended the stairs. "What is going on?" he mumbled. "What is going on?"

He felt the urge to run. In a daze, he left the house and headed for the garage. He turned his old truck's ignition key and nothing happened. "What was I thinking?" he asked aloud. "Of course, the battery's dead." The only way he could get the battery recharged or, he decided when he saw the amount of corrosion on its contact points, to get a new one, was to put air into his bicycle tires and ride a bike into town. His bike was standing at the side of the garage. The tires were flat. He looked for but could not find the tire pump. Frustrated, he returned to the house.

As the sun began its descent behind the Sierras, he went into his music room and sat at the piano. In the dim light, it was impossible to read the sheet music. Niles had played in the prison band for nearly a year before he had had the bone marrow surgery. He tried to remember some of the songs; but he had learned his part in an ensemble version, not in a solo form. He chose instead old standards that he was certain he would remember. He tried *Misty*, but he could not recall the chords of the bridge. He tried *Laura*, but that too stymied him midway through the piece. He had sheet music inside the piano bench but without a lamp the music could not be read. He felt like whimpering in defeat, and he shuddered a sigh and put his head down onto the music rack. Suddenly he heard the sound of a car's motor. A key went into the front door's lock. Aleta, laughing, stepped over the threshold. Niles stood up and yelled, "At last! You're home!" He began to walk into the central room. Aleta stopped, gasped, and quickly turned to prevent someone who was behind her from entering.

A masculine voice said, "What's wrong?" Niles could not see him because the door shielded him from view. "Let me meet him," the man said, refusing to budge. "We're in your car," he said. "How am I supposed to get back to town?"

"Niles!" Aleta called. "I'm so glad you're home, but you should have let me know you were coming early. I'll be back in half an hour. You've waited this long. Another half hour won't matter." She went outside and shut the door behind her.

Niles returned to the music room and in the dark sat motionless at the piano.

Beryl looked at the camera photos of the OM flowers. What a pleasure it was to be remembered on Mother's Day, she thought.

It occurred to her that Akara Chatree, the young Thai-Brazilian priest who currently lived in the little Zen temple with Sensei, might not have remembered to order flowers for his mother. She called him and left a voicemail message to remind him. Mother's Day in Brazil was the same day as it was in the U.S.

Half an hour later, Akara walked down to the offices of Wagner and Tilson Private Investigators. "I am here to respond to your summons," he said, teasing. "And yes, I sent my mom flowers." He looked at the huge OM display of carnations. "But nothing like this. Jack has outdone himself."

"Ah, it wasn't just Jack. It was mostly Groff Eckersley. They two of them scheme together, regularly." She looked at him more closely. "Am I mistaken," she asked, "but are you, George, and Sensei gaining weight?"

Akara sucked in his abdomen. "Well… to be honest, I think I've been a bit sedentary lately." He lowered his voice, "And there's a new congregation member who supplies me with a pastry box of baklava every morning. Sensei got some great Kona coffee and one of those 10-cup coffee makers…"

"And?"

"And George stops by every morning on his way into the office, so the three of us have a little breakfast snack."

Beryl did not attempt to conceal her anger. "I jump through hoops trying to regulate George's diet to keep him healthy and trim, and he pigs out with the two of you on baklava? And I bet he uses sugar in his coffee. Sugar and cream! I don't believe it! Baklava? That's pastry and nuts and honey and butter. Sedentary? You mean you sit around and consume calories. And he never said a word to me. And you don't have the common sense to tell your fan club to switch to a raw vegetable platter?"

Akara protested, "We're gonna do extra exercise at the gym to work it off."

"The only extra exercise you get is walking half a block down the street for cookie and tea breaks. I iron George's shirts. He won't get on the scale for me but I can see that the buttons on his Italian-cut shirts are pulling. So knock it off! All three of you. After all I went through to get him into shape, he's back to his old tricks. He's supposed to lose weight. And you'll start turning into one of those fat Ho Ti Buddhas."

"More to love. More to love."

"Don't count on it," Beryl said. "I will lay the diet and exercise law down with George. You and Sensei better see to it that he keeps it."

"Yes, Ma'am," Akara said, and backed out of the office.

More than a love of Middle Eastern pastry had inspired George to start dropping into the temple kitchen for coffee and pastry in the morning during April, 2013.

Between Christmas and New Year's of 2012, while working on a case in Baltimore, he had been bitten severely on the thigh by a guard dog. He spent the holidays recuperating in a motel, trying to recover sufficiently from the puncture wounds to be able to drive his pickup truck back to Philadelphia. Finally he returned to his home on Thursday, January 3rd, stiff and short-tempered.

He had been in Baltimore to help Dr. Carla Richards, with whom he once had a romantic relationship; and her gratitude for his help took the form of a maternal need to feed him and an almost adolescent attempt to convince him that she was still sexually attracted to him.

In two weeks of being mostly immobilized in a bed watching TV and reading novels, Carla's constant attention had helped him to gain over ten pounds. For breakfast every morning she had brought him a large latté and two expensive coffee shop muffins. ("My God!" Beryl had gasped when she found out. "That's two thousand calories before the morning news is over.") Then there was the lasagna and the chicken *molé*... and the double cheeseburgers and french fried sweet potatoes.

The weight, showing mostly in his jaws, neck, and waist, made him look old and paunchy. Just after Christmas, while George was in Baltimore, Lilyanne Smith, the woman who had brought him so much pleasure and pain during the last three years, had come to his house to leave him photographs of herself and her new baby - who was not related to George - and a note which cursed him for having "abandoned" her.

When George finally drove home from Baltimore on January 3rd, the first thing he did was to go to the kitchen to stretch out his leg on the bachelor's-pad bed he kept there. After a gunshot wound had shattered his left knee, he retired from service and kept a bed in the kitchen during the years in which it was difficult for him to climb stairs. And now, after a rottweiler had sunk its canines into his right thigh, he felt decrepit as he entered the kitchen.

Lilyanne's note, which began by calling him "a rat," was on the table beside his recliner. He picked up her photograph and remarked to himself that she had never been so beautiful as she was then, and then he read the letter in which she said that she'd see the three of them - Carla, him, and her - in hell before she'd let Carla have him. *"Rat?"* he said to himself, "She calls me a rat?" This struck him funny and was so endearing that he collapsed on his bed, laughing and very tempted to call her. But he wondered how old he looked now that he had gotten so much heavier. And when he stood naked in front of his full-length bathroom mirror, he cringed. "How the hell did I let this happen?" he asked his reflection.

He could not risk a meeting with Lilyanne while he looked so unappealing. He was twenty years older than she as it was. He called Beryl who nearly fainted at the sight of him. She had been to his home to water his plants and had read Lilyanne's note. She agreed - too much he thought - that his physical attraction would take a fatal hit if the young woman saw him looking "like an old fat slob." She gave him a scathing look and hissed, "I will get you in shape. Never doubt it." He cowered and submitted to her Draconian regimen. That was in January.

Lilyanne had learned about George's dog bite from Sensei, and she knew when he was expected home. He would read her letter then and naturally, he would call her and they would be re-united. But he did not call. Was it possible that Carla was with him... there in his house? She passed a frantic week waiting for his call... a week and a half... but no call came. Bitter and angry, she called the hotel in Cayman Brac and left word for Claus Van Aken, the name Eric Haffner used, to call her at home. Eric called a few hours later. She asked him, "Do you want to see your son? Your parents were here for Christmas. I have scads of photographs but I didn't want to mail them to you - not knowing whether you were sane or insane or just your normal idiotic self."

"In any one of those conditions I would want to see my boy."

"Then I will open the house in Cape May, New Jersey - I certainly do not want you here at Tarleton - and I will meet you there on Sunday, January 20th. The baby will be two months' old on that day."

"Lily... I can't come there. I'm still being investigated for three missing persons. The authorities have taken my passport. I can meet you in George Town or here at the Brac."

"I'll have to see if one of the nannies can accompany me. Hold on."

Eric could hear her ask the 'day' nanny if she had a passport. She did have one. Was she willing to go to the Cayman Islands for a few days? Yes, she was.

Lilyanne returned to her phone. "I'll call and make reservations," she said.

"Wait!" he yelled. "I don't know that you'd be safe. You were here when the others disappeared. If they see you check in, they may want to interrogate you... or hold you on some charge. It isn't safe for you to come here as Lilyanne Smith."

"I'll have to get a new passport in the name of Haffner. I'd have to present the baby's birth certificate so I can't use somebody else's name. All right. I'm Lilyanne Haffner and we were married... pick a month and day."

"February 25, 2012."

"Excellent. We can say that we were married at sea by Captain Quintero on board the *Santiago*."

"Yes. And please don't refer to me as Eric Haffner."

"Evidently your life of crime hasn't gotten your fingerprints on file with any international law enforcement organization. Hold on while I call a travel agency." She googled a local travel agency that specialized in assisting patrons with expedited passports and made reservations for a flight to George Town on Friday, the 18th of January, arriving at 2 p.m. to return on Tuesday, the 22nd. She would be staying in a suite in the Lamark Hotel. "Call me there," she said and disconnected the call.

Lilyanne immediately went to a jewelry store and purchased a matching pair of gold wedding rings. Then she went to the travel agent's office, had her photograph taken, and paid the fees. She carried her own identification and old passport. She also brought the baby and his birth certificate, and since her family was well-known in the area, no one doubted that her new married name was Lilyanne S. Haffner. Then she went shopping to buy suitably attractive garments for the meeting. One of the new dresses was an evening gown in which she looked, she had to admit, stunning.

Eric, too, sailed his Bermuda sloop, the *Remittman*, down to Grand Cayman so that he could have his hair properly styled, his nails manicured, and his wardrobe brought up to date. He bought evening wear - in case he needed it - and had it fitted perfectly to him. He also bought a business suit and several casual outfits. Wedding rings did not occur to him.

He was waiting anxiously at the jetway as Lilyanne, Baby Eric, and the Nanny deplaned. In spite of herself, Lilyanne smiled when she saw him. He was grinning broadly, with his arms held out to her. He kissed both of her cheeks and then turned to the bundle the nanny was holding. A thin veil covered the baby's face. Eric lifted it and whispered, "He's beautiful."

"Sit down," Lilyanne said, "and you can hold him." She looked at the nanny. To Eric she said, "Our nanny is named Matty. Nanny Matty."

Eric backed into a waiting room seat. As Nanny Matty placed the baby in his arms he asked, "What is his name?" The nanny looked askance at Lilyanne. The baby's father did not even know the child's name?

"Eric Tarleton Haffner," Lilyanne said in a flat tone. "I didn't know your middle name. What is it?"

"August Johann Carl. I'm glad you chose Tarleton." He began to talk baby-talk to Baby Eric who managed to smile and gurgle.

"Here!" she said as she pushed the gold wedding band on his finger that was at the moment cradling the baby's head. She showed him her ring. "You can come back to our suite with us."

He did not look at his ring. "May I carry the baby?"

"Just don't drop him," she said and then added, "and walk in front of me so I can see you at all times." She had told herself that civility demanded that she acknowledge the father of her child... that she was not a mongrel drama-queen who denied a father and his parents the privilege of knowing their own "flesh and blood." But that did not mean that she had to tolerate any degree of mischief. And if Eric, Senior, misbehaved in any way, she would have no compunctions whatsoever in calling the police. Duty. Well, it was a sort of *noblesse oblige*. "Make sure you keep his head supported," she further instructed him, but in a more gentle voice.

George had been forced to do yoga with Beryl for two hours every morning. Every afternoon Sensei had given him martial arts exercises and every evening he had gone for an hour or so to the Police Department's weight room. After two weeks of this intense regimen, he looked "better than ever" Beryl said. "You're ready."

"Would you call Tarleton and see if the Minx is civilized enough to handle a rat?" he asked.

Beryl called and learned that Lilyanne, Baby Eric, and the nanny had gone on vacation to the Cayman Islands. Sanford, the majordomo, delivered the news. He quickly added, "She waited for Mr. Wagner to call and when he didn't, she called that Eric fellow. I'm terrified for her. We all are. But you know Miss Lilyanne."

The call was on speakerphone. Beryl thanked him and disconnected the call. She did not know what to say. George did. "Would you mind leaving me alone now," he said. "And I don't think I'll be doing yoga again so you can fill in your morning schedule with other things. I'll be in the office tomorrow. Please tell Sensei that I'm canceling the afternoon workout, too."

Without saying another word, Beryl left his house. When she returned to the office, she let herself into the rear utility kitchen and sat at the table and cried for half an hour.

SATURDAY, MAY 11, 2013

As though fear were a huge stone that he carried on his back, Frank Goodrich drooped under its burden. He walked like an old man, shuffling rather than stepping. Worry stifled his lungs and he could not take a deep breath. He was too tired to think.

The television was on in his hotel room. He saw the screen but did not look at it. In a moment of clarity he noticed an advertisement for Mother's Day gifts, and he realized that he had identified one problem that he *could* solve. He got out his phone and ordered flowers for his wife and her mother.

He felt so stiff and creaky that it occurred to him that his condition was akin to being frozen, and he filled the tub with hot water, intending to sit in it and melt himself into relaxation. When he lowered himself into the water, he realized immediately that he had made yet another mistake. He had forgotten about the stun-gun's burns on his abdomen; and, touched by the hot water, they flared up painfully. He got out of the tub, flipped the lever that emptied it, and stepped into the shower stall to let cold water drench him.

Then, with a towel wrapped around him, he went to his suitcase and took out clean underwear. He dressed and felt better, cleaner and able to think cogently. His first thought was: what is the best way to raise thirty thousand dollars without anyone knowing? His second thought was: could this be some kind of hoax that was being played on him and Waverly? Were there really going to be blackmail photos delivered to him? That, he decided, was wishful thinking. One thing was certain: if he really was about to be blackmailed, he needed a support system. This was no time to risk an argument with his wife. He called her and invited her to come into town to have dinner with him. "It's the last night of the convention and I'd like to show you off. Everybody thinks I'm boring. I want to give them a dose of Gwen."

She was flattered. She hadn't heard the line before. "All right," she said, "but I don't know how my hair will turn out without a beauty shop appointment. And Frank, this is the day before Mother's Day... Julia Roberts couldn't get an appointment with my stylist."

"Just wear the black dress you wore to that engagement party we went to last month. Nobody will notice your hair."

Someone knocked on the door. Gwen could hear the sound. "Hold on," Frank said. "Let me get the door," then, suddenly realizing that it could be Waverly, he said, "Ah, I won't hold you up. I'll be here in my hotel room. Call me on my cell when you're ready to leave and I'll dress and meet you downstairs at the bar... or you can come up here."

Another knock on the door made him shout, "Just a minute!" He said goodbye to his wife and disconnected the call.

A special messenger delivered a manila envelope. Frank tipped him and sat on his bed to look at the pictures that he knew would be inside it. There were a half-dozen pictures, one more lurid than the next. He could barely look at them. A note was attached: Did you think you could seduce another man's wife and get away with it? Guess again. Be at the Greyhound Bus Terminal at 1 p.m. today, Saturday the 11th, and wait at the line of pay phones at the north side. At 1 p.m. answer the ringing phone. You will be given further instructions then.

His room phone rang. He answered it and heard the voice of an irate Waverly Bryant. "How low can you get? I just got an envelope and a note that accuses me of seducing a good woman's husband." Distorting her voice with sarcasm, she said, "Oh, how you were having trouble with your wife. Oh, she didn't love you anymore."

"Listen! I just got the same envelope and a note that accuses me of seducing you... someone else's wife. We need to talk. These pictures are terrible. And I don't know how the hell I'm going to raise 30 grand. I invited my wife to come in this afternoon for dinner and I just found out that I have to be at the bus terminal at 1 p.m. Are you in your room?"

"Yes. 1217."

"I'll be right up."

Waverly Bryant, looking haggard, opened the door and stepped back to let him in.

"Do I look as beat as you?" he asked.

"I've been up all night," she said. "I'm ruined. If this gets back to my husband, I'm ruined."

"I'm in the same boat as you. I've got nothing to hock. I could tap my friends. Between them and some unexplained charges on my credit cards, I can get the 30 grand. But it may take a few days."

"All I can do is maybe pawn my wedding band... not my engagement ring, the solitaire. But the band has four one-half carat diamonds. They're high quality stones and the band is probably worth around $10,000." She sat on the bed and brought her hands to her face and bent forward until her hands were on her lap. "I thought I'd be a nice guy and give that gal I met on the plane an excuse to get out of feeling like a reject when she wasn't included in the dinner invitation. Why didn't I just keep my mouth shut and let her solve her own problems?"

He patted her shoulder. "I feel the same way. But I can't blame the guy who bailed on my dinner reservations and you can't blame her. Blame won't help us." He looked at her note. "You've got to be at the bus station at 1 p.m., too. Let's not sit here passively. Go take a shower. I'll be out here, and when you're dressed we'll go down to the coffee shop and have some breakfast and see what we can do to resolve the problem before we leave for the station."

She got up and took a few pieces of underwear from her suitcase to carry into the bathroom. She laughed. "Modesty? I'm being modest by taking my underwear into the bathroom so that you won't see my private parts? My God! How could this have happened?"

He stood up and put his hands on her shoulders. "Look... last night... what you said when you hit me with that stun gun. I don't blame you for thinking I had something to do with that holdup. You know that I didn't. I can't tell you how relieved I was to see that the son of a bitch missed your rings when he emptied your purse. And your gold chain, too. That ought to be worth a few grand. But he didn't take it or my watch. Let's focus on the up side of this mess. Go ahead. Take a shower and get dressed."

Mid-May proved to be a difficult financial time for the three friends Frank called. All three had just put large deposits down for summer vacation resorts. Dolph, the last friend he called, had a suggestion. Your name is good and let me tell you, a good reputation is worth plenty. I have a little side business with a Colombian gentleman. We don't need to discuss that now... or ever; but on the strength of your word - and maybe with a little collateral - we can get the 30 grand with no trouble."

"Maybe I can put up as collateral a really nice diamond ring, but if I do, I have to include the debt of the lady who owns the ring. That will make it $50K that I need."

"We'll see the ring and decide. My wife's birthday is next month and if you don't redeem the ring from my friend Hugo, maybe I'll buy it and let him lend me the balance. You can pay me back $3K a month until your $30K debt's paid and your lady friend can pay me back a grand a month till her debt - the difference between the value of the band and $20K - is paid in full. I won't charge you anything extra - but he may have added vig to the debt, in which case whatever he lends me, you'll owe. First, we'll have to find out what the ring's worth. We might not solve all your problems, but it'll be a start."

"Ok. Dolph... I really appreciate this. Let me talk to her and then call you back in fifteen minutes. Maybe we can arrange to meet at a diamond dealer's place and find out how much we're talking about."

Waverly had heard most of the conversation. "They'll advance you money on your name with just the band as collateral? And you can repay the note at three thousand dollars a month? So then all I'll owe is the difference between the value of my wedding band and the twenty thousand dollars?" She sighed. "I guess we can't ask for more than that."

"Your band and my name." He sighed. "I'll call him back and set up a meeting with him, his rich friend, and a jeweler who will appraise the ring."

They waited by the phones at the north side of the terminal. Promptly at one o'clock a phone rang and together they went to answer it. It was Frank who picked up the receiver and spoke first.

The instruction was as simple as it was harsh. "I've got to leave town earlier than I expected," the same man who photographed them said with his French accent. "I feel no shame for having importuned you. Both of you were indulging yourselves in dishonorable activities. You got what you deserved. I rather think you've learned your lesson or, at least, you will have learned it, once you've paid the price. Tomorrow night you will buy thirty thousand dollars worth of chips at the Sweetwater Casino in Joliet. You'll take your chips into the lounge and wait to be given further instructions about where you will deliver the chips. Be there at 7 p.m. Your Jezebel will also bring her twenty thousand dollars to the Sweetwater Casino in Joliet and buy chips. She'll also sit at a table in the lounge and someone will bring her information about where she should go to deliver her chips. I can't give you back the negatives because the photos were shot on a digital camera. You will simply have to trust me when I tell you that I will not contact you again and I will wipe from the hard drive all record of the shoot."

Waverly had listened with her ear next to Frank's. She shook her head negatively. "I can't be here tomorrow night. I've got to be back home tomorrow at dinner time. I have a return ticket already, and I've got to be at my job Monday morning. If I'm gonna pay for this I cannot lose my job or antagonize my husband!"

The intruder's voice responded, "Then Frank can bring all of it and we'll be looking out for only one person. You have your instructions. If I don't get it all, duplicates of the photos will be sent to Waverly's home and office in Cheyenne and to your home in Hyde Park and your office in downtown Chicago." He disconnected the call.

"What are we gonna do?" Frank asked without expecting an answer.

She bit her lip. "Call your friend and see what we can borrow."

They met Dolph and his Colombian friend at a jewelry shop that was owned by someone related to the Colombian.

"Let's see the rings," the jeweler said.

Reluctantly, Waverly produced her rings which she had tied together with a string. She pulled the string's bow and handed the freed wedding band to him. Instead of taking it, he reached for the solitaire that lay on the showcase counter-top, and whistled. He put his eyepiece down and shook his head, smiling as he looked at the solitaire. "Gorgeous," he said. He continued to study it. Waverly began to protest that it was the other ring that she wanted to offer as collateral, but the jeweler said, "Shhhh. Don't spoil my pleasure. This stone is exquisite." He spoke privately to the Colombian who then spoke to Dolph.

"He says it's worth between sixty-five and seventy thousand dollars. You'd have to leave the stone with him if you want a more precise appraisal."

"No!' Waverly said. "What about the other one... the band?"

He examined the stones with his jeweler's loop and gave another rough estimate of the value. "Three thousand a stone. High quality. A total of twelve thousand dollars. But those prices are retail. For the set together, eighty thousand. Maybe more. Maybe less. Hugo," he said to the Colombian, "I can give you a more precise value but I'd have to look at the stones under a special microscope we use... I've got one in the back. It'll only take a minute."

"Go ahead," the Colombian said. He looked at Dolph. "You still interested in giving your wife some diamonds?"

"Yeah. I am. She's never let me down. She'd go crazy seeing this stuff on her finger."

The jeweler went behind a partition and began to move equipment around. They waited, hearing only a chair scrape the floor. Finally he returned and said, "Seventy-five thousand for the pair of them."

"And you need only fifty thousand?" Dolph asked.

"Yes, fifty thousand," Frank answered. "Thirty for me and twenty for her."

Waverly picked up her rings and started to put them in her purse.

"Here!" the jeweler said, producing a velvet ring box. "Don't leave them loose in your bag. Protect them properly." He took the rings from her hand and placed them in the box. Then he snapped the box shut and handed it to her.

"Let's go talk about this in the coffee shop," Hugo said.

They thanked the jeweler and went out into the busy Saturday afternoon street.

"You trust this Frank?" the Colombian asked Dolph.

"Absolutely."

"You wanna give your wife both rings for her birthday?"

"Sure, if you'll trust me."

The Colombian looked at each of them. He spoke directly to Dolph. "I know you're good for it. So I'll tell you what I'm willing to do. I'll lend you seventy-five thousand for you to pay the little lady here. She can pay off her twenty thousand dollar debt. She's out of the picture. I'll also lend you thirty thousand for you to lend Frank. That's a hundred-five thousand you owe me. I'll give you sixty days free but then I'll charge interest on the debt. So, on your debit side you've got the rings and an accounts receivable of the thirty thousand that Frank owes you. On the credit side, you owe me a hundred five thousand, or the rings plus thirty thousand in cash. Do we all understand this transaction?"

Waverly gagged. "I can't do it," she said, wretching into a napkin that was in a dispenser on the table. She bolted for the ladies' room. Nobody said anything until she returned. Her eyes were red and she shuddered and hiccoughed, hardly able to restrain herself from sobbing. A little fleck of toothpaste was at the corner of her mouth. Frank reached across the table and wiped it off. Pathetically, she looked up at him "It's the only thing I own in the world," she whispered.

"You'll have all that money," Frank consoled her. "You can start that new life without worrying about what other people are going to do to you... firing you from your job... divorcing you... you'll be free."

"Well," Dolph said, "what's in gonna be?"

"I'm in," Frank said, as Waverly weakly nodded her head.

"We'll do business in my car. It's a block from here in my parking place."

Waverly wiped her eyes. "Let's get it over with," she said.

In the spacious Lincoln sedan, the Colombian gave Dolph one hundred and five thousand dollars. Dolph gave thirty thousand to Frank and seventy-five thousand to Waverly. She handed him the ring box. He opened it, making sure the rings were still there. She handed Frank twenty thousand dollars, saying, "I'm trusting you to keep that appointment and pay my debt."

"I will," said Frank Goodrich, not knowing what trouble he had just gotten himself into.

Aleta Portmann did not return on Friday night. When she left the house at sundown she said that she'd return in half an hour. But she had mistakenly thought that she'd only be going back to Tonopah, but instead her destination was Beatty, ninety miles farther.

Niles had waited until he lapsed into "jailhouse stasis" and lay upon his bed in a zombie state of no-mind, a vacuous state akin to open-eyed unconsciousness. He was not aware of his surroundings until he heard birds chirping outside his window at dawn. As he rolled over and yawned, he could smell for the first time the perfume of the woman who had left the long blonde hair on his pillow. He showered and tried to rekindle in his mind the joy he imagined he would feel when he did the simple things like sleep in his own bed or shower in his own shower.

There was no fresh food in the house. No eggs, butter, milk, or bread. He made coffee and found a pack of camper's rations which he ate for breakfast. He worked on his truck, removing the corroded battery, and at noon, Aleta returned. He cautioned himself not to forget that the next day was Mother's Day, a particularly difficult day for a childless woman who had had five miscarriages.

She parked the Buick in the garage and came to his truck. "I'm sorry I wasn't here when you got out. I would have gone to meet you... at least at the bus stop in town."

"You haven't picked up the mail. I wrote but you didn't stop at the post office to pick up the mail. People have been sleeping in the house.

People have been partying in the house. I saw strange underwear in a silk pouch in your sewing room. 'Satan's Lure' was written on it. It looked like something a hooker would wear. What is going on, Aleta?"

"First, I don't like to get the mail because I don't like being stared at. People point their finger at me because my husband is a convicted saloon brawler. They think your fight was about me, not horses. I'm the troublemaker.

"You want me to give you an explanation for what's been going on when you left me alone? What was going on that you had to go into the bar that night? What was going on that you had to beat up Joe Gregory and cost us half a million dollars in legal fees and investment returns? After what you did to me and my life, you don't have the right to criticize me for the way I've had to live alone out here." She turned and marched into the house. He put down his tools, wiped his hands, and followed her.

"Let's go over this one more time," he said, sitting beside her at the kitchen table. "I stopped in the bar because I was getting the oil changed in the truck. I drive the twenty year old truck. You drive the new Buick. I did not hit Joe Gregory first. I defended myself against a drunken lunatic. If you've decided that I'm a liar, then I guess you've decided that I'm not fit to be your husband."

"Living alone out here has not been easy for me!"

"It was a lot easier then being caged for something I didn't do. I was innocent, and I didn't care about the money I lost. I cared about not being with you. You at least could go to your folks. You were free to move around. You know what I was doing for two and a half years. I'm still your husband, and I'd like to know what you were doing for those two and a half years."

"I joined a religious group, The Sisters of Gethsemane Garden. I'm taking my vows and turning my life over to Christ. That's what I've been doing."

"Who are these people? What does a getup like 'Satan's Lure' have to do with serving Christ? Tell me, Aleta. I'm listening. I want to understand."

She poured herself a cup of coffee. "It's easier for some people to understand than it is for others. I don't have a college degree like you. I can't express myself the way you can." She busied herself with the coffee.

"I'm listening," he said. "I promise I won't get angry or argue with you. Just explain it as best you can."

"We pose for a picture while wearing the Satan's Lure underwear to show a personal commitment that a good Christian woman makes to prove that she is ready, willing, and able to face Satan down. The whole idea of free will is that all people are free to do sinful sexual things, but that a good Christian has the willpower to choose not to do them. But you have to understand... if a person is unable to do something, he just can't say that he chooses not to do it. If a woman is homely and no man will look at her no matter how hard she tries to attract a man, then she can't say she has no man in her life because she chooses not to have one. Can you understand that?"

"Yes."

"It's the same with sin. Many people want to sin but simply don't have the courage to sin - and this means they don't have the courage to be righteous, either. So as part of the initiation phase, a Sister poses in front of the camera looking like the kind of woman any man would want to be with... to sin with... and he'd pay a lot of money to be with. So I can look at that picture and know that if I don't run around and do sinful things it isn't because I can't do them or because if I did them I couldn't attract anybody to do them with. That picture shows that I can be as wantonly sexy as any tramp on the street. But I have free will and I choose not to do those things. That photograph is the proof that I could sin if I wanted to. But I don't live like that at all. I thought you'd be away for six years so I turned my life over to God."

Niles was moved by her ingenuous expression and the childish explanation. It seemed bizarre to him for any Christian pastor to require his followers to pose in such a licentious way. "How often do you have to dress like that?"

"Just the one time the picture was taken. Go look in my vanity drawer. You'll see all that makeup that I bought a year ago. I used it only one time for that picture. Look at it if you don't believe me."

"I believe you." His voice softened. "I'm sorry I doubted you about that underwear."

"I know how hard you worked to accumulate the wealth that you brought to our marriage. I brought nothing. And aside from the miscarriages, we did have a few great years together. But I want to take my religion seriously. I want to preach the Gospels."

"Living at home and going out occasionally to preach isn't the same as being a traveling Evangelist. That's a very difficult life."

"I know it is and that's why I wanted to use our home as a kind of headquarters for the ministry. It's really too large a place for only the two of us; and the Sisters of Gethsemane Garden could put it to much better use. I had started to make the place a retreat for us... them and me. I made the commitment because I thought you'd be gone a long time. Let's face it, Niles. We're husband and wife in name only. You're still young enough to get yourself another wife... maybe down in Texas with your brother and his friends you'd feel more at home. There's no life for you up here now that you've got a criminal record."

"Are you asking me for a divorce?"

"Well... would that be so unusual? Prison separated us. I wouldn't be the first wife of a convict to obtain a divorce. The process is automatic when one person is jailed for a felony. I did talk to a lawyer down in Pahrump, but I haven't signed any papers, yet."

"I'm not out on parole, Aleta. I've been effectively pardoned. You had your chance to get an automatic 'jailbird' divorce, but you didn't take it. I won't stand in your way if you want to divorce me, but I won't pay you to do it. That man who was here? What was his name?"

"He's the pastor of our ministry."

"Avery Christian?"

"I see you've been going through my things. So you've learned his name. He was there for me when I needed someone. You were away."

"And he wants to marry you?"

"Yes, he does. The fact that I can't have children is, for the first time, an advantage in my life. There is no room for children in an Evangelical ministry. I finally feel wanted and needed. Avery Christian says he loves me and wants me beside him to help preach the Gospels. I don't know what to do."

Niles moved his chair closer to her and put his arm around her shoulder. "I don't have the right to criticize the man. Why don't you go with the group for a tryout period? If that's where your heart is now, follow it. See where it leads. I'll still be here, waiting for you."

She stopped crying. "I want to go tomorrow if that's all right with you. I made those plans before I knew you'd be home. And one thing more… you know how you taught me to make venison stew? Well, I made it for the Sisters and they loved it. There's a young buck who keeps coming around to eat the vegetables I planted. He's really destructive. Could you take him down in the morning early and dress him. You can keep half and I'll take half when I go to our temporary place in Beatty tomorrow." She got up from the table. "I have to start getting my things together."

"Could you run me into town so that I can get a new battery?"

"I guess I could do that little thing for my long lost husband," she said, flicking her finger playfully across his nose. She stood up. "Let's go if you're going!" she said, and Niles Portmann, no longer feeling anxiety, but overwhelmed with loss, followed her out to the garage.

SUNDAY, MAY 12, 2013

For a reason he did not understand, Niles Portman had begun to experience low blood sugar while he was in prison. He would awaken every morning angry and nervous, and not until he drank coffee and ate breakfast did he feel like a normal human being.

On this Sunday morning, he awakened early and was just as angry as he had been in his cell. Aleta was in her bed in her room and this separation was not what he thought about for thirty months of cell life. He knew he'd feel better once he ate. But the deer would be gone by then. He loaded his rifle which, miraculously, had escaped her "garage-sale" of his equipment.

He saw the handsome buck from an upstairs window. The animal was happily munching on Aleta's carrot tops. Niles tiptoed down the stairs and went out the front door and checked the direction of the weather vane. He turned to the downwind side of the house and quietly approached the animal. As soon as he sighted him, he fired a shot and the deer collapsed in place.

He went into the kitchen and got his best knife and a bucket and went to the animal and began to gut it. The innards steamed in the chilled air. He put them into the bucket and then walked to the edge of his property and dumped the bucket's contents on the ground. He admired wolves and there was talk that some wolves had moved into the area. He returned for the head, neck, and four shanks and dumped them for the scavengers to eat. There were bears, too, in the mountains. "Better than bears or coyotes, I hope the wolves get'cha," he said and returned to skin and quarter the animal and to carry the lot into the kitchen. Wolves were faithful to their mates. They mated for life.

It irritated him that Aleta had surely heard the shot and knew what he was doing, but had not bothered to join him to help. "Not even this," he said bitterly. He started up the gasoline generator so that the freezing compartment of the refrigerator would be sure to reach the desired temperature. He put each quarter in a plastic bag and put them into the refrigerator.

He had worked for nearly two hours and still Aleta had not come downstairs. He heard the water running in an upstairs bathroom. "She's up," he muttered. There still was nothing to eat besides a camper's ration pack. "To hell with it," he said. He would drive into town and eat breakfast like a normal man. No... more. He had a few geodes and fossils that had escaped her sell-off of his personal possessions. He'd go down into Vegas and see a few old friends and maybe sell a few items for some spending money. Two could play that "disappearing" game. He'd leave and let her come down to an empty house. And if she missed him or didn't miss him, what the hell was the difference?

He put the rocks into a bag and climbed the spiral staircase up to the second floor to get a change of clothing from his room.

On the way into Tonopah, he could feel the carburetor struggle. He had thought it sounded funny when he started the engine after he had put the new battery in. But that was something else Aleta cost him... fretting over her when he should have been attending to his truck's engine. He decided not to risk driving to Las Vegas with the sluggish carburetor. A bus left at 10 a.m. He'd get breakfast and take the bus. He'd pick up some carburetor cleaner while he was in Las Vegas and attend to the neglected engine when he got back in a day or two.

Not wanting to confront Niles, Aleta had purposely stayed in bed. She believed that she had been summoned to the ministry, a calling that she could not deny. Yes, she was disturbed by some of the unusual methods that Avery Christian, the man she had fallen in love with, used to organize his followers and to enlighten them to a new way to approach the divine.

Avery wanted a spiritual marriage as well as a legal one, but propriety had forbidden him from making her even a spiritual wife until she divorced Niles. She envisioned the ceremony. Her father walking beside her down a cathedral's aisle, being led by her sister who would be her maid of honor and the Sisters who would be her bridesmaids.

She had a nagging suspicion about Avery's goal in insisting that she be divorced. She had seen that he interacted intimately with the other sisters and one, in particular, the older Sister Hope, had turned over to him the settlement she had received when her husband had been accidentally killed. Sister Hope had acted as though she were Avery's fiancée. But now she was gone and Aleta did not know the reasons for her absence. But if Avery were true to his word, he would accept her without any deeds to property. He often said that she needed no dowry. She could preach beside him anywhere. Yes, anywhere they were together would be their church.

She had wanted to stay upstairs until Niles got tired of waiting for her to come down and went out in his truck. He could drive it now. But it grew later and she began to prepare for her trip to Beatty. Avery Christian was going to pick her up in Tonopah at noon. She still had a little personal shopping to do and she wanted to get vegetables to add to the venison stew. When she heard the pickup truck leave the garage and start down the road, she hurried downstairs. It was not yet 10 a.m. She had time to go shopping, return to pick up the venison that was waiting for her in the kitchen, and drive back to Tonopah to meet Avery.

She went into town, bought a pair of shoes and some underwear and stopped at a grocery store. Then she came home and tried to cut the meat into smaller pieces so that they would fit in an ice cooler. She got a knife and began to cut through a shoulder joint. The knife slipped and she cut herself, a two inch superficial slice that went from her inside left index finger down to the top of her palm. The wound bled more than she thought it would. When it didn't stop bleeding under the cold water that she ran over it, she went upstairs and tried to staunch the bleeding with gauze. Finally it stopped and she applied a few Band-aids and finished cutting the meat. She tossed the knife into the cooler and dragged the cooler out to the Buick's trunk. She unloaded the meat, placed the cooler in the trunk, and then replaced the venison parts. She drove as quickly as she could into Tonopah. Pastor Avery Christian arrived at the same time that she did. She parked the Buick at the far end of the gas station, leaving the keys under the seat for Niles. Avery helped her to transfer the cooler into the Escalade, and they left.

Her great adventure had begun.

Frank Goodrich opened his eyes and lazily viewed the morning light. Gwen, her back to him, lay closely beside him. His arm was around her and he tightened his grip and whispered in her ear, "I'll never be able to tell you how much you mean to me. Last night was wonderful... you at dinner... dancing... singing along at that old piano bar... and then here beside me in bed. What a wonderful night. I love you."

She had heard him. "You still sing off key and ruined the entire experience!" She grinned and he mussed her hair. She turned around. "Since the kids are home and it is My Day after all, how about if we go out for breakfast? I'll race you to the shower!"

He made love to her in the shower stall. "I'm like a dead guy, cobbled together with mismatched parts. I'm Frankenstein's monster and you're the electricity that makes me work."

"Good grief, Frank!" she laughed. "You ought to put that on a Valentine card."

His teenage kids were already eating breakfast. "Well," Frank said, "let's all have breakfast together at Frank's Place. Pass me the corn flakes and a banana... and don't forget the lady."

Frank Jr. said, "Mom, have you looked in the laundry room? You better go look!"

Gwen went into the room and gasped at the flowers Frank had sent! "You fool!" she cried. "You wonderful fool!" She carried the three separate vases into the kitchen. "One from each of you!"

"Mine is the nicest," Frank Jr. said. "Mom likes tulips best. Thanks, Dad, for remembering that."

The kitchen phone rang. His daughter ran to it and shielded it from being answered. "That's got to be Dougie and his merciless hoard. No way am I spending time with them today! I get one weekend home from school and I don't want them anywhere near me."

Doug had called from his cellphone. He pulled into the driveway and blew the horn before he turned off the ignition. While the Goodrich family silently looked at each other in alarm, Doug opened the kitchen door and asked, "How come you're not answering the phone? Look! I've brought you a surprise. Gwen's mother was climbing up the kitchen steps.

"Mom!" Frank exclaimed. "Come on in and have some corn flakes with us. They're particularly flavorful this time of year. Robust! With just a challenging hint of spice to tantalize the palate."

"Funny man," his mother-in-law said. The kids waved goodbye and went upstairs to bathe and dress and make themselves unavailable for the rest of the day.

Frank saw no reason why he could not be cordial to anyone in the world. He knew precisely how he would be able to repay three thousand a month. He'd say he was on a corn flakes diet. Instead of stopping at the coffee shop every morning, he'd save the money. Instead of going out for lunch, he'd save the money. Cornflakes with peaches, strawberries, bananas, or even just raisins. "By the way," he said, "I have to sign off on a contract after dinner. I'll only be gone an hour or two. I forgot to mention it yesterday."

He went into the den and turned on a basketball game. Doug joined him. So did Doug's children. One stood in front of the screen and shouted, "What the Sam Hill is the key they keep talking about? I don't see any key." Frank did not answer. He had tuned them out. "What's the key, huh? Why do they keep talking about a key?"

The other one shouted back a comment. "What a stupid game. You're really stupid for watching a stupid game!"

"Ten months of corn flakes," Frank was thinking. "Please God let it be only ten months of corn flakes that my idiocy cost me."

He spent the day in blissful prayer and contemplation. Doug was staying for dinner. He was ordering six pizzas and a whole case of Cokes. Gwen's mother had already brought an assortment of pints of high quality ice cream for dessert.

At 5 p.m. he checked the trunk of his car to be sure his briefcase - the case that held the fifty thousand dollars in cash - was still there. He opened the case to be doubly sure. It was all there. He closed the case and carried it to the front seat. And then he drove to Joliet to keep his appointment with the chip cashier at the Sweetwater Casino.

At 7 p.m. he sat in the lounge and a waiter delivered a sealed envelope to him. He opened it and read: *Take the elevator to the tenth floor and leave the package in the big ashtray between the elevator doors. Then get back into the elevator before the doors have a chance to close.* A heavy cotton bag accompanied the envelope. He tipped the waiter, put the chips into the bag, went to the elevators, entered one that was standing open, pushed the tenth floor button, stepped out of the doors when they opened, put the cotton pouch in the ashtray, stepped back into the elevator, went up to the fifteenth floor to pick up someone who had just rung for it, and rode down to the ground floor again. It was all over. He left the casino and went home. The only thing he wanted was to find Doug's car gone.

Doug, the two monster-kids, and his mother-in-law were not at his house. Frank parked in the driveway and felt like skipping to the front door.

MONDAY, MAY 13, 2013

Frank Goodrich intended to dispose of the photographs in the men's room. He had feared tearing them into little pieces and tossing them into someone's trash in case one of the ubiquitous surveillance cameras would record the disposal. He did not want to do it in his own toilet for fear that some fluke in the plumbing would regurgitate one of the pieces that he couldn't explain. But the toilets in his office flushed with more verve than his own. They would do the job. He pulled into his place in the multi-floored parking garage next to his office building. Dolph was waiting for him and Dolph did not look happy.

"What's up?" Frank asked, getting out of his car.

Dolph handed him the ring box. "Zircons," he said. "You've been had, but you ain't gonna have me. I'm on the hook for a hundred and five big ones. I did you a favor and now you're gonna do me one and take my place on that hook. Hugo expects me to pay in 60 days. He don't wanna know more than that."

Frank opened the ring box and stared at the rings. "It was his jeweler who said they were real diamonds! I didn't examine them." His hands began to tremble. "I paid the debts we owed last night. Everything went smoothly at the pay-off. How did the stones get switched?"

"Maybe when Waverly went to the ladies room... you know... when she suddenly felt like throwing up."

"Maybe the jeweler switched them. He had them in his hands and they were out of our sight..."

"The jeweler is Hugo's cousin. Don't even give that possibility a split second of thought. I'll pretend I didn't hear you say it. If you say it again and somebody hears it, you're a dead man."

Frank looked at the rings again and leaned against his car for support. "She's probably back in Cheyenne now. She works at the University."

"What kind of asshole are you, Frank? She said she'd be going back to Cheyenne on Sunday afternoon. Well, she checked out of the hotel five minutes after we dropped her off there on Saturday. I took my wife out to dinner last night. The rings looked good under those night-club spot lights. So do rhinestones. But when she woke up this morning and looked at them in the sunlight, they didn't look so bright. Her sister comes over and says, 'These ain't diamonds, girl. Dolph's been played.' I already talked to Hugo and we showed them to his cousin. He says they're good quality zircons. He'd give me a hundred bucks for the pair."

"I can't believe this. I don't understand what the hell is going on."

"You better start thinking, Frank. I'm gonna call the loan in and for scammin' Hugo, his cousin, and me, you'll be lucky if we don't come after your widow for the money. Keep the rings. They're on me. When you think up a way to solve the problem, call me. I'll be waitin' for your call." He turned and walked to the elevators, leaving Frank speechless.

Frank slowly went to his office. He barely acknowledged his secretary's greeting. When she came into his office to review the day's events with him, he waved her off. "Shut the door," he called. "And see that I'm not disturbed."

He called the University of Wyoming. Waverly Bryant did not work there. Neither did her husband. He did a net search for Waverly Bryant. There was a woman by that name who lived at the correct address; but she was 80 years old. Was Waverly in on the photography scam, too? Was he up against two thieves or only one? He buzzed his secretary. "Get Martin Mazzavini on the phone for me. Tell his secretaries it's urgent."

The office phone was ringing as Beryl Tilson returned from having lunch with George at the health food store.

She answered the call. There were no witty opening lines between her and Martin Mazzavini. He was grim. "I'm sitting here with a client who has problems. Can you come here immediately?"

"Does it sound like a two-man problem? We're breaking in a new operative. If you think we need him, I can try to find out if he's available."

"Go ahead. I think we'll need him for this mess."

While Martin waited on the line, Beryl called the temple and asked Akara if he wanted to go on assignment in Chicago. He answered with an enthusiastic,"Yes!"

"Hold on," Beryl told him and again spoke to Martin. "When do you want us?"

"I'm making reservations for the two of you now. Your flight leaves Philadelphia at 1:30 p.m. American Air. We'll meet you at the gate. Don't bother to pack. You can get stuff here. You better hurry. Ciao."

"Akara!" Beryl switched to her iPhone. "Get down here immediately! I'll get George to take us to the airport."

Martin Mazzavini's law firm, Mazzavini O'brian Mazzavini, had been the corporate attorneys of the company for which Frank Goodrich worked. It was not until young Martin got out of law school and expressed a desire to practice criminal law that his father and grandfather expanded into this otherwise neglected area of jurisprudence. Through the corporate connections, Martin and Frank Goodrich had become good friends.

Now, as criminal attorney and client, they waited nervously at the gate for two business class passengers - who looked more like they belonged in steerage - to come down the jetway. Akara's jeans were tattered at the knees and the hems at the rear of the pants' legs of Beryl's low-cut jeans were flattened a half-inch by dragging under the heels of her tennis shoes.

"Armani meets the Flintstones!" Beryl said as Martin hugged her.

Beryl began the introduction ritual. "This is my associate, Dr. Akara Chatree, a PhD in computer science and a Zen Buddhist priest."

When everyone knew everyone else's name, Martin asked, "Did you remember to bring your contract forms?"

"Yes. Where do you want to talk?"

"Anywhere private," Frank said.

"Let's go to my apartment," Martin said, and led them out into the temporary parking lot to get into his car.

When they were finally seated around Martin's kitchen table, Frank reviewed the entire weekend's events. Beryl then began the interview. Akara took notes in a little blue spiral tablet.

"How old would you guess Waverly was? And did she have any distinguishing marks... moles, tattoos, scars?"

"Twenty-five. I could be wrong. No marks."

"Jewelry or watch?"

"No watch. She did wear a gold chain around her neck. It had some kind of disk pendant... about an inch wide. There was engraving on it but I didn't look at it closely enough to tell you what it said or what it represented."

"Since, ultimately, you're on the hook for the money, let's say that she conned you out of $55,000 in the car and $50,000 in the Casino."

Frank protested. "That's only true if Waverly was involved in the photography. We don't know that! She was a victim, too."

Beryl sighed impatiently. "She was involved, Frank. Do not doubt it."

Martin said, "You heard the lady. I would have considered the possibility that these were two discrete events. But she's the expert. I, for one, know better than to contradict her. Waverly was in on the photography. That is now a fact we have to deal with."

Beryl asked, "Did her hair look artificially colored?"

"She had blonde hair."

"Was it dark at the crown... all the way around the crown of her head and lighter at the ends, or was it uniform in color?"

"Uniform."

Beryl nodded to Akara. "A bleached blonde." She turned to Frank. "What color of eyes and what was her general complexion?"

"She had blue eyes and her skin was light... like my wife's."

"Any marks of sun tan? And how tall would you guess she was?"

"No tan lines. About five feet six."

"Did she speak with any kind of regional accent?"

"She said a couple of words funny... she said 'orange' as though it were one syllable. Ornge. A couple of words she said like that."

"Southwest," Beryl said to Akara who noted it in the tablet.

"The man who came in to photograph you. Tell me what he looked like."

"He had an obvious wig on... a cheap black shoulder-length wig and he wore an animal mask... it looked like a mouse or rat. I guess he was about six feet tall... well built... like a male model."

"Did you see his hands? His teeth? His lips and chin? His eyes behind the mask?"

"He wore latex gloves - the thin kind, like a surgeon's. I think his teeth were straight... at least I'm sure none was missing. His lips were like normal... like Marty's. He had the mouth and chin of a good looking man. I'm pretty sure his eyes were light colored... blue or grey... maybe hazel. He had a French accent."

"Do you have any dramatic or linguistic training, such that you could, with a knowledgeable ear, detect a fake French accent from a real one?"

"No. It sounded French, but it could have been an act. I wouldn't be able to tell. And he knew how to look up a person's own phone number on his iPhone."

"Try to remember the skin on his neck. Was it creased or sagging?"

"No. It was like Marty's or Akara's. Tight... the skin of a younger man, but the way he spoke was not with a kid's voice. He didn't use any unusual words... he pronounced 'rather' like 'rah-zer' and he said 'importune' like 'amportune' - aside from that I don't remember anything unusual."

"Did you see the camera? Was it like a cellphone, an iPad, a video camera, or a regular single-shot camera?"

"A regular one. It was on a strap around his neck. But I didn't recognize the brand."

Beryl looked at Akara. "Get out your iPad and call up high-end cameras. This guy is a pro and he'll want high quality prints from a reliable camera. He wouldn't have used anything cheap." She asked Frank to look at all the cameras Akara showed him and to see if he could recognize the one that the man used. When shown the Hasselblad Digital, he responded, "That looks like it."

"Top of the line," Martin said. "He must be a pro."

"Now," Beryl said, "let's compare what you've told us against what the pictures reveal." Frank had not wanted to show anyone the pictures, but he had shown Martin who had put them in his briefcase, promising him that he wouldn't show them to anyone without his permission.

"Ok to show them?" Martin asked Frank, who nodded his assent.

Beryl and Akara made no comment about the content. "Check bleached hair and blue eyes. Her pubic hair is not very dark. She's probably a natural blonde whose hair got dark as she grew up. She has calloused toes... probably a corn problem. She'll have seen a podiatrist. She hasn't had any breast augmentation that I can detect."

"Let's get an image pro to enlarge the disk on her chain. Maybe we can get a readout... if we think we'll need it."

"I don't want anyone else to see these images," Frank protested.

Martin calmed him. "I'll make copies of the photos and we'll cut out the actual disks from the originals. We'd lose resolution in the copies. But we need the photos." He looked through the pictures. "Only two of them show that disk in any detail."

"Then go ahead," Frank reluctantly consented. Beryl nodded her approval.

"Well," Martin asked Beryl, "what do you think?"

"Frank must reveal everything to his wife. Everything."

"No way!" Frank objected. "I can't do it. I just can't do it. It will cost me everything."

"Frank," Beryl said gently, "it has already cost you just about all you can lose. They have the pictures. The only thing you've got going for you is that one of them is in the pictures, so they won't be quick to use them. But we don't know how ruthless this guy is. If he's afraid of getting caught because his partner - or one of his partners, since we don't know how many people we're dealing with - is recognizable, he can kill her off and not have to worry about seeing her arrested for extortion. They move around. He can dispose of her in a thousand ways and not have to worry about the dangers her face in those photos present.

"You're standing in the middle of a shooting range. And you will be standing there for years with shots being fired all around you and you don't know when you'll be hit."

"For what my opinion's worth," Martin said, "I agree. Tell your wife the truth. Then together you can figure out how to pay the money back."

"I can't tell her. I can't bear to think of what she'll say... of what my kids and my in-laws will say. No. I wouldn't even know where to start."

"Then let me talk to her woman-to-woman. I can't move forward with anything unless she knows what's going on. This is my way of saying that for so long as she doesn't know, she's at risk. So are your kids. I'm not gonna have that on my conscience. You've gotten mixed up with dangerous people and your wife has a right to be warned. Get her on the phone and tell her we're coming by and to be alone for the next few hours."

"The kids got an extra day off from school. They're home."

"Akara can show them tricks on the computer while I talk to her, and you and Marty can wait outside until it's safe to come in."

Marty handed him his cellphone. "Call her."

Frank spoke to his wife. His voice registered abject fear. He disconnected the call. "She's alone now. Let's go."

Beryl gathered the photographs to take with her.

Gwen Goodrich answered the door. She looked at the two sloppily dressed individuals and incredulously asked, "Did my husband send you? What is going on?"

"Mrs. Goodrich," Beryl began, gesturing with a large manila envelope, "may I present Dr. Akara Chatree, a private investigator with my firm,

Wagner & Tilson." She handed her two business cards: hers and Martin Mazzavini's. "Out there, in that Caddy by the curb, sit your husband and his attorney, Mr. Martin Mazzavini. As soon as I tell you what you need to be told, they'll come in. Are your children home?"

"No. They're visiting friends in the neighborhood."

Beryl asked Akara to wait in the dining room while she followed Gwen Goodrich into the living room. Gwen repeated, "What is going on?"

"First," Beryl said, "I want to explain that a few hours ago I was in Philadelphia, getting ready to clean my office, when Martin called and told me that Akara and I had forty-five minutes to get to the airport and get on a flight he had booked for us about this matter. I have no luggage with me and I was not exactly prepared to travel. That said, I'll continue."

Gwen stared at her, unable to detect the slightest clue about the matter, although she wondered about the manila envelop that Beryl held.

"All men," Beryl began, "are idiots. Some are rarely idiots; some are often idiots; and some are consistently and at all times idiots. Do you agree with that?"

"I don't know."

"I do. Your husband is in the first category. He loves you desperately but since he is a man he is also an idiot. In a very rare moment he made a terrible mistake. This is not a small mistake. This is a big one. Martin Mazzavini, as you know, is not your neighborhood attorney. He's a very high priced attorney, but he's here more as a good friend, today."

"Why does my husband need Martin?" Fear had come into her voice. Beryl was gratified to hear it.

"Frank made a dreadful mistake and sought his counsel because when you make a big mistake you need a powerful lawyer to fight for your side. Marty's sitting out there now... free of charge... he actually went to the personal expense of flying Dr. Chatree and me here, in business class yet, because he knows and admires and respects Frank. And Frank's in trouble. So I came to investigate the trouble and my first response was, 'Tell your wife the truth.' I don't think you should be left in the dark about this."

"What is it?"

"Last Friday night Frank had a dinner appointment with one of the men in the convention. I don't know who it was. He can tell you. Frank had dinner reservations for two, and while he waited at the bar, quietly getting drunk as he looked at his watch, the man called and regretted that he couldn't make it. Frank thought the news added to the angst he's been feeling about what he perceives as your father's desire to replace him in his position with the business, and the competition from your brothers - I don't know any of these details - and from what he perceives is your mother's desire to replace him here at home with a gentleman named Doug.

"Men, as I've already said, are given to fanciful thoughts. They can't always distinguish real from false. So when he was stood up by his friend and he was a little drunk - I think you know what's coming next."

"A woman."

"Right. Not just a woman, though. A con artist. And in all my years of criminal investigation, a damned fine con artist. One of the best I've ever come across. She played him as a virtuoso would. He didn't want his reservation for two to go to waste, so he invited her to dine with him. After all, she wore a lanyard and photo I.D. around her neck. He thought she was a colleague, a research assistant from the University of Wyoming... interested in robotics. She said her name was Waverly Bryant and there is in fact, in Cheyenne, Wyoming, a Waverly Bryant living at the address she gave. The real Ms. Bryant is 80 years old. So we begin with identity theft.

"She told your semi-drunk husband that she had a shaky marriage and everything was in her 'professor' husband's name except her wedding and engagement ring. She kept the rings in her purse, but when they got up to dance, she didn't want to leave her rings in her purse there on the table so she put them on. All eighty thousand dollars worth of diamonds."

"My God! What are you telling me?"

"The diamonds are as nothing compared to the rest. Still a little drunk and very vulnerable, he took her to a cottage type suite the business maintains on Lakeshore Drive."

"Yes. I know the place."

"He was in bed with her and a man came in and photographed them and then sent him copies of the photos - terrible photos - and demanded that Frank pay blackmail. Waverly claimed to have gotten a set of photos, too. Frank was to pay $30,000 and she was to pay $20,000. Waverly claimed to be penniless, except for her rings. Frank's friend Dolph lent him $30,000, and the good Waverly got some of Frank's associates to buy the rings for $75,000 - except she switched the diamond rings with Zircon fakes. The blackmail payoff was to be made at an Indian casino near Joliet. Frank took his $30K and the $20K that Waverly gave him, and made the payoff. Dolph wanted to give the diamond rings to his wife, and in the morning light the obvious switch was detected, and now Frank has to pay back the money... all $105,000 of it. He didn't make the switch and technically he is not involved in *that* crime; but his associates do not care to be fair about it. The debt is his. The worry about you seeing the photographs is his. The fear that he will be replaced by Doug is his, as is the fear that he will lose his job and every material thing he owns which, I can tell you, means nothing compared to losing you. He is wracked with shame. Martin knows the kind of people Frank has been involved with, and he fears for all your lives which is why he brought me here. You are the aggrieved party. As I see it you have the right to respond in any way you wish. You can be a divorcee, a widow, or you can forgive him. It's up to you."

"Are those the pictures you're holding?"

Beryl acted as though the photographs were much worse than they were. "Yes. I'll show them to you if you're sure you want to see these dreadful images."

"Show them to me."

Beryl handed her the envelope. Gwen looked at each one and then put them all back into the envelope. "He really is an idiot. You're right about that. One look at her and I can see 'con' written all over her face. What should I do?"

"All I can say is if you divorce him, make it a clean break and let him visit the children... don't keep them away from him. I don't think he'll survive losing you. He has no chance at all if he loses the three of you."

"I would never do that," Gwen countered.

"And if you decide to forgive him, you have to become his partner in solving this problem... you have to be prepared to face down that bitch in the photographs if she ever shows her face... and you'll have to help him get out of the debt he owes a mysterious gentleman from Colombia."

"What is the debt again?"

"One hundred and five thousand dollars... if he doesn't pay it, they'll kill him... or maybe break his legs... I don't know what these people are capable of."

"Oh, dear God!" She began to cry. Beryl handed her a tissue. "And he's waiting outside now?"

"Yes."

"Tell him to come in and tell me to my face what he's done."

Beryl got up and went to the front door and signaled them to come in.

Gwen sat stiffly in a chair. Frank came in and dropped to his knees in front of her and began to sob like a baby. At first, Gwen did not touch him, but his remorse was so disconcerting, that she had to touch his hair. He blubbered explanations that were unintelligible, he huffed, and shuddered, and wailed, and gasped.

Beryl looked at Martin. "This is like being bound to a chair and having to watch a puppy drown." Frank finally raised his head, revealing the mess of snot, saliva and tears he had left in her lap. Beryl took her the pocket pack of tissues.

Akara whispered, "Geez, he's really sorry. No fakin' there."

Frank Jr. suddenly came through the front door. "What's goin' on?" he asked, alarmed.

"Your father has done a very bad thing," Gwen said.

"What? Like treason?" He was serious.

Frank stood up. "Come here," he said, and as Frank Jr. got within grasping distance, Frank hugged him. It was an awkward moment. "Where's your sister?" Frank asked. "I want to tell her I love her."

"For god's sake, Dad, Patrice is right behind me with two of her friends. Don't let her see you like this when she's with her friends. She'll die. Go sit on a chair."

The front door opened as Patrice entered with her chattering friends. "Dad! What are you doing home so early?" she asked.

Gwen answered, "If you must know, we're meeting with the caterers to plan our anniversary party. Now stop interrupting." The girls giggled and went upstairs.

Akara took Frank Junior by the arm. "Let me show you a few tricks on the old computer. What system are you runnin'?" They left the room together.

"Frank," Gwen said, "Enough. A hundred five thousand and now you've just about ruined this dress. I hope the cleaner can get it all out."

Gwen Goodrich seemed to have resolved all of the problems during Frank's abasement. She made Frank sit on the couch and promise to be silent. "First," she said, "I'll make it clear that Doug is never to set foot in this house again. If my mother doesn't like it, she can stay away too. I will tell my father that he either makes you CEO, and stipulates that you are to succeed him as president or we will move to Cleveland and you can take that job you were offered there...or another job any place else. Tomorrow morning we will go to the bank and cash in our U.S. savings bonds and some other securities we can liquidate easily, and tomorrow you will pay off your friends and get a receipt or have two reliable witnesses to the transaction. The kids hate prep school and would much prefer to go to high school here at home, so that will save us a bundle in tuition. All this accommodates your interests, Frank. I have my own. I want the woman in these photographs caught. I'll pay for the investigation, but I want her to be put in the same room with me. For six years I've taken self-defense classes to keep in shape. Now I have other plans for those katas. That's all I have to say. Find them and bring them to justice... my justice."

Martin called Akara who came into the room with an ebullient Frank Junior. "Mom! Dad! You should see what he did! He hacked into the academy's records and I saw what all my teachers had to say about me. I thought my math teacher was a real dick, but he says I have great potential. The rest gave me a passing grade but said I lacked polish. I hate that school. I don't wanna go back." The adults all looked at each other, not knowing what to say.

"Sorry about that," Akara said sheepishly.

Beryl finally went to Gwen and whispered, "I told you they were all idiots. It's not a question of kind. It's merely one of degree and frequency."

"I believe you," Gwen said, and then she asked, "Don't I have to sign a contract?"

"No," Martin answered, "your husband is my client and the investigators are under an agency agreement with me."

"Ok," she called. "Just send him the bill when it's ready."

They all waved goodbye. Akara, Beryl, and Martin got into Martin's car. When the doors were shut, Martin said, "Tell me that you didn't change any grades when you hacked into the school's computer."

"Not a jot or a tittle," Akara replied. "And I didn't let him see how I did it."

TUESDAY, MAY 14, 2013

Beryl and Akara sat in Martin's office. They had gone to an all night Wal-Mart and purchased new shirts and jeans. They displayed, Martin insisted, sartorial splendor - compared to how they looked when they got off the plane. He, too, wore western attire.

From two of the photographs, Martin had cut out the pendant that was on the gold chain Waverly had worn. He had given them to an expert in image clarification. The image showed something circular and possibly a Cross inside. He could not raise the image to a higher degree of definition.

"Ok. Where do you want to start?" Martin asked.

"Cheyenne," Beryl said. "It's one thing for an identity thief to steal while hidden behind the curtain of internet distance. They buy over the net or they put some disguising make-up on, a wig, and glasses and empty out your bank account at ATM machines. But when they've stolen an identity and intend to use it in public, to shake hands and say, 'Hi, I'm Jane Doe from Peoria,' they usually know that the real Jane Doe isn't going to walk in and disrupt the impersonation. We've got to find out how the fake Waverly Bryant came to know the real one."

"It'll take us a little over two hours to fly there. We know where she lives, so with any luck we'll be home tonight."

"Here's a key to my apartment," Martin said, removing a key from his key ring. "If you get home in time, let's all have dinner with my grandfather. We'll go down to Joliet to that Indian Casino that Frank went to for the payoff. We can kill two birds with one stone. They have a western-style restaurant and saloon, and the old man wants to show off his line dancing. He's been practicing."

"Is he askin' me out on a date? I don't know... it sounds like he's askin' me out on a date." She quipped, quoting *A Few Good Men*. "Ok. There are a few things you could do here. Can you get one of your investigators to find out whatever he can about Waverly Bryant's stay in Chicago? Get a copy of her phone and room charges. Maybe her mouse-faced partner ate dinner with her. The staff may know something." Beryl stood up. "We'll take a cab to the airport and another cab when we get back."

"Do me a favor? Call me and let me know when your flight gets in. I'll pick you up at the airport."

Tuesday, at noon, the bus from Las Vegas stopped in Tonopah and discharged the last of its passengers, Niles Portmann among them.

He carried several cans of carburetor cleaner and a gas additive, and at the edge of the bus station's parking lot, he worked on his truck for half an hour. Then he drove home to find his wife, two deer quarters, and the Buick gone. He walked around the house dazed. He didn't know what he expected to find in the house, but something told him that he would feel terrible if something had happened to Aleta and she had lain critically ill in one of the rooms that he had neglected to look in.

In her bedroom he found a pair of tennis shoes, old ones that she had recently worn. There was blood on them... downward drips... a few drops, nothing more; and in her bathroom trash can he found a few bloodied bandages. He correctly assumed that she had cut her hand while cutting the deer quarters into smaller pieces. He returned to the kitchen and looked at the likely place that she had cut herself. In front of the sink he saw drops of dried blood and he reasoned that, yes, she must have cut herself when she was cutting the quarters into more manageable pieces. He muttered resentfully, "I guess her new boyfriend doesn't like to get his hands dirty." Then he remembered that he had forgotten to ask her about the barbed wire Crown of Thorns. He sat at the table and cursed himself for having forgotten to buy some groceries in town.

And then, suddenly, he got what he would later call, "a brainstorm." He said to himself, "This is perfect. Nobody knows she was going with the preacher. She told me that she kept that quiet. So I'll report her missing. The crooks in Tonopah are still making money selling horse meat and they want nothing better then to pin another crime on me. When they come to question me about her absence, I'll leave her bloody tennis shoes in an open trash can out front. That will really start their juices flowing. I hope it's that bastard Becker who finds her blood on the kitchen floor. He'll grill me again like he did the last time, and he'll lie and cheat and enjoy doing it. He'll do everything he can to railroad me, and then when she turns up safe and sound just preaching the Gospels, I'll sue him for false-arrest. It will be my turn to make him squirm and spend his money trying to defend himself.

He decided first to bury the bloody bandages that had been in her bathroom trash can and then to go into Tonopah and phone her parents in St. George, purporting to be looking for Aleta. They would say that she wasn't with them, and then he would call the sheriff's station to report her missing. And then, to help the process along, he'd go to Death Valley Junction and anonymously call in a tip that he had killed his wife and dumped her body down a mine shaft.

The perfect way to make an anonymous phone call would have been to use a voice altering device; but no local stores carried such a specialized piece of equipment. A well-disguised accent with something that would muffle the mouthpiece would work, especially if he recorded the one line he needed. He got an old cassette player and practiced saying, "That Niles Portmann has been bragging that he killed his two-timing wife and threw her down a mine shaft in Ryolite where she'll never be found." When he played the piano in the prison band they had done the highlights of *My Fair Lady*. Various cons had sung the leading roles using a British accent. The band even sang a chorus of many songs during the performance. He'd have to change his intonation and make his voice "creeky" like an old-timer's voice. He practiced and soon was able to say the line with what he thought was an acceptable British accent. He repeated it a few dozen times and then made a fresh recording that he would use when he called the Sheriff's station.

He got into his truck and drove to Tonopah, called St. George, learned that Aleta was not with her parents and that they did not know where she was, and then he called Sheriff Alex Hornsby's office to report Aleta missing. The Sheriff told him to give her another twenty-four hours to get back and that she'd probably turn up by then.

Niles thanked Hornsby for his encouraging words and drove to a gas station in Death Valley Junction and called the Sheriff's station again. He did not realize that the sheriff had recently installed a recording system. Had he known, it would have made no difference. The euphoria he felt at the prospects of getting even made him see probabilities where no possibilities existed. He was completely confident that his voice disguise could not be traced back to him. He stood outside at the pay phone and played the single recording of his one line accusation.

The sheriff and the deputies played the recording repeatedly, each time laughing at the voice they were certain was Niles. Why, they wondered, would he have made such a call? What was he trying to accomplish by accusing himself of killing his wife? They knew the source of the call and immediately the one deputy that Niles hated, Deputy Bill Becker, drove to Death Valley Junction and interviewed the gas station attendant and obtained a statement that Niles was present when the call was made.

The deputies had also known that in Tonopah, Aleta's car had been parked at the far side of the gas station, obscured by a pile of used tires. This fact had not been known by Niles.

Satisfied that he had set the trap, he returned home to wait for the deputy to come. He put a box of trash outside in the gutter of the road and made sure that Aleta's bloody tennis shoes were easily noticed on top. The knife he had used to gut the deer was now in the kitchen under a pile of bags that contained salts and other chemicals used to preserve the deer hide. He'd leave it there for them to find.

He went upstairs and watched the road from a bedroom window. In half an hour, two cars kicked up dust as they approached his house.

He watched the deputy find the tennis shoes and put them in an evidence bag. He put the whole trash box in the trunk of his car. Deputy Becker knocked on the front door. Niles answered, "What do you want?"

"We'd like to come in and talk to you about Aleta. You reported her missing."

"Well, I haven't found her yet, and you're not coming in... unless you've got a warrant."

The deputy, afraid that if he seemed too aggressive, Niles would hide evidence, turned and left quietly. He spoke to the driver of the second car and immediately the car turned around and headed back to town, no doubt, Niles thought, to get a warrant.

It was a lovely spring day in Cheyenne, breezy as it often is, but warm and filled with the colors of blooming trees.

Beryl and Akara got out of the cab and smiled at the old lady who was rocking on her front porch getting some "after lunch sun," she said, inviting them to join her.

"Miss Bryant?" Beryl called. "Miss Waverly Bryant?"

"Indeed I am. Come and tell me what I can do for you."

Akara thought that she was sincerely friendly - the kind of disposition that someone evil could take advantage of. As they came to her porch and sat beside her, rocking, too, she rang a dinner bell, summoning a houseboy and ordering iced tea for the three of them. "Now," said the real Waverly Bryant, "what brings you to my house?"

"Someone in Chicago recently used your name and address. She had a credit card in your name and possibly charged some hotel expenses to your account. We've just begun our investigation."

"Oh, dear. It's happening again. A couple of months ago a bill came for one of my boarders for eight hundred dollars. She protested to the credit card company and they took it off her bill. It was for two nights at a ski lodge in Lake Tahoe. The poor woman's been in a wheelchair for the last ten years. She wasn't likely to go skiing. She had some smaller bills from credit card companies that she didn't even have an account with. And now, you're saying, my name's been used?"

"I'm afraid so," Beryl said. "But that at least begins a measurement for a window of opportunity. My experience tells me that the person doing this knows you personally or has had access to your social security number. You have a boarding house. Perhaps it was a boarder."

"Nearly all of my boarders have been with me for years. And they are on the elderly side and don't do much traveling around."

"What about hired hands? Gardeners or cleaning ladies or laundresses?"

"My church sends over younger women, some of them single with kids, and they help out once a week. We have an institutional caterer come every day to deliver dinner. It's awful stuff, but you don't have to clean the greasy stove and pans."

"Who has access to your mail? Does your social security check get deposited directly into the bank or does it come here?"

"Here."

"Before several months ago - before the first credit card identity theft occurred - did you always bring in the mail? Think back. The box is pretty far from the front door. Maybe when it snowed..."

"Now that you mention it, last winter I had a Christian group as tenants in the house next door that I rent out month-to-month. I keep it that way so that if we don't get along with the people we can get them out faster. They regularly got the mail for me. But these were wonderful people. They wore pioneer dresses and I told them to come back again for Frontier Days at the end of July."

"Tell me about them."

"They were a group of sisters - not biological sisters - but, they said, 'Sisters in Christ.' No children. Just a pastor... a nice lookin' fella they called Father... Father... I'll call Jasper out here. He'll know." She rang the tinkling dinner bell and the houseboy appeared in the doorway.

"You wanted me?"

"Do you recall the name of that Christian group who stayed in the house for a month last winter... in January?"

"The ladies belonged to The Sisters of Gethsemane Garden and the man was their pastor by the name of Avery Christian. The pastor said

64

that his mother gave him a special name since you could say, 'A Very Christian kind of man.'"

"Where were they from" Beryl asked.

"They went all over and they were from all over, but the car they drove was a big Cadillac Escalade and it had Utah plates."

"They left a book for us to read," Miss Bryant recalled. "An elderly pastor wrote it. Pastor Marlowe... Lamont Marlowe. He had died in 2011 they said. We showed his book to our pastor and he lent it to someone who left it out on the porch and ruined it when it rained. It had to be thrown out. A broken gutter spout just squirted so much water down on it that the pages were mush. Those sisters were all so sweet... plain with those old fashioned dresses. We had a lady tenant who asked them where their bustles were. I told her to be quiet."

"Did they have a logo? You know, an insignia that they used just for their group?"

"If they did, I didn't see it," Ms. Bryant said.

Beryl removed the cut-out face of the fake Waverly Bryant. "Do you recognize this girl?"

"I don't have my glasses on, but Jasper would know. Show him."

Jasper recognized her. "Yes, she was one of them, but I don't know her name. They were like the Seven Dwarfs with their names. One was Sister Prudence. One was Sister Faith. There was a Sister Charity. Names like that; but I never put a name onto any one of them. But she sure does look like the woman."

"Did they leave anything behind that might have their fingerprints on it?" Beryl asked.

"No, they cleaned out the house good. And it's been painted inside and out since they left."

"Do you know what they were doing here in town?"

"Visiting congregation members. They said they often go to a town to help someone who had to care for an Alzheimer's patient, to give the person a break. They'd take the patient on long drives. Same thing with young mothers who had a new baby. They go and clean house and watch the baby while the mother took a day to go shopping or to visit friends."

Beryl thanked her for the information and left her card. "If you think of anything else, or if you hear from them again - which I personally doubt - don't hesitate to call. And reverse the charges. That's the least we can do."

Akara called a cab.

When the car returned, Becker and two other deputies pushed Niles aside, handed him the warrant, and forced him to wait outside while they and a forensics' tech came in and searched anything that was relevant to the demise of Aleta Thurman Portmann. The bloody knife that Niles had used was taken into evidence and samples of the blood on the floor in the kitchen were also taken. Niles was told that he could come in willingly "like a man" or stay there and wait for a warrant for his arrest to be issued.

Niles went with them to the station.

He jauntily refused counsel. "I've spent enough money on lawyers," he laughed. "You guys have vivid imaginations." He insisted that he had not seen her since Saturday and that Sunday he had taken the bus to Las Vegas and had not returned until noon of that day, Tuesday. When he found that she was not home, he went into town and called her parents and when she wasn't there, he called the Sheriff's station to report her missing.

It was after 10 p.m. He pretended to be tired. They asked if he would prefer to sleep there in an open cell and finish questioning him in the morning. He agreed to stay.

Niles hoped that someone would falsify evidence... *that* would be a criminal offense. He'd give all that he owned to see Becker jailed... Becker, the deputy who was married to Joe Gregory's sister... Gregory, the man whose jaw he broke and who nearly bankrupted him for the pleasure of doing it.

"I will even the score," he told himself as he finally fell asleep.

When they were picked up at the airport, Beryl insisted that Akara sit up front in Martin's Cadillac so that she could sit in the back seat with his grandfather, her favorite dance partner and famous corporate attorney, Massimiliano Mazzavini.

They giggled about Martin's love life and dished the latest news about the Calvino family, subject of the investigation that Wagner & Tilson Private Investigators had once conducted in Chicago for Martin.

In the hour it took them to drive to Joliet, they discussed the results of their separate investigations. Martin's investigators had learned nothing about the fake Waverly Bryant. Beryl's trip to Cheyenne, however, yielded considerable information.

When they were seated in the Casino's lounge, one of Martin's investigators came to their booth and revealed that he had spoken to the head of hotel-casino security who had shown him security camera views of Frank Goodrich buying fifty thousand dollars worth of five hundred dollar chips and receiving a note while he sat in the lounge and entered the elevator which he momentarily left to place the bag of casino chips outside the elevator and immediately returned and then left the casino. Footage showed him getting into his car in the parking lot. The tenth floor security cam showed a Stetson-hatted man pick the bag up from the large ashtray that stood between the elevator doors. His face was obscured by the hat's brim and no one at the reception desk remembered anyone having checked wearing a Stetson hat. The investigator did obtain a photo of the man picking up the bag of casino chips. Since literally thousands of people walked through the lobby of the impressive hotel-casino, it was impossible to locate a man whose face they had never seen before.

Beryl, though exhausted, found the energy to dance several times with the elder Mazzavini and while the rest applauded their performance, they curtseyed and bowed and called it a night.

In January, George had returned to his normal work schedule. As before, everyone knew not to mention Lilyanne Smith's name. For nearly

two months nothing changed. And then late in March, while Beryl was on a case in Suriname, George was searching her desk looking for an old form letter they used. He found an envelope on which was written "Herr und Frau Eric Haffner and the scion of the House of Haffner - Ha Ha. Cayman Islands 'vacation' January 2013." The envelope was hidden in the back of a drawer. He opened it and found three photographs. One photo was of Eric and Lilyanne, dressed in evening wear, posed in the doorway of a country club dining room. Lilyanne was smiling and Eric was transfigured - no longer the trig chauffeur or grubby wheelbarrow pusher that George remembered, but elegant, handsome, aristocratic. George's hands were trembling as he looked at the next photograph. Lilyanne, Eric, and Baby Eric were sitting on a couch. Eric was holding the baby as upright as a two month old baby could sit, on his knee. And a third photograph of the happy family wearing nautical garments. Father and baby son in white pants, navy blue double breasted jackets - and even caps. Lily in a white pleated skirt and navy blue jacket. They were standing before the wheel of a sailing ship. All three of them, even the baby, were more than smiling... they were laughing.

George's hands were shaking so badly that he had difficulty returning the photographs to the envelope. He replaced the hidden cache of photos and went back to his desk and propped up his face with his hands until his heart's beating slowed and softened. He sat there for nearly an hour and then he finally sighed deeply and returned to Beryl's desk to look for the form letter.

And then, a few weeks later, every morning a girl in the sangha began to deliver a box that contained three diamond-shaped pieces of baklava to the temple doorstep. Her family owned an upscale bakery. Akara naturally shared the pastries with Sensei and George. Sensei was also under severe romantic stress. He had not been able to locate the love of *his* life, Sonya Lee.

As they sat in the temple's little kitchen, they did not have to acknowledge the fact that comfort food served with commiseration was a far more pleasurable way to self-destruct than drugs or alcohol.

Only Akara found "a fly in the soup." The baklava presented a problem in reciprocity that he did not quite know how to solve. He thought the girl who gave the gift was nice, but definitely not his type. She was a computer geek... a nerd. His libido shivered. *Brrrr.* He wanted poetry; she recited specs. Maybe he'd take her to the movies.

WEDNESDAY, MAY 15, 2013

In Tonopah, the forensics' technician who tested the knife issued a report that stated that the blood on it belonged to a deer and no human blood was anywhere on the blade or handle. Fingerprints on the handle were exact matches to Niles Portmann. He put the report on the Sheriff's desk and went home.

At 7 a.m. Niles left his cell and went into Sheriff Alex Hornsby's office. Hornsby read the report and saw no reason to detain Niles. "Killed a deer, eh?" he asked.

"Yes," Niles replied, "it was eating Aleta's garden. She put up scarecrows - as if they were going to deter a ruminant from eating spinach and carrot tops. I'll be getting some wire to string around it... or maybe, since the sight of an animal hung up on wire upsets her, I'll build a fence around it. It'll be a big job. She's got half an acre planted."

"Well," the sheriff concluded, "we're still looking into a few things. So don't leave town. And I hope Aleta gets back safe and sound."

"How am I supposed to get home?" Niles asked. "Your guys brought me in. The least they can do is take me back."

"Don't you have keys to the Buick? It's parked behind the gas station."

"Aleta's Buick? I didn't know it was there."

"Let's look," the sheriff said, "At least I think it's hers. I saw it but didn't run the plates."

They walked to the gas station and saw the unlocked blue Buick parked behind a stack of used tires. Niles opened the driver's side door. "The seat's all the way forward," he said, "the way she always positioned it." He groped under the seat and felt the key ring she used. "Here are the keys," he said. "I'll be damned. I didn't know it was here."

The station attendant approached, saying, "I was wondering when this was gonna be picked up."

"There's a lot of dust on it," the sheriff noted. "How long's it been here?" He looked inside the Buick and found nothing amiss.

"Since Sunday, somewhere around noon."

"Did you see her park it?"

"No, I went out to lunch and when I got back it was there."

Niles offered an explanation. "She must have left it there when she got picked up by those Evangelicals. I don't know why they didn't pick her up at the house. They've been there before." He opened the trunk. "Nothing but a spare and a jack, here." He closed the trunk. "She must be with them. She got religion in a big way while I was upstate. She had plans to go preachin' with a group of ladies. Sisters of Gethsemane Garden. She didn't pick up the mail and didn't know I'd be home. I thought she ought to postpone the trip. I guess she didn't want an argument with me and left quietly."

Sheriff Hornsby put his hand on Niles' shoulder. "Cappy's Cafe is open. Why don't you get yourself some breakfast," he suggested.

Niles walked back towards the sheriff's office and then, when they came to the Cafe, he thanked the sheriff for telling him about the Buick and went inside.

Semi-retired attorney Liam MacDonald sat alone in a booth, and since the other booths were taken, he invited Niles to sit with him. "I heard Aleta's gone missing," he said.

Niles sat down. "She said she planned to go preachin' with her new Evangelical group. I didn't think she meant this week." The waitress came and he ordered a big breakfast. While he waited for his food to be brought to the table, Liam conveyed the latest hijinks of the "horse meat" gang.

Niles had eaten only half of his breakfast when Deputy Becker entered the cafe and stood at the booth, looking down to watch Niles eat.

"There's room at the counter," Liam said curtly, "if you want to sit down."

"Oh," the deputy said, "I'm just gonna wait until Niles swallows what's in his mouth and then I'm gonna take him in for questioning. Aleta's body is back in the morgue. She just got brought in. Highway patrol found her in a ditch and judging from the maggots in her, she was there awhile."

Niles looked up, not knowing if Becker was making a grotesque joke or whether he was stating the truth in the most crude way possible. He gulped down his mouthful of food and said nothing, leaving his mouth hanging open in confusion.

Becker continued, "We've called in an entomologist to give us an exact time that somebody dumped her naked body there. My guess is that she was dumped just when you supposedly went to Las Vegas. Funny coincidence, eh?" He then spoke harshly, and touched Niles' shoulder. "Let's go, Cowboy."

"Don't put your hands on him," Liam said, "unless you're effecting an arrest."

Niles was barely aware of what was happening. His mouth stayed open and he was not breathing. *"Let's go!"* Becker shouted. Niles slowly stood up. Liam went to the cashier and paid their checks.

Niles, confused and afraid, muttered frantically, "Stay with me, Liam."

His plan to trap Bill Becker had been created on the premise that Aleta was safe and sound. Now, he feared that he was the one who had stepped into his own trap.

When they entered the station, Liam said to the desk sergeant, "Put me down as Portmann's attorney of record." He went with the deputy and Niles towards an interrogation room.

Niles stopped walking. "I want to see my wife," he said.

"No, you don't," a lab technician countered. She looked at Liam, "Her body's not been cleaned up yet."

"Show the man!" Deputy Becker said, pushing open the door that led into the morgue. "Let him see his handiwork - or should I say 'knifework.'

We're testing the knife we found in your kitchen, and I wouldn't be surprised if the tech finds that it's got Aleta's DNA on it."

Liam grabbed Niles' arm and pulled him back. "Let's get this interview over with. You go in and sit down and say nothing. I'll go back and verify that it's Aleta."

"Where's Sheriff Hornsby?" Niles said unable to comprehend what was happening. "He told me the tests showed only deer blood."

Becker grinned malevolently. "That was somebody's opinion, my friend, not an actual test result. We're getting it tested now, along with the blood samples we found in your house. We're also looking into your attempt to divert our investigative resources with your stupid phone call, and a few other things." He lowered his voice to a whisper. "This time, Brother Niles, you're gonna go up and not all the bone marrow in the world is gonna get you out."

Beryl, Akara, and Martin sat in Martin's kitchen in the morning as Beryl began the formal presentation of the direction their investigation would take. "We're dealing with a pro, so we shouldn't expect rookie mistakes. She wouldn't have left any records unless it was for something routine. What we need now are Utah listings... property... eleemosynary organizations... tax exemptions... the usual stuff of residence. We need to find Pastor Avery Christian and The Sisters of Gethsemane Garden. We know they drive a black Cadillac Escalade, at least they did last winter. We need the list of Escalade owners.

Beryl asked Akara to access the list of licensed drivers in Utah. He connected his iPad to his "sixteen-server cluster" computer system back in his room in the Zen temple in Philadelphia and determined that there was no one by the name of Avery Christian licensed in Utah. No vehicles of any kind were registered to Avery Christian. "It's such a convenient name for a preacher," Akara said. "It's no doubt made up."

"But we have another problem," Beryl said. "The car had Utah plates. Getting the list of Escalade owners will not be easy to obtain."

Akara asked, "How are your printing capabilities here in the apartment?"

"I've got a laser black and white," Martin said.

"Get online and set up your printer while I access the lists."

"Can you get into DMV files?" Martin asked.

"If you give me a few minutes... I just have to finesse a few portals."

Beryl and Martin looked at each other and shrugged. Beryl solemnly announced, "As it says in *The Hagakure*, 'Continue to spur a running horse.'"

Akara worked while Beryl and Martin talked about business and pleasure. An hour later, Akara came into the kitchen with several long lists. "Let's clear the table," Akara said. "Here are several printouts. The first is a list of Utahans who are current owners of Escalades."

Martin looked at the list. "We're never going to get through this list tonight. I don't know how the hell to get started."

Beryl opened her laptop. "Let me tell you about a movie Lana Turner once made. In it she pretended to be a long-lost heiress who had been kidnapped as a child. According to the plot, the child's grief-stricken father put her favorite doll - a doll she constantly carried and even slept with - in a wall safe; and for fifteen years every few months some young woman would show up at his door claiming to be the missing heiress. The kidnapped little girl had a bedroom in which nothing had been touched in all that time. Her bedroom was huge and had windows on three sides; and along those windows, about a foot below them, was a running shelf that was lined with her dolls... dozens of dolls... all kinds of dolls. Whenever a young woman showed up claiming to be the long-lost heiress, the father would go to the safe, remove his daughter's favorite doll, place it among the others on the long shelf, and then ask the claimant to go into the room and pick out her favorite doll. Invariably the fake would-be heiress picked the wrong doll. But then it was Lana Turner's turn.

"She enters the room and starts at one end of the shelf. One by one she eliminates the dolls. 'This one is too big to be put in the safe. This one has too many hard edges to it and we know she slept with the doll.

This one is faded on the back so it has not been in the safe, but rather has been sitting out here with its back to the sun.' There were troublesome places... the spaces between the windows which did not sit directly in front of the sun-exposed glass. On the dolls that were positioned between the windows, it was still possible to see that one side of the dress was slightly faded by the sun as it moved seasonally through the year and struck the side at a slanted angle. So she continued. 'This one is slightly faded on the left... this one slightly faded on the right. This one is dressed too nicely - she never played with it to wrinkle its clothing.' She looked at each doll and continued on. 'Too new and unused; too faded; too hard edged; too big'; and then she came to a doll that was worn, small enough to fit into a safe, not faded, and soft enough to sleep with. She picked it up and held it to her heart. 'My dolly!' she said. And naturally her would-be father replied, 'My baby girl!'

"So whom can we eliminate? An Escalade is not a single guy's sports car. It isn't even the family type car. But it is an organizational car bought usually for legitimate commercial or social groups. If there's any question, we can do net checks on them as we write them off. Let's start with the Elders of the Latter Day Saints. They often drive around with visitors so they need big cars." She accessed a list of Latter Day Saints' elders and important members of the Mormon Church and checked off these entries. Next she did the same for all established religions, hospitals, nursing homes, country clubs, political organizations, universities, and anyone who would have purchased the car in the name of a known business or eleemosynary organization. The list shrank. With Akara's help, each questionable entry was double checked in a cross reference that established long organizational standing or a commercial license.

"Let's look up day care centers, private schools, and group residences for the elderly or other specialized groups." More were checked off. "Now check scouts and athletic organizations." More were checked off. Soon she eliminated all but six owners. She asked Akara to access the driver's license photos of each of the six. "Let's hold them aside and turn to the property tax records. The group in Cheyenne gave the landlady a book by Pastor Lamont Marlowe. They said that the woman who gave them the book said that he had died in 2011. Look up the 2010 property tax records."

They found property Marlowe owned both as Tenants In Common and as Joint Tenants with Margaret Cromwell, the registered owner of a black Cadillac Escalade. "Now see who inherited Marlowe's property." The most recent owner of nearly all of Marlowe's properties was Jebel Kitchener. A search of his name in driver's licenses revealed a handsome blonde man who was born in 1977. Beryl said, "Bingo!"

Akara added, "He sure fits the description of the pastor of those Sisters in Cheyenne. He's probably our mouse-faced guy, too." They now had his official home address in St. George, Utah.

"I guess that's our next stop," Akara said. "St. George."

Evidence against Niles began to accumulate quickly. Tuesday's voice recording in which a mysterious person accused Niles Portmann of killing his wife had been taken to an audio expert for voice analysis and for a comparison to the earlier recording that was made when Portmann reported his wife missing. There was no doubt, the analysis concluded, that the two voices, despite the obvious attempt to fabricate a foreign accent on one recording, were the same voice.

The tech, who had originally reported that the knife found in Niles' kitchen contained only deer's blood, issued a second report "completing" the initial evaluation. In addition to deer's blood, he found that there were deposits of "Visceral adipose" tissue that were being submitted for DNA analysis.

The blood samples along with hair follicles taken from Aleta's hairbrush had already been submitted to a lab for DNA analysis before her body had been found. Additional DNA tests were ordered.

During Tuesday's initial interview Niles stated his alibi: he had been in Las Vegas for two days surrounding her death. Investigators had been unable to account for long stretches of time during which Niles could have returned to wherever it was that Aleta had gone and had murdered her there. The two hundred miles between Las Vegas and Tonopah were of no significance if she had been murdered closer to Pahrump - a mere seventy miles from Las Vegas - near where her body had been found.

Sheriff Hornsby refused to comment on any of the information that had been leaked to the public, but his request that people suspend judgment until all of the facts had been ascertained was ignored.

Niles Portmann remained in a dazed state and did not express surprise when he was told his attorney wanted to confer with him. He was in the same daze that he had entered when he had been told Aleta had been murdered. He could comprehend nothing.

"Niles," Liam began, "you've got serious trouble. Give me a dollar if you want me to represent you. You've had deputies crawling all over your house."

"They took my money and my watch and my belt."

"That may just be temporary. You may get a day or two out of here while they formalize the procedure and gather the evidence. The autopsy will be conducted tomorrow - but if the coroner officially calls the death a homicide, you'll be formally charged - and I wouldn't look for bail. Instruct the property clerk to bring your envelope back here so that you can give me the dollar. I want you to tell me everything you know about this religious group Aleta was going to join."

Niles tried to relate as cogently as possible things that he did not understand. He told Liam about the venison, the books, the photographs, and the two pastors, Lamont Marlowe and Avery Christian, associated with the Sisters. As far as Niles knew, she had been going to meet up with them in their temporary quarters in Beatty; but evidently, they had come to Tonopah to pick her up because her Buick was left at the gas station. He also related Aleta's odd story about posing for a racy photograph in sexy underwear called "Satan's Lure" but that he also had found in her closet home-made long pioneer type dresses that he supposed was their normal uniform.

"There is one funny thing I guess I ought to tell you about. This pastor has a photograph of himself holding a barbed wire ring... like a

Crown of Thorns." Beyond that, he knew nothing about her plans except that she would be traveling around to preach the Gospels.

In the afternoon, Liam MacDonald returned to consult Niles again. "When she asked me to give her venison to take to them," Niles said, "I thought she was on her way to their place in Beatty. But she didn't have to be with them when she was killed. She could have been waylaid by a stranger."

"They located the place in Beatty where that religious group had been. The place is empty now and Becker says that there's no indication that Aleta was ever there. Joe Tuffs, the man who rented the house to them, is a guy I know and respect. Becker just went up and talked to him and says it's a dead end. No proof that she was there. Her body was found near Pahrump. But I'm gonna go up now and talk to Joe."

"But that still doesn't mean that some stranger couldn't have gotten her as she went there."

"Niles," Liam said forcefully, "please do not form opinions about anything. You've gotten yourself in enough trouble with that British accent shenanigan you pulled. They're bringing experts in to testify that the voice is yours. It looks like you were trying to distract them and divert police resources by sending them to Ryolite so that you could retrieve her body and dispose of it properly. It's as if you had her in the truck and saw some highway patrol cars up ahead and just dumped her body in a ditch. And then reported her missing and invented that story about Ryolite so that you could go back and bury her where no one would find her.

"I won't be able to get back from Beatty until late. So I'll see you tomorrow morning. I'll talk to the sheriff myself tonight to see what the hell is going on with that knife. First it was just deer's blood and now they're talking like it's the murder weapon. I can't get anything out of the lab tech. He's strangely mute on the subject of the knife. If I can't get anything out of the sheriff, I'll ask Millie down at Cappy's to keep her ears open for me. They're building a strong case against you now that they have the body. Niles, you're gonna be indicted."

"How are they saying Aleta was killed?" Niles asked.

"There's been no official post-mortem conducted. Officially, they'll have that tomorrow when the pathologist gets here. Unofficially, the talk is that you stabbed her. We'll see."

Liam drove his white Lincoln and stopped at one of the gas stations in the small town of Beatty. He knew the owner and while he filled up the Lincoln, he asked him if he knew anything about the religious people who rented Joe Tuffs house. The only thing he learned was that the group paid cash for gas. He then called Joe Tuffs and told him he was in town and would meet him at the house.

He parked in front of the old wooden Victorian style house and found Joe Tuffs waiting there for him. It was late in the afternoon, but he was eager to talk to Liam. He had just been interviewed by Deputy Bill Becker and he was not particularly fond of the lawman and resented the way Becker had conducted the interview.

"A high school kid could have conducted a better interview. I've known Niles Portmann for years," Tuffs said. "I didn't know him well, but nothing I ever knew about him indicated that he had a short fuse. But Becker? He's always seemed like a conniving rat to me."

"What did he ask you?"

"He showed me a photograph of Aleta that had been taken before Niles went to prison for hitting the Gregory kid. He asks me if I ever saw Aleta Portmann on my property. I tell him that there were half a dozen women in the group. They dressed alike in those long home-made dresses. All but one of them were Aleta's age. I couldn't tell one from another. 'So,' he says, 'you cannot identify Aleta as a member of the group.' I say, 'Don't make it sound like I'm saying she wasn't here!' That's what he was doin'."

"What else did he ask you?" Liam asked.

"He asked me when had they come and gone. I told him it was the first day of April that they moved in and I couldn't say for certain when they left since I didn't even know they had moved out until Becker contacted me. They left an undated note on the kitchen counter-top saying that I should hang onto the security deposit, since they expected to be back this way again soon. Incidentally, they left the place immaculate."

"How did he know to contact you?"

"I asked him that and he said that in a box of trash that had been left in the road in front of Niles' house, they found hand written notes by Aleta giving this address as the meeting place of the Sisters of Gethsemane Garden. I asked him if he wanted to come inside and inspect the house. He came in and looked around and said, 'Maybe the reason you don't know when they left is that they weren't here to begin with. This place doesn't look like anybody was here at all.' That made me mad so I just stopped tellin' him anything."

"Tell me what you didn't tell him."

"He never asked about the guy who was the pastor of the group. His name was Avery Christian. They drove a big black Cadillac Escalade. Utah plates." He reached into his shirt's breast pocket. "I wrote the license number down which I always record. It's just common sense." He handed Liam the paper. "And they did something strange about where they drove the car. I used to live in this house and what is the garage now used to be just a carport. I had a hobby of restoring old race cars so I started to keep a lot of tools outside and figured I ought to enclose the carport. I didn't want to cheapen the place by working on the cars out front... you know... as if I were the 'Shady Lane Mechanic.' I built a wall on one side of the carport there and I put those retractable garage doors on both the front and back. I'd work in the yard out back and then just roll the car into the garage at night or when the weather was bad. Now, the funny thing is that you can get to the main road from the back way - if you want to drive over a bumpy trail. But apparently that's what they did. I could tell by the crushed weeds that had grown in the path. I could figure only one reason anybody would take a Cadillac over that lousy trail and that was to avoid being seen. I don't know why they didn't want to be seen. There could be a reasonable explanation for it. All I know is that they were clean and quiet people. I had no complaints about them."

"What about Becker's intimation that they weren't here?"

"That's crazy. Rigg's Pig farm came by every two days and picked up their edible waste. They get everybody's edible waste in town. There's no garbage disposal unit in the sink, so people throw the slop in a plastic bag that fits inside a bucket Riggs supplies. The driver was here on Saturday, the eleventh, and took the bag. But when he came back on Monday, nobody was home. No slop."

"Do you recall how they paid you? Credit card or check?"

"Cash. They paid the security deposit and a month's rent in advance. That was on the last day of March. Then on the last day of April, they paid another month's rent for May. They had no kids or pets and they didn't smoke. What the hell else could I ask for?"

"What did the guy look like?" Liam asked.

"Nice looking. Thirties. Strong and in good physical condition. When I met him and introduced myself, he said his name was Avery Christian. He laughed a little and said his mother had been guided by heaven to give him that name... since he could pronounce it as 'a very Christian' kind of man. I didn't do a background check. When they pay up front as well as he did... in cash, I don't bother. But the women called themselves, *The Sisters of Gethsemane Garden.*"

"Do you know if they had work done on the car or bought anything locally that might have required a credit card?" Liam asked.

"No. No work done on the car and they paid for gas with cash. I just talked to the guy who owns the gas station thinking that Becker would have talked to him, too. But Becker never asked him anything. I did hear that they went to the laundromat and washed a bunch of bed linens and clothing on Sunday night. I furnish the bed, but not the pillows or sheets. They brought their own linens and blankets."

"I take it," Liam said, "they were not the religious type you usually get - by that I mean they had no big bake sales or revival tent meetings."

"No... they didn't participate in any county fair type of selling home-made merchandise and they didn't have any public prayer meetings.

But that doesn't mean they didn't come here for a few weeks to help someone. I've had tenants who came just to support a new mother who was overwhelmed with those Baby Blues. The ladies would go and clean house and take care of the other kids in the family and help the mother get on her feet."

Liam thanked Joe Tuffs and left his business card with him. "If you think of anything else, call me. Niles could use all the help we can give him."

As he drove away, Liam MacDonald called a friend of his who worked for the State Police in Salt Lake City, Utah, and asked if he would do him a favor and run the plates and also the driver's license for Avery Christian. While he waited on the line, his friend got the information: the Cadillac Escalade was registered to Margaret Cromwell on Abington Road, St. George, Utah. There was no licensed driver in Utah by the name of Avery Christian.

Niles had said that Aleta's family approved of her religious pursuits. They lived in St. George. Their phone number was unlisted. He'd have to ask Niles for it.

It was ten o'clock when he returned to his home in Tonopah. "Luella," he said to his wife, "I think I'll be driving to St. George tomorrow."

THURSDAY, MAY 16, 2013

Liam MacDonald respectfully conveyed his condolences to Aleta's grief-stricken parents who were not inclined to be grateful to a visitor who turned out to be the attorney of the man they believed murdered their daughter.

Aleta's father went to the front door and opened it, indicating that the interview they had mistakenly granted him was at an end. "And you can tell that jerk you represent that we hope he rots in hell."

Liam returned to his Lincoln sedan and instructed his navigating system to lead him to the address of Margaret Cromwell, the registered owner of the black Cadillac Escalade associated with Pastor Avery Christian and the Sisters of Gethsemane Garden. While he drove, he called Sheriff Alex Hornsby in Tonopah, hoping to learn if the autopsy results were in.

"It's not good news for your client, I'm afraid," Hornsby said. "Aleta's injuries indicate that she had been placed in a chokehold and died as a result of it."

"What about that adipose tissue on the knife Becker talked about?"

"I don't know where the hell that came from... maybe it was some kind of cross-contamination or just sloppy work in the lab. But that knife never killed anything but a deer. It's no longer considered evidence."

"I saw a lot of cuts on her body when I briefly looked at her yesterday. What were they caused by?"

"They were all post-mortem cuts. She had been tossed into a ditch that had a lot of broken glass in it. She had a cut on her hand that was made approximately twelve hours before her death; but her body was so full of maggots and bruising that nobody could tell from looking just what had happened. It wasn't until the entomologist estimated from the development of the larvae that her body had been there for approximately forty-eight hours. We also learned that the lividity pattern indicated that she had been killed elsewhere and dumped in the ditch. There was one peculiar injury that the pathologist couldn't explain. It was the damnedest thing you ever saw... really disturbing. It looked as if she had sat on a cactus plant... like ring-shaped rows of maybe ocotillo cactus. There were fresh puncture points around her rectal area, the inner top of her thighs, and even up front to the pubic area. And there were old, healed tiny puncture wounds in the same areas. So, this wasn't the first time she sat on a cactus."

"What did it look like? Sexual self-mutilation?"

"My guess is that the bruising on her upper arms and shoulders indicated external force. There were fresh lacerations leading up to the punctures on the recent injuries, but none of the old ones had any of those drag marks. I didn't know what to make of it.

"I can tell you that among child-abuse victims, sexual self-mutilation is common," Hornsby said. "The other cause of such mutilation is two-party arousal. The person who causes the blood and the infliction of pain gets a high from the triumph and control. The one that's bleeding experiences the pain as an extreme intensity of orgasm. Look... the main thing here is that if she didn't like the first experience she wouldn't have gone back for the second."

"I don't see self-punishment in this," Liam said. "She may have been sad and frustrated about the miscarriages, but she wouldn't have felt guilty or responsible for them. She would have known what to blame them on. With no history of child abuse, we can rule that out. Maybe we're looking at some kind of ritualistic sexual gratification - at least with the first experience. That her death is associated with the second experience suggests that it's somehow related."

On an avenue lined with the homes of St. George's most affluent residents, the white-columned mansion with its meticulously kept lawns seemed to be at home among its neighbors. All the houses, though different in design, formed a pleasant unit, like faces of so many Dutch masters sitting around a long table. The only thing that seemed out of place was the rented Honda that was parked across from the mansion and the two people who sat in it, looking up at the house.

Beryl Tilson and Akara Chatree were surveilling the Cromwell residence. There had been no traffic in or out of it, and there was no more movement in its facade than could be detected in a painting of it.

Liam parked at the curb, but wondering who they were and what they were up to, decided not to pull onto the driveway. For several minutes they stared at each other until Beryl asked Akara to go to the rear of his car and record his license plate numbers. It was intended to be a provocative act, and it succeeded.

Akara stood behind Liam's car, noting the plate's number in his little blue tablet, and Liam, still ruffled from the treatment he had received from Aleta's parents, was in no mood to tolerate such a brazen act. He got out of his car and asked, "Just what is your problem?" Akara looked to Beryl for direction.

Beryl got out of the car and crossed the street. "We got a little tired of waiting for you to do something beside stare at us."

"The plates are from Nevada," Akara said.

"And just why are my license plates any business of yours?" Liam countered.

The out-of-state plates indicated that he was probably not a resident and might have an interest in the house that was similar to hers. Beryl gave him her business card. "We're working on a case."

"Private I's? And the case concerns Margaret Cromwell? The lady is of interest to me, too. I'm an attorney."

"Let's go someplace and talk, counselor," Beryl said. "We've just checked into a motel a few blocks from here. Follow us back. It's time for lunch, and there's a western-style steakhouse down the street from it."

Because Liam had to find a bigger parking place than the ones that were closest to the entrance, he entered the restaurant a few minutes after Beryl and Akara had been seated.

The white haired sixty-something gentleman carried himself like an elderly version of a young man, an appearance he had cultivated since his college days. He spoke in an educated, unaccented speech, and used the glasses that hung on a silver and turquoise chain around his neck only to read the menu.

He was dressed somewhat dramatically in black western garb and boots and wore a watchband and two rings that matched the design of the eyeglass chain. As he leaned back to gain access to the small watch-pocket in his jeans in which he carried his business cards, he revealed the full beauty of his large silver belt buckle. He slid his fingers into the pocket and withdrew a couple of business cards. As he extended them, Beryl said, "I just know this is gonna read, *Have Gun - Will Travel*."

In mock seriousness, MacDonald intoned, "*Wire Paladin, San Francisco*." Beryl immediately began to sing the *Ballad of Paladin*, and MacDonald joined in the chorus. Nearby patrons turned to smile and a few of them - much to Akara's amazement - sang along.

Beryl looked at the menu. "Ah, broiled trout," she murmured.

Akara had been sitting at the table totally ignorant of the subject that had caused so much merriment. He did appreciate that the little jaunt down memory lane was an expeditious way to forge a good working relationship, but, that being conceded, the interlude, he suspected, was one of Beryl's diversionary tactics, one that she was probably using to get his mind off the menu's great wasteland. "I could eat a cow," he said, his voice edged with malice, "if it were not made of meat. I'm starving."

Clearly pleased that he did not have to be alone in avoiding meat, MacDonald drew upon his Paladin persona and portentously read the note at the bottom of the menu: "'The trout served at the steakhouse is flown in daily from Jackson Hole.' But," he said philosophically, "as Cervantes noted, *La mejor salsa es la hambre*. Hunger is the best sauce."

As the waitress recorded their order, he explained, "Whenever I have one of these business dinners, my wife asks me what I ate, and I just can't lie to the woman. And then she gets upset. And then I feel guilty. I don't mind eating fish if everybody else is eating it... especially if I'm as hungry as I am now."

They ate broiled trout and steamed vegetables and no mention of the case was made until they were drinking Galliano on the rocks with sugar cookies for dessert.

Liam began the working part of the lunch. "Now that we're old friends who've shared a meal together, suppose you tell me what your interest in Margaret Cromwell is. What's your client's problem?"

"We're following up an extortion matter involving a nominally religious organization," Beryl replied.

"The Sisters of Gethsemane Garden?" Liam asked.

"You got it. What's your interest?"

"Not extortion. Murder."

"Oh, Jesus!" Akara whispered.

They talked openly about their diverse but common interest in Avery Christian and the Sisters. Beryl filled him in on their blackmail scam. He filled her in on the peculiar photograph his client had seen, a photograph in which Avery Christian was holding next to his chest a ring of barbed wire, configured exactly in the shape of a Crown of Thorns. "I don't know what these Sisters are up to."

"There were six of them," Beryl noted, "five pretty young ones and one older one, staying in Cheyenne for a month last January. They wore long pioneer dresses. Everyone thought they were so sweet and they still think so even after the identity thefts occurred. The amounts were not large enough to warrant professional investigation by the credit card companies; but especially in light of the thousands they got out of our client, just enough to evidence the need of a thief to steal - no matter how little - from any mark he or she encounters."

"The group of women my client's wife, Aleta, got mixed up with were also odd. They stayed in Beatty for a month and a half; and the owner of the place they rented said that they drove their big Cadillac Escalade down a dirt trail to the highway, rather than go down the street where they could be observed. In residence, they also wore those old-fashioned, home made dresses. Maybe they went down to Vegas to scam a few marks and didn't want folks to see them all dressed up in glamorous outfits."

"At least our client is not as yet in trouble with the law. Your guy was railroaded before and it looks like he may be railroaded again."

"As long as our interests are dovetailing, why don't I officially engage your agency to work on the case for me. My guy is seriously in trouble. That bizarre phone call he made makes him sound like a lunatic. But after you've spent two and a half years in stir for a crime you didn't commit and you come home to find your wife has joined a religious cult and is getting ready to leave to go preaching, who knows what you'll sound like?"

"A cult?" Beryl asked.

"I just talked to the sheriff just before we met and he told me the autopsy was completed and she had been choked to death but there was one strange thing about the body. She had two different sets of puncture marks around her genital area... One set was just punctures and had healed, and the other was fresh...with drag scratches up to the puncture point, as if she had maybe been forced to sit on a ring of cactus. The points went back to her rectal area and the inside of the thighs... like a big ring."

"Like a Crown of Thorns?"

"Oh, my God, yes!" Liam suddenly connected Aleta's wounds with the Avery Christian's photo.

"Your guy will have quite a story to tell."

"But listen to the tale of the knife. She asked Niles to kill and dress a deer because she wanted to take venison to the group... venison. What does that tell you?"

"That she bought into their pioneer style."

"Right. If she had thought they were the extortionists that you've encountered, she'd have brought them truffles and filet mignon. But she wanted venison. And he killed and dressed a young buck, hoping she'll think so kindly of his generous act that she'd stay home and cook it for him. But though she hears the shot she won't come out of her bedroom; and he's so hurt that he just takes off and heads down to Vegas; and two days later, when he gets back and finds her and half the deer gone, he's really steaming. This guy says that he feels like he'd been marinating in battery acid for two and a half years. He blames everybody who had a part in his being sent away. He thinks they're all responsible for Aleta's joining up with that religious group. So, sure, he's not thinking straight. He wants revenge and you know what that gets you."

"Yes," Beryl said with mock gravity, "'He who sets out for revenge should dig two graves.'"

"Wisdom that Niles Portmann never learned!"

"That deputy was all set to fabricate evidence but, just in time, the pathologist determined that the cause of death was choking, so he dismissed the knife that he had smeared with Aleta's tissue as being of no value to the case."

Beryl nodded. "And I suppose the knife and the second report have vanished?"

"Yes. Exactly. Strange how that happens. And I know that if the tech wants to keep his job, he won't disagree with anything the deputy says."

"You've not only got to prove Niles innocent, you've got to prove Deputy Becker guilty," Akara offered.

"I'd be happy just to get the charges dropped. He's being held for a routine 72 hours and I personally think he's better off being in custody than off on his own in his state of mind. So, where do you think we should start?"

"According to Margaret Cromwell's driver's license, she's an elderly lady who probably doesn't know what her big black car is being used for," Akara said.

"Then let's split the questioning into two independent lines of inquiry," Liam suggested. "I'll take her and you take Avery Christian a.k.a. Jebel Kitchener."

"And Aleta's parents?" Beryl asked.

"They won't give you anything. I don't know whether or not they truly believe Niles to be guilty, but they're second beneficiaries to a million dollar life insurance policy on her life. He had two million on his life."

"That's a nice incentive for them to believe that he's guilty. I guess they see themselves as generous grandparents... lavishing gifts on their grandkids."

"No. They don't have any grandchildren. They had five children. One died of leukemia and Aleta had five miscarriages, her sister never got pregnant at all, and her two brothers are apparently sterile. They spent a lot of time at a ranch that was right in the line of the jet stream's delivery of radioactive dust from Nevada's nuclear tests. The feds don't like to talk about it. So there's no grandchildren in the family.

"And now," Liam said, "I'll get ready to interview Ms. Margaret Cromwell."

"Knight takes rook," Beryl said.

"Damned straight," he answered.

Acting at Liam's request as his secretary, Beryl called the Cromwell house and asked if Ms. Margaret Cromwell was available for Mr. Liam MacDonald to call upon her that afternoon.

The person who answered the phone put her on hold and several minutes later returned to say that if Mr. MacDonald would call promptly at four o'clock, she would be happy to receive him. Beryl thanked him and relayed the message.

Beryl and Akara drove past the address listed as the registered location of Jebel Kitchener. It was not a large two-storey house, but, Beryl noticed, it was extremely well-kept. The lawns were freshly mowed, the shrubbery trimmed, and the paint fresh. Yet, for all that, the house did not have a lived-in look. There were no tell-tale signs of occupancy: no mail in the box, no motor oil drips on the driveway, no trash cans waiting to be put away. Like the other houses on the street, it had a six-foot cinderblock wall around the rear of the property. Other than that, there was nothing noteworthy about the home of Jebel Kitchener.

They drove past Margaret Cromwell's white columned mansion. Liam decided that he should be groomed for the occasion. "Let's go back to the motel. I'll register there, and then I'll get some new garments."

"Can you drop me off at the nearest beauty parlor?" Beryl asked Akara. She took the photograph of the fake Waverly Bryant and the pendant as well as the Stetson-hatted man with her and a picture of Aleta that Liam had provided. "A beauty parlor is like a reference library."

"What do you think I should do with my hair?" she asked the beautician. "I put myself in your hands. Do whatever you think will improve the mess."

"I see grey and I see darker roots. Not much... but just a touchup. You've got a great cut, but I could give it a more youthful style."

As the beautician worked she made small talk. Eventually she asked Beryl what she was doing in "our neck of the woods."

"I'm trying to find a guy." She showed her the driver's license photo of Avery Christian which had been enlarged.

Suddenly the beautician grew cautious. "You a friend of his?"

"No, I'm afraid not."

"A relative?"

"No, I'm a P.I. I'm searching for him in connection with a gal who was last seen with him."

The beautician sighed with relief. "Well, lemme' tell you, girl... that's Avery Christian, and you'll have a hard time findin' him. He gets around."

"A moveable feast?"

"Yeah... like Easter Sunday. How old is the girl?"

"Twenties."

"Between you and me, he's the leader of a cult of mostly young women."

"Polygamist?"

"I ought to say, 'Is there any other kind in this part of the world?' but I can't say that because they really aren't like any other kind. They're supposed to do a lot of good... visiting their congregation members all over the Southwest. And they don't have the usual compound... no schools... no teenaged boys being dumped on street corners, homeless and abandoned because they compete with the patriarch. They don't have any kids at all that I know of."

"Do they dress in that old-fashioned polygamist way? 'Polygamy chic?' Gingham dresses and calico aprons?"

The beautician laughed and nodded. "I like that... 'Polygamy chic.' They don't come in here to get their hair done. And you never see them wearing those dresses on the street. I only know of them because of the car."

"Ah, the Cadillac Escalade?" Beryl asked.

"That's the one. They often keep it over at the big Cromwell house on Abington Way."

"Ah, I've seen it. Big white columns," Beryl said as she removed her iPhone and showed the beautician the blow up of Margaret Cromwell's driver's license photo.

"That's Margaret Cromwell. She looks like she just had her hair done... but nobody in this salon did it. God! That finger-wave style went out in the Thirties. People who work at her house say that sometimes she wears a huge black wig. She's Avery Christian's mother. What a character she is!" She looked again at the Pastor's picture. "Ain't he the best lookin' guy you ever saw? And girl... that picture does not do him justice."

"Is his real last name Cromwell?" Beryl asked.

"I think he's a son by one of her many marriages. Kitchener was his father, but he was raised in Nevada. He was fully grown when his mother bought that white house and then married a preacher who lives in the neighborhood."

"Would that be Lamont Marlowe?"

"It would. He died a couple of years ago. Nice man. Nobody could figure what he'd be doing married to Margaret Cromwell. She's a nut... a crafty nut. Some people say she employs parlor maids who don't do an awful lot of dusting." She laughed. "I'll be nice and just say she must have married well. She's not exactly destitute."

The conversation turned to other subjects and finally Beryl's hair was finished. When she left she gave the beautician a twenty dollar tip. "It's on my client's tab," she whispered. "You've been really helpful. And frankly, I love what you did with my hair."

While Beryl was getting her hair done, Liam went to a western outfitters shop and bough new black western garments and some toiletries for an overnight stay,

Liam MacDonald had gauged the quality of the inhabitants of the Cromwell house by the quality of the fastidious landscaping. "This is not the domicile of a person of ill repute," he told Beryl when they met back at the motel and she conveyed to him the opinions of the beautician. "If you put a scissors and comb in a woman's hands you create a gossipy old busybody... a harpy," he said, criticizing the beautician's suggestion that the parlor maids were actually employed in a much older occupation. He suddenly felt obliged to defend Margaret Cromwell's honor and the hairdo she wore in her driver's license photo. "All the ladies in my family, as I recall, wore their hair in that plain but attractive way. No doubt, Miss Cromwell uses the services of a rival beauty shop. I'll give you a more professional opinion of the lady's character after I meet with her." Liam polished his western boots into a nice shine, insisting, "A gentleman never calls upon a lady with dusty boots."

He admired himself in Beryl's full-length bathroom door mirror. "I keep a gentleman's 'presentation' with the ladies," he said. "We call it 'chivalry.' I'll have a pleasant chat with her and learn what I can about the Gethsemane Sisters. Ah, you'll see," Liam said, using a wet cloth to take the packing folds out of his new shirt, "that civility thrives in soil that is nourished by civility."

The sun was beginning its western decline when Liam, assuming his Paladin demeanor, set out on his quest to interview the old lady.

"Please don't forget that your mission is not to socialize," Beryl felt it necessary to remind him, "it is to learn all you can about the movements of Avery Christian and his religious group."

They signed agency agreements and Beryl transferred all of the relevant photographs into his iPhone. Liam said simply, "Wish me luck."

The afternoon sun struck the side of the mansion and dazzled off what Beryl was certain were mirrored windows. Having more faith in the integrity of hairdressers than Liam had, she immediately wondered if these were two-way panes of glass. She drove the white sedan up the driveway, turned and stopped in front of the house. Liam got out, and as he began to climb the steps of the columned portico, she continued down to the street and parked half a block away.

Liam lifted the white door's brass knocker and let it fall several times upon its striker plate. He extended his business card to a servant who answered the door. "I have an appointment with Miss Margaret... Miss Margaret Cromwell."

The door swung open and Liam disappeared into the dwelling.

The white-jacketed houseboy led Liam through the foyer and knocked on a door which apparently was locked since he made no attempt to open it until a buzzer sounded and a clicking sound indicated that the knob could be turned.

The houseboy did not enter the room. He merely pushed the door open and flattened himself against the jamb as his extended arm held the door back so that Liam could enter.

For a reason he knew that he would never be able to determine - and certainly not for the remainder of his natural life - Liam MacDonald was thrust into a concretized vision of hell. He, a lawyer, instantly imagined his name and crime in the docket of an asylum's court. It was his Judgment Day's nightmare, a fearsome rendering of a place envisioned by Hieronymus Bosch.

Open mouthed, he looked around the garish room which he could clearly see in the light that flooded it. Heavy drapes on the windows had been pulled back and tied with golden cords, leaving apparently bare windows to let in light and the prying eyes of outsiders - at least until the drapes were untied. He saw the four-poster iron bed with its metal crossbar head and foot boards, and the hand cuffs and manacles that were affixed to the crossbars; the purple and red velvet Victorian settees that had ropes trailing from their ornate legs; the artificial flowers and *cat-o-nine-tails* whips that jutted out from the lava bowls mounted on the walls; the cloying stench of pachouli that thickened the atmosphere; the gaily painted carpenter's horses on which were mounted saddles, stirrups, and clamps; the coiled bullwhips; the lamp bases that were large and anatomically correct copies of a scrotum and penis that ejaculated silk fabric that flared out to become lampshades fashioned to look like overarching buttocks; the metal chains and tools and leather implements of sadomasochistic pleasures that hung from the fireplace like so many Christmas stockings, all combined to terrify him.

Liam MacDonald, a knight of somebody or other's realm, heard a clicking sound as the door closed behind him and he stared uncomprehendingly at the place in which he correctly assumed he was now imprisoned.

A bell tinkled and a door at the rear opened. Miss Margaret Cromwell entered the list to joust with her knight errant. If not actually dead, she looked at least ninety years old and she was naked except for an insouciantly opened bouffant blue and white brocade redingote. She carried a walking stick and wore a massive jet black curly wig that rippled against her shriveled breasts with their downward pointing nipples - which she clearly rouged - and hung on her chest like the clappers of church bells. She wore red high-heeled shoes and powder blue stockings secured by long black garters that hung from a black waist belt, creating a kind of proscenium arch around a bushy clew of pubic hair.

At such times of trepidation the human mind is apt to seize upon some trifling detail; and Liam MacDonald's eyes fixed upon the black triangle at the top of her thighs and he repeatedly asked himself if there was such a thing as a pubic toupée.

He might have pondered this curious possibility for another hour or more if the lady who owned the item had not ended his musings by whacking his thigh with her walking stick and speaking to him in a voice that crackled like a Tesla coil. "Eh, Liam, you old stud! We meet again! Comin' here to satisfy your sweet tooth, eh, Liam? Still got that Star of Texas tattooed on your pretty little ass?"

Liam MacDonald gasped. The Star of Texas that once proudly crowned his gluteus maximus had been relegated to a place hidden beneath a flap of sagging skin. But how did this witchy creature know he had ever inked his behind? He could not remember ever having been in such a predicament that would have allowed her to observe his naked tush... not shipwreck, not surgery, not initiation in his college fraternity. He could think of no scenario - no, not even the drunken weekend over Mardi Gras in New Orleans when he had got the tat - that allowed for her to have seen it. It was then a simple act of lawyer-ship to extrapolate non-existence from an inability to establish provenance. He said to himself, "If the absence of evidence is not the evidence of absence, what the hell is it?" He said, "I... I... I..."

"You what?"

"Was born in... Oklahoma City!" And the words began to gush forth like arterial blood. "I am an Oklahoman and I assure you, Madam, I do not have the Star of Texas tattooed anywhere on my body!" An adjacent dam of memory broke and suddenly Liam MacDonald recalled where he had seen an image similar to the one that now assailed him. "My God!" he said, "You look like Louis the Fourteenth! I saw his portrait in Paris!"

"Do I, now?" she said, flicking the long crimson acrylic nail of her index finger in his face. She took a step nearer to him, and he backed up and frantically groped the door seeking its precious knob. He stared fearfully at her... at the eyelashes that looked like large black caterpillars rippling on her lids; the scarlet wound of a mouth, and the powdered-over crevices that were stuffed with "foundation" creams. And again one of those inconsequential thoughts seized his mind and he wondered how much all the makeup on her face would weigh if it were scraped off. A pound? His fumbling hands found the doorknob. He needed to leave. The knob would not turn. He could not remember what his quest had been; he knew only what it was now, and that was to get the hell out of there.

The Tesla coil crackled. "It's five hundred a visit... baby cakes. And I don't take checks."

With trembling hands he opened his wallet and snatched bills from its fold. Five or six one hundred dollar bills... he could not be sure. Her withered fingers with their curved and painted bear claws snatched the money.

Margaret Cromwell turned away from him and pressed a button under a nearby table and the door lock released. Liam ran, without breathing, out of the house and into the street.

Beryl could make no sense of his stuttering explanation. "Wait here," she said, motioning to Akara to take care of the hyperventilating attorney. She proceeded to walk to the house.

She knocked on the door, handed her business card to the houseboy, and followed him into the foyer.

The houseboy knocked on the sitting room door, the buzzer sounded, and Beryl entered.

"Good evening, Miss Cromwell," she said, completely ignoring the woman's outrageous attire. "I'm Beryl Tilson. Would it be too much of an imposition to ask for your guidance about a man I'm seeking?"

"Please sit down," said the old woman. "Would you care for tea?"

"I'd like that very much." Beryl smiled.

Ms. Cromwell flipped an intercom switch and ordered tea and cookies. In another minute a tea cart rolled into the room from another door. The maid who pushed the cart served the tea.

"Who is the man?" Margaret Cromwell asked.

Beryl produced the driver's license photograph of Avery Christian. "Ah, Avery," Ms. Cromwell said, "my favorite son. You just missed him. He and the Sisters were here for a few days. They left yesterday. Plucked my pantry clean like a chicken. My freezer, too."

"Ah... my son and his friends do the same to me. When they leave, the freezer is empty and the trash can is full."

"They're all alike. Why did you want Avery?"

"I have a client in Philadelphia who's got a daughter he'd like to place with the Sisters, but my job is merely to find Pastor Christian. Do you happen to have his itinerary?"

"Oh, my goodness. Place his daughter with The Sisters? First, can you tell me why he has chosen Avery's ministry?"

"People rarely tell you the truth about their motives. I do know that she's a young woman of about twenty-six who has been a problem to the family for years. Teenage rebellion and more. They tried placing her in a variety of Christian schools and organizations, wanting her to develop a spiritual life and settle down - maybe get married and raise a family. But nothing worked.

"Then, several years ago, she joined a little Hindu Tantric group - a handful of women and one male leader who was called a 'guru,' and her personality underwent a kind of miraculous change. She became obedient and respectful and learned all kinds of crafts - things the members sold to support themselves. Of course, her folks really didn't know what Tantric religions did - all that sexual stuff - or that she had gotten her tubes tied and couldn't have children. But they certainly welcomed the change in her demeanor. She wrote to them regularly and sent little gifts. Then after a couple of good years everything changed. Some of the women in the group had prevailed upon the guru to allow a few men to join. In no time at all, there was fighting and resentment and jealousy. You can imagine the problems. Her behavior deteriorated terribly. She left the group and came home in a state of constant anger. That's when the family learned about what really went on in that Tantric group. They threatened to disinherit her if she left Christianity again. Then she became completely depressed. My personal feeling is that she missed all that sexual excitement. You'd think with more men around, there would have been greater opportunities for adventure, but it didn't work out that way."

"Oh, it never does," Miss Cromwell offered, "since it's like putting two or even three foxes in the henhouse. They not only tear the hens apart, but they wind up tearing the hen house and even themselves apart.

A sad story, but unfortunately, a common one. She's lucky she got out when she did."

"And then somebody gave her a copy of one of Lamont Marlowe's books and the girl expressed a definite interest. This led her to Avery Christian's Sisters of Gethsemane Gardens. She tried to locate Pastor Marlowe, but he had recently died. And she couldn't find Avery Christian, either. So they engaged me to see if I could locate his group or any other old-style Christian group that was similarly devoted to Christian service. So here I am. My client is eager to get his daughter placed. She's a hard worker, and when she's in the right hands, an obedient girl."

"Ah yes... an obedient soul is a perfect soul in the eyes of God. So what you're doing is checking him out."

"Essentially, that's exactly what I'm doing."

"May I see your driver's license?"

"Of course." Beryl took her wallet out and displayed her Pennsylvania driver's license along with several credit cards and her investigator's license. Margaret Cromwell pretended to be able to read them, but about all she could distinguish was that the Pennsylvania driver's license was just about the same size as the Utah license.

She returned the cards to Beryl. "Avery makes a more or less routine series of stops to see the various members of his congregation... he calls them 'beads on a necklace.' If I'm not mistaken, he was on his way to our place just north of Pahrump, Nevada. We have a converted property on Route 95... which used to be part of La Casa Serena, a motel-restaurant complex near Pahrump. I don't know how long he'll stay there. Summer is on its way and Avery loves to lie on the beach and sail."

"A sailor, too? A man of many talents."

"Ach! Talent? What talent is required to sit under an awning and drive a boat the way you drive a car? A 'putt-putt' we used to call them. Motorized things... no sails... no skill. When I was a girl we had sailing ships and captains who knew how to read the ocean... the swells... the winds... the currents... the clouds... what the fish were doing that gave a clue. He knows nothing about water. I raised him in desert country. So he has one of those putt-putts. 'Darien' he calls it. I won't put my toe on it. It stinks to heaven; and Lord... if you're running before the wind... look out. The fumes will gas you."

"Oh... so many of the old ways are lost to us. Where does he like to sail?"

If Margaret Cromwell had heard the question, she did not acknowledge it. Instead she sighed, "Horsemanship. Now there my Avery excels. Not in dressage, of course. And not in those trick rider show-off stunts. He just looks so elegant cantering on a horse. English saddle. Boots and breeches. Ah, I did well with him. Well, you don't want to know all that. I believe he was on his way to La Casa Serena. When he's not here in the Kitchener House in St. George, that's his alternate headquarters. I'm sorry to say I don't have his exact schedule. Sometimes he tells me and sometimes it never comes up and I don't hear anything. Is that how your boy is, Miss Tilson?"

"Yes. I'm afraid so."

"Then I don't have to tell you how they are. For every thing they tell you, they keep ten things secret."

Beryl laughed. "And it can be worse. Sometimes for every truth they reveal, they tell you ten lies!"

Margaret Cromwell tossed her head back and made a noise that was between a yell and a laugh. Her upper plate showed in its entirety. "Ah, men! They train early to be deceivers! Maybe they're just born that way. Avery doesn't use cell phones, and the place doesn't have a land line. He has a short wave radio. The place is on a dirt road that leads back to the California side of Mount Charleston. You'll have to search for the road, Take the road up to Pahrump and go another ten miles north east... you won't miss it. There's not much else around. No doubt that old buzzard who was here just before you arrived is with you. Will you be taking him with you?"

"No," Beryl said with regret. "Liam will be going home to Nevada."

"Are you a religious woman? Hmmm... My Avery is quite the handsome fellow, and as a Christian, he has no equal."

"Are you asking if I wouldn't like to leave the rest of the world behind and live in an environment where I could simply be a woman... who depended on a man to make all those nagging decisions for her?" She chuckled and conceded, "Ah, I've reached the age when my decisions are nothing but stupid guesses. Well... I won't lie. Christianity's life of spiritual service has a certain appeal to me. I've been on my own for so long and frankly, I'm getting a little tired of it. But nobody's asked me to join so I guess I'll just have to keep on truckin' alone."

"Maybe Avery can do something for you," Margaret said.

"I'll look into it. As long as I'm checking him out for someone else, I might as well try to do myself some good. Thank you for the suggestion."

They finished their tea. Beryl curtsied. "Madame, your hospitality and your tea share the same excellence."

"You are so kind," the Louis Quatorze look-alike mewed.

Liam MacDonald said that he needed a drink; but Beryl rejected the idea, and gave him a Valium instead. When he was once again calm and could bleach the sight of the black pubic toupée out of his mind, they went out to a delicatessen for sandwiches. "I'm never gonna look at beavers the same way," he grumbled.

"She's slicker than okra, and I wouldn't trust a bloody word that came out of her mouth." He was still trembling.

"I would," Beryl said. "She kept moaning, 'Liam... Liam... show me that tattoo. I dream about it every night.'"

Liam MacDonald began to laugh at himself. "Honest to God. I thought I was in Louvre-Hell or something... like I was a piece of aged filet mignon and Louis XIV was coming to dine."

Beryl laughed. "She tried to interest me in joining the Sisters. I told her I'd consider it."

As Beryl told him all that she had learned from Margaret about Avery Christian and his semi-headquarters in La Casa Serena near Pahrump Liam interjected, "I remember that name. That place is an old combination whorehouse, restaurant, and motel. They even have a swimming pool. The locals call it Cazarina. It's been years since I was there. I'm surprised it's still standing."

"As long as I've got to pass Pahrump on my way home, why don't you ride with me?"

"Then follow me up to the car rental," Akara said, "and I can turn the Honda in."

As they left the shop and got back into Liam's sedan, he announced, "I am never going to say an unkind word to my wonderful wife again... never in my life. For her peace of mind, I will never eat animal fat. I will never have another alcoholic beverage. And I will never smoke another cigar. So help me God."

"And the reformation cost you only five hundred dollars!" Beryl said. "You must send Margaret a 'Thank You' note."

Before she went to sleep that night, she called George and Martin and got them on a conference call and told them both about the murder connection to Frank Goodrich's blackmail scheme. "Incidentally, we're sort of under contract with another attorney who represents the victim's husband who is about to be indicted for his wife's murder - one that we believe this so-called Sisters of Gethsemane Garden and the Mouse-faced photographer, Pastor Avery Christian, choked to death."

"Oh, boy!" Martin said.

"This is a serious bunch of professionals," George said. "I'm glad Akara's with you. I don't have to tell you to be careful and to call me tomorrow."

"And me, too," Martin said. "Meanwhile I'll let Frank and Gwen know we're hot on the trail."

FRIDAY, MAY 17, 2013

Liam dropped Akara and Beryl off in Pahrump so that they could each obtain a rental car. He then drove home to Tonopah to be with Luella and check in with his client Niles.

As Beryl finally prepared to go on her mission, Akara made sure that he could track her iPhone's GPS before she left to find Avery Christian's La Casa Serena or Gethsemane Garden residence. He arranged a signal that she could make by hitting his number on speed dial. Akara would find her and pretend to be her son Jack.

She went shopping in the early afternoon to buy suitable garments for the interview. It had first been her intention to use some kind of ruse to gain admittance to Cazarina; but then she decided that subterfuge was unnecessary and planned to use the direct approach and simply lie. She had put make up on and a sheer blouse that had a suitably low neckline. She wore a jacket over the blouse so that if a more chaste appearance was advisable, she could readily affect it.

Gethsemane Garden was a large log cabin made in a style not mentioned in the Bible. A bulldozed area, wide enough to park two cars and no more, had been leveled at the base of the hill on which the cabin was situated. The Cadillac Escalade, not expecting company, hogged the center of the parking area, forcing Beryl to park her rented sedan with two wheels on the driver's side in the gutter of the road.

An unlocked, short gate barred the path up the walkway. She could see smoke rising from a chimney and she could smell meat being grilled on an outdoor barbeque. "Hello!" she called. No one responded, although she could hear laughter. She opened the gate and walked forward for another twenty feet and called again, "Hello!" This time she was heard.

A young woman dressed in a long green gingham dress came down the walk. "Are you looking for someone?" she asked.

"Avery Christian. I was told I could find him here."

Another red gingham clad woman came down the path. "And who told you that?" she asked pleasantly.

"Madame Margaret Cromwell of St. George, Utah."

"Just a minute," the first woman said, and, while the second woman stayed with Beryl, she went back to the barbeque.

An exceedingly handsome man of between thirty-five and forty came down the path. "I'll take it from here, Sisters," the blonde, blue-eyed Apollonian creature said to the women. To Beryl, he extended his hand and said, "I'm Avery Christian. You have found what you sought."

"That makes me an unusual individual," she replied.

"So you've seen my Mamma? When, may I ask?"

"Yesterday. My name is Beryl Tilson. I'm a private investigator from Philadelphia."

"And she led you to me?"

"I was investigating you - but only to the extent that you in fact existed and had - let me recite the specifics of my mission," she said, opening a little blue tablet, "a Christian group that believed in the Biblical requirement of a strong male head of family, weren't loaded down with children, and were happy doing God's work... service being your spiritual purpose." She closed the tablet. "I think that covers it," she smiled.

"Not entirely," Avery said cryptically, taking her arm and leading her up to an outdoor picnic table.

They sat side by side on a picnic table bench while they discussed Beryl's "client" - the one with a wayward daughter.

"Is that all you discussed with my mamma?" Avery asked.

"Your mother," Beryl said, "inquired about my religious background. She asked me if I were a Christian and also interested in a life of service."

"And you said?"

"I confess... I never really thought about it before. But she was such an unusual woman."

"How was she dressed?"

"Like the Sun King."

Avery Christian began to laugh. Suddenly he reached around and grabbed Beryl and hugged her to him. Then in one swooping gesture that nearly elicited an automatic defensive move from her, he twirled her over his lap so that her face was in the neckline of his shirt and he had his face in her hair while he shook with laughter. "Louis XIV!" he continued chortling. "I know that portrait of him. It's in the Louvre. Those gosh darned blue stockings and red shoes... and the walking stick and..." he began to laugh so hard it was difficult to speak, "that immense black wig. I tell her that pterodactyls could nest in it!"

He was wearing cologne, but Beryl could not identify the scent. "Whoever created your perfume deserves the Nobel prize in chemistry," she said. "It's a scent not of this world but of some far-off Eden."

Avery put one arm under her knees and picked her up as he stood. After he had carefully placed her on top of another picnic table, he brought a chair to the table and seated himself directly in front of her. Her knees were against his chest. It was an awkwardly sexual arrangement, but he hugged her legs as a child would and took no advantage of the arrangement.

"My mother! She's amazing!" he grinned. "She was forty-five when she had me! She ran a whorehouse in New Orleans for years, and then she moved to Nevada and ran one there. Pleasuring men is in her blood! I swear! I liked growing up here in the Silver State. I lived down the street from the only Nevadan who ever won a Nobel prize. Honest to God! Michelson's his name. He proved something or other about space... density or ether... I never understood it. I was home schooled and we never got around to physics. At any rate, my mom named me Avery Christian... A Very Christian... and the cologne I'm wearing is called *Christian Number One*, by Clive Christian - no relation."

Beryl was astonished by the man's boyish manner of speaking and the way he seemed to regard Albert Michelson's 1880's experiments as current events. "I didn't know that about Nevada and the Nobel laureate," she said, "but the perfume is a winner."

"Where are my manners? You must be hungry and thirsty. Did you drive here from St. George?" He stood up and lifted Beryl off the table and stood her on her feet.

They returned to the first table and Beryl put some food on a heavy paper plate. "I'm a vegetarian," she explained. "But don't let it get around. Sometimes I am sufficiently tempted and forget that I don't eat meat."

"You're an educated woman. I can tell."

"You sound as though you're accusing me."

"I am hoping, that's all. Name ten plays by William Shakespeare!"

"What?"

"It's a test. You get nothing if you win, and you get nothing if you lose. But I run the risk of being wrong about your being educated. So, go ahead, name them."

She swallowed some cole slaw. "*Hamlet. MacBeth. Julius Caesar. Othello.*" She stopped to chew a delicious medallion of beef. "*Romeo and Juliet. The Taming of the Shrew. Richard III. Henry IV. Henry V. Twelfth Night. The Tempest.* King Lear. *As You Like It.* How am I doing?"

"What does Mercutio say to Romeo when he has just been stabbed and Romeo wants to know the extent of the wound?"

"Everybody knows that. He says: *'tis not so deep as a well nor so wide as a church-door, but 'tis enough, 'twill serve.'* And then he dies. It's a great line."

"Do you realize that there is not a woman here who can name three plays? Except you, of course."

"I'm not such a rare bird."

"Yes, you are. Don't fly away. Stay with me."

"Then I am a rare working bird. I have, as the poet says, 'Promises to keep and miles to go before I sleep.' I also have a son waiting for me at a motel in Pahrump. He'll probably come looking for me. He doesn't think much of my driving abilities and will imagine I'm in a ditch someplace."

"And you quote Frost. That's so neat! And you say you want a life of service? What does your son say? He sounds protective."

"He probably says, 'Ah... the house to myself!' But let's see... what I want, I already have. I might like to change the kind of service I do. I admit it. I'm often bored with my life. My little boy is all grown up. I'm no longer needed maternally. So while I was here checking you out for a client, I thought I'd do a little reconnoitering for myself."

"Do you know what a patriarch does... in the sense that our little group requires a patriarch?"

"Gives the orders, I expect."

"Could you follow orders?"

"You know I'm going to answer that that would depend on the orders."

"Would you come quietly if I asked you to watch a movie with me? No pornography, if that's what you're thinking. I've got Depp, Cruise, Streep... take your pick. I've got martial arts' movies, too."

"I can't. My car is half-parked in the road."

"Give me your car keys. That's another order."

"*You* want to move it?"

"Sure. I'm not going anywhere tonight. You can block the Caddy in. Ok. Come on. You can drive it yourself. I'll just walk you down so that I can move the Caddy."

She gave him the keys. The women were beginning to clean up the tables and put the left-over food into plastic containers. "I'll stay here and help with the chores. You can provide the valet service."

It was dusk and getting cold in the mountains. As he walked down the path she called, "But just don't block me in while you're at it."

The woman who had first come to answer her call approached her. "My name's Sister Faith but you can call me Annie. Would you like to join us inside for tea and home made pie?"

Beryl smiled. "I'd like that very much."

They all went into the cabin and sat in the large all-purpose room. The fireplace was a working fireplace. Ovens were built into its masonry walls and long wrought iron swinging arms, notched to hold a pot's handle, extended over the fire. A kettle was now boiling.

"Usually, we eat in here," Annie said as she set a large plank table with porcelain cups and saucers that contained the logo of the Sisters of Gethsemane Garden: a Crown of Thorns surrounding a Cross.

"That's a beautiful logo," Beryl remarked.

"We have small ones made in gold that we wear around our neck." She reached inside the collar of her dress and pulled out a gold chain with the logo, now reduced to about an inch in diameter, etched into a gold disk.

"It's lovely," Beryl cooed, delighted at last to see the actual pendant that was such an indistinct image in the blackmail photos. As she studied the clothing that the young women wore she could tell that they had no underwear on. Breasts jiggled as they walked and the impression they made on the bodice fabric was not of normal skin. The women, Beryl suspected, were all wearing nipple jewelry, heavy rings of some kind. Also, when they bent over it was often possible to see the skirt fabric settle into the cleft of their backsides. She also noticed that all of the women had acrylic nails. They were not exaggerated in length or polish. All were pale pink and appeared to be well-maintained in a conservative style. Four of them had professionally bleached or colored hair.

Another Sister, whom Beryl immediately recognized as Frank's nemesis, introduced herself as Sister Charity and began to cut a pie. "Ah," she said as she drew the knife in a series of diameters, "We're back up to eight. No left-overs."

Beryl counted eight place settings. Avery was evidently going to sit in the master's chair at one end, while the youngest woman sat opposite him in the mistress's chair.

"Do you ever number more than eight?" Beryl asked.

"No. Seven Sisters and our Holy Father," Annie replied.

"I'm the newest Sister in the *Sisters of Gethsemane*," the girl in the privileged chair said. "My name is Sister Prudence. Not too long ago we were down to five."

"Do the Sisters leave to attend to other duties and then return?" Beryl noticed a nylon stocking that was filled with golf balls and tennis balls hanging from a hook on the back of a door. She wondered what it was for. Since there was no place in the mountain setting in which anyone could play tennis or golf, she guessed that it was a battering instrument of some kind. Hanging beside it were two riding crops, and beside these, hanging on another nail that protruded through a hole in its handle was a long board that measured about five inches wide and three feet long. Something was written on the wood. She strained to be able see it, but not until she later stood up could she read, "Board of Education."

"You mean, do we ever get a 'leave of absence'?" Annie asked and then immediately answered, "If we explain to Father why we're needed elsewhere, of course. But we-" she indicated the others, "always come back no matter how far away we go."

"That's good to know," Beryl said. "I imagine you come from many different places and that you value your positions here."

Sister Prudence quickly answered. "Who would want to give up a life like this? So in case you ever do join us remember there's always somebody who's happy to replace you. When our group lost Sister Hope, our Number Six, I was right there to take her place."

"Why did she leave you?" Beryl casually asked.

"She got sick and her doctor wanted her to have surgery."

"Will she be back after she has the operation?"

"I doubt it. She was older than the rest of us, and Father Avery thought she should stay home and get some rest."

"Where's home?"

"She has her own house near the entrance to Nellis Air Force Base."

"Air Force bases are noisy, but if she lives there I guess she's used to it."

Avery returned to the kitchen and handed Beryl her keys. "Both cars are now out of harm's way."

"Dirty work for a *dauphin*," Beryl whispered, and Avery once again laughed.

"Those red shoes! I've begged her... We absolutely need to talk in private." He picked up her hand and led her into a room on the ground floor of the cabin. "The Sisters sleep upstairs... it's more like a partitioned loft; but I stay down here. I have a fear of fire. It's crazy, I know. But I prefer to be downstairs even if a grizzly bear sticks its head in the window."

He handed her a clean folded home-made "polygamy chic" dress. He opened the bathroom door and said, "You can change in here. That way, when you leave, your clothes won't be all wrinkled." She had carried her tote bag into the bathroom. She left the door ajar and slid her hand into the tote bag, took hold of her phone, looked down and hit the signal for Akara to come.

She put the dress on and when she opened the door and showed him the dress, the two of them laughed. Now, as she faced the wall that contained the bedroom door, she could see that his bed's headboard was against the wall and that above the bed was a kind of "Stations of the Cross" box that contained the infamous barbed wire "crown." On a shelf that protruded from the base of the box sat a row of seven votive candles. "Good grief," she told herself, "they venerate the damned thing."

Avery went into the kitchen to get a bottle of wine and two glasses. "Tell me," he called on his way back to his bedroom, "what's this client of yours like? Is she pretty?"

"She's not my client. Her father is. I've only seen one photo of her and she seems to be pretty enough."

He sat on the bed as he poured a glass of wine for Beryl. "What color is her hair?" he asked.

Beryl affected a look of surprise. "I have no idea. The photo was taken at the ashram and she was wearing a chuddar - one of those Indian shawls - with a lot of dangling gold jewelry on her forehead." Having invented the client and his daughter she was not in a position to describe a girl she might eventually have to hire to play the part. "Look," she said instructively, "my role is not that of a matchmaker or a beauty-pageant consultant. My function is to locate a suitable Christian group with a charismatic pastor. You fit the bill. The next step is for me to report back to my client and describe your ministry and for you to decide if there is room in your organization for her, and if he and his daughter are interested, and if you give it some thought and decide you want to interview her, then I'll set up a video conference. Do you have a computer out here?"

"I go down to a motel near the main highway... they have a kind of 'internet cafe' corner in the lobby."

"Ok. Let's take one step at a time. Can I leave word for you at your mom's house?"

"No, I have a disposable phone. Before you leave I'll give you the number. How's that?"

"Fine." Her eye caught the case of a professional camera - a Hasselblad digital - on a desk. That was the camera Frank had seen. A professional photo printer was on the floor beside the desk. He had to own a computer. She thought about his denial and said to herself, "Internet Cafe, my ass."

"Now," he said, pouring himself a glass of wine, "it's time for you to pick a flick! We had a deal. It's movie time! You promised!"

"Do you have *A Few Good Men?*"

"*It's one of my faves!*" He selected the plastic case from his movie library and inserted it into the DVD player.

Beryl sipped her wine and blinked. "This is a first rate burgundy."

"Nothing but the best for you," he said. "Turn around. I'm going to put loose clothing on. No peeking." He removed his outer clothing and, she could tell, his underwear, too. Then he put on a pair of hospital scrubs and plopped down, sitting with his back against the headboard.

They sat propped up on the bed as the DVD began to run the FBI warning. As the film rolled, he commented on it. Like Beryl, he knew many of the lines by heart. In awkward stages, he began to put his arm around her shoulders. By the time the film ended, she was comfortably leaning into his encircling arm.

She was tired and sleepy. The moon was shining brightly through the window. Night birds were singing. A wolf... a real wolf... howled in the distance. Another wolf answered. There was something magical about the setting and the presence of this handsome, funny and altogether charming man-boy. Beryl thought, "Whoever this guy is, there is absolutely no mystery about the way he can keep seven women in line... probably as sex slaves... or worse." She knew professionally colored hair when she saw it, and manicured acrylic nails, and the implications of women who wore no underwear under loose dresses. The women, she suspected, were probably pimped out by him. How he did this... with only a CB radio that was now pretty much passé and a disposable phone remained a question she would have to answer.

He sat up. "Pick another flick!" he squealed like a child. "That's an order!"

"*Donnie Brasco.*" She began to worry about Akara. The first film had taken an hour and a half. Surely that was more than enough time for him to have found her.

"Coming up." He put the disk into the player and jumped back into bed. Then he reached for Beryl's wine glass and refilled it. As she thanked him, he took it from her hand, put it on the nightstand, and leaned forward, trying to kiss her. She turned her face and he gently kissed her cheek.

He clearly wanted to kiss her more intimately, but his attempt was so awkward that she was reminded of a Norman Rockwell painting of a pubescent youth attempting to get his first kiss. "This man," she thought, "knows absolutely nothing about normal male and female relationships. He must be like an oriental pasha lying on a couch while harem girls perform sexual acts on him... a pimp who has probably never gone out on a date. Home schooled? Hah! Brothel schooled is more like it!"

She began to find his fumbling attempts to interact with her in some kind of socially ordinary way disturbing. "Where the hell is Akara?" she asked herself, smiling as she put an index finger against Avery's lips.

She watched Donnie Brasco begin to act out his part in an undercover operation. "How," she asked herself, "do these guys do it... month after month."

Avery turned onto his side and stared at her. "So, do you think you'd like to change your mode of service?"

"I admit, I'm tempted. My mind's a veritable Tempest."

"Ah... Shakespeare. I miss being able to talk about him. One of my mother's best clients was an old actor. He said he had been with the Royal Shakespeare Company. I never verified that. But he did know his Shakespeare, and he taught me about all the plays. He'd cast me in various roles and we'd do the scenes together... sometimes we'd each have three or four roles in the same play. I'd like to do that again. Suppose I cast you in a play of Shakespeare. Would you enjoy *Titus Andronicus?*"

The suggestion shocked her. "I think not." A feeling akin to a high speed elevator's sudden stop came up from her toes. Avery's charm evaporated and she breathed in an air of nauseous reality. She was an investigator and this man was quite likely a murderer. "Why was I finding him so charming?" she asked herself, without attempting to supply an answer.

It required disciplined effort to talk to him without revealing a change in attitude. "Of all the plays, *Titus Andronicus* is the worst. It is so bloody and cruel... why on earth would you pick that one?"

"Because service isn't always pleasant."

"I know," she said simply. Then she feigned a yawn. "Think of another play. I've had such a long day."

Ten minutes into the film, Akara sounded the horn of Liam's Lincoln. She sat still, listening. "That's my son," she said. "I'm sure of it."

Akara bounded up the path into the picnic area and knocked loudly on the cabin door. "Mom!" he called. "I'm home!"

"My son, the comedian," Beryl said.

Avery grabbed her. "When will you contact me again?"

"Give me your disposable phone number."

"Ok." He reached into the drawer of a bedside table and withdrew a business card. "The number's written on the back. Don't give it to anyone else. Call me tomorrow."

"Ok. I will." She went to the bedroom door, unlocked and opened it, and went into the main room to let Akara in. "Wait here," she said. "I'll go get my regular clothes. I was sitting on a bed watching movies... and changed for comfort."

Akara smiled coyly as she left him. The girls upstairs were bending over the loft's railing to look at him. "Ladies," he said, "you have a lovely home." They giggled.

Avery came into the room. "So you're Beryl's son."

"I have the honor to be him."

"Excuse me for asking, but you have a definite Asian look to you. Tilson doesn't sound like an Asian name."

"It's my mom's second husband's name. He died and she retained it for professional use. My dad was her first husband. My last name is Chatree. It's a name well-known in Thailand."

"I'm glad you explained. Where is your dad?"

"He's also deceased. She's footloose and fancy free... or so I keep telling her."

Avery laughed. "That's good to know. So, what's the rush with getting your mother? She and I were enjoying a couple of flicks."

"She's officially working. I'm officially beginning a vacation tomorrow morning. There's the obligatory list of 'do and don't' to discuss. Besides, she's got to get to an ATM. I need some 'mad money.'" He grinned.

Avery smiled and nodded. "I know how it is. I've been there."

In the bathroom, before she changed her clothes, she looked inside the medicine cabinet and saw vials of estrogen and hypodermic needles. There were other vials but she could not read their labels.

She came into the living room, dressed now in street clothing. She stopped to kiss Avery on the cheek. "Until tomorrow," she said.

Akara followed her back to the motel. She went into her room and got into bed. But it was nearly three o'clock in the morning before she finally drifted into a light and fitful sleep.

SATURDAY, MAY 18, 2013

Before Beryl and Akara headed out for breakfast, Beryl called George and Martin to bring them up to date about the tangential line the investigation had taken.

"I've located Waverly who is part of that group that scammed Frank. The guy who heads the group, the mouse-faced photographer, is a phony Christian pastor of a group of women called The Sisters of Gethsemane Garden, based in both St. George, Utah and a place northeast of here called La Casa Serena. Incidentally, I've been able to identify that pendant Waverly wore in the photographs. It's a Crown of Thorns around a Cross. They venerate a barbed wire crown and they apparently use it in some sexual initiation ritual. I've got to call the pastor in an hour or so and then I need to head down to North Las Vegas, near Nellis Air Force Base to try to find a former Sister who left because, supposedly, she needed surgery. Got any tips on how I could go about finding her? I don't even know her name or what she looks like, except she's older than the others."

"What about that gold necklace? Was she ever given one?" Martin asked.

"Damned if I know."

"Well, given the price of gold," George said, thinking aloud, "if she's got one and she's flush, you've got a problem; but if she's hard up for money, there's a good chance she hocked it."

"My source indicated that she owns a house there."

"Usually, around a military base," George said, "especially a noisy air force base, the real estate is not high-end. So she's probably living in a low-end development. Try the pawn shops first."

"That was fast work, *Lieutenant Caffee. So this is what the inside of an investigation looks like.*"

"May I remind you again that we're under contract with another attorney. Yes... you've got competition for my services. *We just might plead Mr. Mouseface down to a misdemeanor.*"

George groaned. "Are you two ever gonna stop talking about *A Few Good Men?*"

"*Nobody likes him very much,*" Beryl said, laughing.

"Oh, Avery, I wish I were calling to say, 'Hello,'" Beryl said, "but I'm afraid it's 'Goodbye,' for now, anyway."

"Why are you leaving?"

"My dear... We're in Pacific time. Back east, my business partner is already trying to figure out what to do with this piece of mail and that piece of mail. I have a report to prepare. I should have asked you this before. But suppose you wanted to interview or at least look over a candidate for admission to your order, where and when would it be convenient?"

"Hold off on that until you decide whether or not you'll join us. I can try to bribe you. You can have the mistress's chair at the other head of the table and I'll even let you wear my *Christian Number One.*"

"Avery Christian... if you were familiar with the *Hagakure* you'd know the admonition: 'People will become your enemy if you become eminent too quickly.' If I joined you, you'd not be doing me a favor by making a pet of me. What should I tell my client?"

"Set up a video interview. But you'll have to contact me when I'm someplace else. I like to start my summer skin-exposure season in a controlled environment - which is another way of saying that before I go to a beach resort or out sailing, I like to get a gradual tan, poolside if possible. I'm fair, and skin care is important. If things are ok in the video call, can you get her down to Las Vegas in a week or so?"

"I can get the process started. I'll call you on your secret cell!"

"Yes. We'll set up the meeting with the other girl. But make sure you leave time for us to talk... we can talk more about Shakespeare."

She sighed. "I will, *Votre Majesté*."

He giggled and disconnected the call.

"Let's get moving!" she announced. "We have to get in touch with Liam. He's got contacts with P.I. agencies in the area. We need him to find a young P.I. who can act the part of our client's daughter. We've also got to get down to North Las Vegas to look for the sick sister."

She and Akara drove their rental cars to North Las Vegas, some seventy miles southeast.

On the highway, George called Beryl. "Give me some background on this guy. What do you think his problem specifically is? Is he in some kind of arrested development or just your garden-variety Peter Pan?"

"As you could see from his photograph, he's extremely handsome... beautiful even. He's like a blonde Greek god... something you'd see carved in stone or painted on an urn. But he is a boy-man. Not even an adolescent-man.

"He must work out. He's lithe but muscular. Not that muscle-bound stuff you see in 'body builders' contests. No, he's slim and tall and fair. He's what you'd call 'a youth.' He's a youth going on forty. Not a blemish on him. A Charmides type. Strangely sexy.

"I described his mother to you... she's right out of a vision of hell. But this is the thing... she was able to talk to me in a woman-to-woman business-like or neighborly way. Yet, with Liam MacDonald, she lapsed into some kind of whorehouse tart... as if nobody would notice that she was pushing eighty-five or ninety. That's bizarre to the point of insanity. Grotesque.

"Avery says she was forty-five when she had him. She was the madam of a whorehouse and he grew up completely inside that whorehouse. He was home schooled. The only male models he's had were the johns who paid to be serviced by the women. I'm guessing that there was a lot of sadomasochism involved. Her mansion 'workroom' was filled with SM instruments, and I noticed a few whips in his Cazarina cabin - that's what they call La Casa Serena. But to him, sex must always have been equated with money... lucrative sexual exploitation. I don't think he ever hated living in a whorehouse. I don't think he realized that there were other ways to live. I doubt that he ever had any friends his own age. He looks at me as if I were a pal of his age group.

"So I don't see him as just another Peter Pan. He's infinitely more complicated than that. I've only seen the artless child in him. My gut tells me that his other identity - the one that I can only surmise from the artifacts - is that of a sadistic monster. To get them to perform he pumps them up with hormones - no matter how dangerous that might be to them. And they surely don't get their hair and nails done to please him. No, those Sisters are groomed for work. And that work has got to be extremely profitable.

"His mother has probably raised him to be a greedy, abusive, megalomaniac. His Crown of Thorns! It's coiled barbed wire the women apparently sit on for a really memorable climax and to give him the thrill of power. They venerate that ring of wire. I think Avery is probably stark raving mad in that refined but insidious way of a *Schutzstaffel* officer. A delightful sociopath."

"What you're describing is a dangerous man. Be careful."

In North Las Vegas, after they checked into a motel, Akara sat on Beryl's bed and asked, "If you were one of the Sisters and you were dumped for some reason here, why would you be dumped, and where would you go when you were dumped?"

"First, she may have left by her own choice. Maybe she has a relative who truly needs her care. Maybe she's going through menopause or something and doesn't have the nervous system for so much excitement. According to Joe Tuffs and the real Waverly, one of the Sisters was older... in her forties. Since none of the women at the cabin was that old, this one has to be the older one. That he just let her leave says that he probably doesn't regard her as threatening. She must be insanely loyal, or maybe terminally ill, or too scared to speak the truth."

"Scared? Why scared?"

"He didn't have a professional camera because he likes to photograph sunsets. In order for them to live the way they live, they have to be pimped out. He probably had a zillion compromising photographs of each of them."

"To use in case she objected to being dumped?"

"Yes. He would have plenty of photographs of each woman... videos maybe... in which she performed sex acts on him or on another Sister. He'd know where she came from - her family, her school, her former jobs. Oh, he'd see to it that she never exposed his racket to anyone.

"But if he did dump her purposely, the inability to produce money would be the principal reason. He would probably measure the time it took a Sister to get a man to come to her in the bar and buy her a drink. She couldn't look like a pro or the hotel security people who know which pros to allow and which to flag, would get rid of her. So she'd have to be checked-in as a legitimate guest.

"The operation would have to be done with precision. The Sister would have to get the mark back to her hotel room on a tight schedule. To run six girls at a time, Avery would have to plant video cameras in several strategic places in the room. The Sister would not charge the mark, so he'd be feeling pretty good about the evening's entertainment. He'd probably get chummy with her... talk about himself and get her contact information. But suppose he had the room next door and nixed the idea of going back to her room. Then Avery would have to follow them wherever they went, maybe by her phone's GPS transmission. It could get complicated. So think about it. How would you run the operation?"

Akara laughed. "This is what I love about this work. It isn't mathematics, it's something with infinitely more variables than any problem. Ok. I've got six girls, and each one is all dressed up and sitting alone at a bar or 21 table. I'd give each of them a really sensitive GPS transmitter or some kind of beacon I could follow. I'd know when she was headed for her room or another room. If it was another room, then I'd have to time the operation carefully. If I pretended to be room service when I knocked on their door... well, maybe they already called room service so I'd have to get the pictures before the real room service guy arrived. Wow. She'd have to keep a tight schedule. If her performance was erratic, the operation could get risky. No profit in that. I'd have to dump her."

"Exactly. And what would make a woman less attractive?"

"She could look old and tired."

"Right. The subtleties that might make an older woman sexually desirable would take too long to appreciate. Avery would want quick and reckless attraction. So age is a factor, as is a physical inability to perform due to a disease or some other medical problem. Problems that could be solved with antibiotics or lotions would be one thing. But surgical problems could get expensive. Speaking in terms of profit and loss, it probably wouldn't be worth keeping her."

Akara nodded. "Then there are the personality problems. Maybe she was argumentative and made life miserable for the others. If she were sufficiently angry and threatened to expose the group, he'd have to do away with her."

"Right. Everything depends on a Sister's devotion to him. He's got to keep punishing and rewarding her... like a card game. If you win all the time, you won't want to play. There's none of the excitement of chance. So he's got to keep them guessing. He requires harmony, teamwork, loyalty. If he can't depend on her devotion to him or her fear of those photographs to keep her quiet about the operation, he won't risk dumping her. She'll disappear... maybe down one of those abandoned mine shafts Niles Portmann talked about."

Akara made a list of all the pawn shops in the area. One after the other they visited them and asked the pawnbroker if he had such a gold necklace available. The first seven of them did not. They pushed the door open on the eighth.

The proprietor greeted them and Beryl announced, "We're looking for a gold chain and a pendant that is a gold disk that has a Crown of Thorns and a Cross etched on it. Do you have one?"

"Yes," the owner said, more surprised even than Beryl and Akara. "I didn't figure there was much demand for this sort of thing. But since the price of gold keeps going up, I thought I'd hang onto it." He produced the chain and pendant.

"This is it," Beryl said. "What we want is not the chain, but the woman who hocked it."

"I can't tell you that unless you've got a warrant, and I don't think you have one."

"How much is the chain and pendant?" Akara asked.

"Two thousand dollars."

"Here's five hundred," Akara said. "You keep the chain and pendant and we just happen to see the name and maybe the address of the woman who hocked it."

"No. A local lady pawned this and I'm not going to give her up for a few bucks. If you want to buy it, it's yours."

"Two thousand dollars is a lot of money," Beryl said. "I'm sure the piece is well worth it, but since you know that we've already described the article, you can appreciate that we're familiar with the religious group that uses this logo. Membership in it isn't anything that someone has to be ashamed of, but a new member customarily uses pseudonyms which doesn't help us to locate her. If the previous owner of this necklace wore it, she was proud of it. The point is, we need to contact her. She's due to come into some money. If she doesn't need it, fine. We'll move on. But if she does need money - and I'm guessing that she wouldn't have parted with the necklace if she didn't - I think she'd appreciate your giving us her name and address. Think about it. We'll buy it, but please... try to give us a little direction. The group is The Sisters of Gethsemane Gardens. We know her only as Sister Hope."

Akara went into his 'mad-money' cache in his wallet and withdrew two-thousand dollars.

The pawn broker wrote up the sale. As he boxed the necklace, he said, "Diedra Swanson. 4820 Jenkins Way. Tell her I hope I did the right thing in giving you her address."

Diedra's modest tract home showed the unmistakable signs of neglect. What once had been a lawn was now clumps of sere wisps of grass, frost-heaved stones, and leafless shrubbery. A tree, that apparently sent its roots into the neighbors' watering system, provided the only sign of life and source of shade. The house faced west and the curtains on the windows were bleached and tattered by the strength of the afternoon sun.

Akara rang the bell, but no interior noise was heard.

"Listen," Beryl said, "the air conditioner's not on."

"She must not be home," Akara said, stepping to the side of the house to look at the back yard. "She's got sheets hanging on a line," he said. "Damn! You only get to see laundry hanging outside in movies... in the States, anyway."

"Try knocking," Beryl said. "Maybe her electricity has been turned off."

Akara knocked on the door and almost immediately Diedra answered. "If you're selling something or trying to get me join your group, you're wastin' your time."

"We're not salesmen or missionaries," Akara replied.

"What then? I don't owe anybody any money. All my accounts are paid up."

Beryl smiled and said, "We're here on behalf of the Sisters."

"Oh!" Diedra gasped. "Oh, I've been waitin' for you for so long. Come on in." She began to flutter around the living room, pumping up pillows and straightening lampshades. "Let me turn on the air conditioning. I keep it off to save expenses." She adjusted the thermostat on the wall and immediately air began to blow through the ducts. It occurred to her that they may have wondered about the door bell. "I disconnected the bell months ago when I did a long devotional service and didn't want to be disturbed in my prayers."

"Oh," Akara said. "That's a good reason. I can sympathize."

Considering that she had been "lost" to the group, Diedra Swanson did not appear to be distraught. Beryl guessed that she was in her late-forties. Her hair was completely grey, her eyelids crinkled, her upper lip creased, and her facial skin badly sagging. If acrylic nails had ever been applied over her own, they had grown out beyond the tell-tale ridge. Even with make-up and given a stylish hairdo, she would never have attracted a man with or without money. It puzzled Beryl to know that someone this unattractive could have been so recently dumped by Avery. Why had he held on to her for so long?

Beryl furtively turned on both the voice recorder and the camcorder in her tote bag and carefully placed the bag on the couch beside her, pointing the hidden camera lens directly at Diedra who sat in a single stuffed chair across the room. Akara sat on the couch, too. He removed a small tablet from his pocket and affected a serious expression as he looked at Diedra. "Pastor Christian insisted that we be certain that we have the correct Diedra, his special Sister Six. Would you mind answering a few questions?"

"Oh, my goodness! He called me that? He's so wonderful. Ask me anything you like. You know, I had just about given up. Eugenia kept telling me to be patient. Patience is such a virtue, but I was beginning to think I had no virtue left!"

"Who is Eugenia?"

"Father Avery's cousin!"

Akara made a note. "Do you have your copy of the Satan Lure photograph?"

Diedra giggled. "That's a trick question! I never had my photograph taken in Satan Lure underwear. Besides, Father Avery kept all the photographs. Nobody ever got a copy."

Akara nodded, smiled slightly, and made another check.

"How long were you with the Sisters?" Beryl asked.

"I met Father three years ago when Eugenia lived in Las Vegas. I used to clean house for her. It was love at first sight. I adored him right away and secretly wanted to join the Sisters of Gethsemane Garden. But I was just a cleaning lady. My husband - he was a lot older than me - was walking in a hardware store and a bin that was up high tipped over and killed him, so I got a settlement. I wanted to donate money to the ministry and Eugenia said why don't I invest in my future, and that she'd talk to Father Avery about taking me on as his personal assistant.

I could live in style with the Sisters. When I was younger I worked in a department store so I knew how to present myself. Oh, it's a long story."

"We're here to listen," Akara said. "Please tell us... and don't leave anything out."

"Well, since I was a widow, I was free to become a missionary. I made the decision to do God's work. Father took me to the Gethsemane Garden house in Utah. We were alone together for a whole week. The sisters were at the special place in Nevada. Cazarina. I've never been there but they say that that's where they recharge their batteries. Isn't that funny? Recharge their batteries. They get massages there and they swim. I think that's where they learn their missionary techniques. It must be heaven."

"How big was the settlement you got?" Akara inquired.

"Three hundred thousand dollars. Father Avery was going to buy a beach house and a boat for just the two of us. I had put this house up for sale, but nobody bought it, and then I got sick. I had a bad Pap test and my doctor, Doctor Lassiter, wanted to operate."

"A hysterectomy?" Beryl asked.

"Yes. But I didn't have health insurance and my husband didn't get Social Security benefits because he was always 'odd-job' contract labor. He got paid 'under the table' and so did I, but then I didn't have a job anymore because Eugenia moved away. Father Avery said that I should have the surgery done in Salt Lake City so I would have to wait. And then Father had a revelation that God would cure me after a forty-day silence in the desert. I didn't have to leave the house. I just had to stay inside and pray eight hours a day for forty days. And then to see if my prayers were answered - which would prove that I was worthy - I had to have another Pap test. I thought for sure I would be cured, but it was no better. I tried again to keep silent for forty days, but I was running out of money. Then I got a job cleaning two gas stations regularly. I make enough to buy groceries, pay the insurance on my car, and buy gas and all, but I have to watch my electricity and water use. Those bills are just too high. So I'm not starving and I'm not complaining. I knew Father Avery would never let me down. He told me to think about being on the sailboat." She pointed to a framed photograph of a sailboat. "I tore a page out of a magazine in the doctor's office. I didn't think they'd mind. This is such a pretty boat. I hope we buy one just like it."

Akara stood up to look more closely at the picture of a new two masted yacht skimming over the water with its spinnaker billowing before it. Diedra evidently did not know that her $300,000 donation to Avery might have served to make a down payment on the ship, but it wouldn't have come close to buying it.

"I think that's why everyone loves Father Avery so much," Beryl said. "He fills us all with such happy thoughts. Tell us about your experience with the Sisters. What role did you play?"

"You mean as Father's assistant?"

"Yes. Can you start by telling us what Father Avery did with the ring of barbed wire?" she asked.

"The initiation ritual? I never went through it. I will, though, after my surgery. So all I did was assist at the ceremony and take pictures." She hesitated and seemed to be uncomfortable discussing it.

"If you took pictures as you say, then you must know about the ritual. I'm afraid you'll have to be more explicit. Father insists that we must be thorough."

Diedra smiled. "Father told us not to discuss such things. But if he asked you to ask about it, he must want me to answer. You know how when you get hot enough down there you just want to feel the pleasure and pain of the blood sacrifice? Father has a lingham and yoni... that's a penis and vagina that they use in India. We put the Crown of Thorns... the ring of barbed wire... we just call it the Crown of Thorns... on the ring of the yoni and the candidate rubs up and down on the lingham and when she's ready she drops down on the ring in ecstasy. It's a beautiful ceremony."

"I bet– uh, better let a woman talk to you about that," Akara quickly recovered from his original enthusiastic intention to say, "I bet!"

"I was good with the camera. My husband was a photography buff... that's what you call people who have a hobby about something... a buff.

So I knew a little about lighting and composition. I would take the "Confront the Devil" photographs."

"Like Satan's Lure?"

"No. Father took those pictures."

"Describe the 'Confront the Devil' pictures."

"Oh, I don't know if I should. They were personal demonstrations of love for Father and defiance of Satan."

Akara got out the necklace. He dangled it for Diedra to see. "I'm not supposed to show you this as an inducement to get you to be truthful. But I think that you know that if you want to wear this again, you have to answer all the questions that Father Avery insists that we ask."

"Oh!" Diedra's eyes welled with tears. "I'd give anything to be able to wear it again. I had to sell mine. I never thought I'd have the honor to wear that symbol of righteousness again. All right. I'll tell you. A sister would have to take her vows once a month, every month. All the sisters would participate. Nobody was allowed to be absent. They would have a contest to see who could challenge Satan most. The whole idea of free will is that all people are free to do sexual things, but that a good Christian has the ability to do them but also has the will-power to choose not to do them. So the Sisters would pose in front of the camera doing sexual things to Father and to each other and sometimes to themselves. It was like 'thumbing your nose at Satan.' It was like saying–" she pointed her finger at Akara, "'*I can sin better than your most ardent devotees, Satan, but I choose not to sin because I have free will and I am a good Christian woman.*'"

"Wow," Akara said.

Beryl gave him a silencing look and resumed the questioning. "Did you ever meet a woman who was considering joining him? Her name was Aleta."

"Oh, Aleta Portmann!"

"Did you like her?"

"She spent time with us in Gethsemane Garden in Utah and in our temporary place in Beatty. I liked her. She could cook. She made the best venison stew. It was unlike any venison stew you ever had. So sure, I remember Aleta. She was nice, but a little thick headed."

"What do you remember about her?"

"She just couldn't see the wisdom of using the Devil's money to fund our ministry. I never went on a Sacrifice trip, but the Sisters tried to explain to her that it was wrong to take money from hard working Christians - the way that most churches do - when for a small sacrifice we could get so much more money from people who serve Satan. Father Avery gave money to orphanages... to soup kitchens... to needy people. I told Aleta that every woman makes a sexual sacrifice when she sleeps with her husband and he wants sex but she's tired from raisin' the kids and doin' housework. No matter. She has to drag her body into bed and then bump and grind a man for his pleasure. I was married twice. My first husband had two little kids. I was a kid myself. By the time I was twenty I looked and felt older than I look and feel today."

Beryl nodded in sympathy. "Why couldn't Aleta understand? It was so obvious. Really! Aleta must not have been too bright if she couldn't understand that, or maybe she just didn't like sex."

"We got regular injections... 'divine elixir' Father called it but would make you feel like one of those nymphomaniacs. Father Avery gave her an injection and in a couple of days she started to warm up to the idea; but then the Sisters made a mistake. It was their job to test her to see if she was ready for the initiation. He started the process and a couple of Sisters went in to help with sex toys... you know... to get her so hot that she'd want the Crown of Thorns pressed into her flesh... down there... to bring her to the agony and ecstasy of the blood climax. The first time she seemed to like it, but she wasn't quite ready I guess."

"Was that what the last argument was about?" Akara asked.

"Yes! Father Avery loved her house. He wanted her to divorce her husband and get the house in the divorce settlement. At first she agreed; but then she said it wasn't possible to get it. She must have changed her mind. She said she'd just come to be one of us. No house. No alimony. She wouldn't explain. Father Avery had picked her up in Tonopah and brought her to our rented place in Beatty, and then she told him that there would be no house. He was so angry! She got nasty, and then he blamed us for not having given her a proper initiation with the Crown of Thorns and she went wild."

"What happened to her?"

"I don't think I'm supposed to talk about it..."

"Ah, ah!" Akara said, waving the necklace.

Beryl held a hand up, indicating that Akara should cease the demonstration. "We can talk about the 'accident.' I'd hate to see you fail to be united with the group because you refused to discuss it."

Diedra immediately began to plead. Her eyes brimmed with tears. "I'm so sorry. I know how Father Avery is. If he told you to ask, the least I can do is answer. Aleta came to the house in Beatty and acted so shocked. Then she got nasty. She called him names. Vile names. We have a paddle for getting spanked. It's called 'The Board of Education.' Aleta tried to hit him with it. That's when he blamed us for not initiating her properly. So we held her legs and made her sit on the crown. She really got nasty then. He tried to quiet her... to calm her down. But she was so feisty... kicking and screaming."

"What did she call him?"

"Oh, my goodness! She said, 'You are a pimp... a whore master. You made love to me and told me you wanted me for your spiritual wife! But the whole time all you wanted was my house... that and to peddle my ass to drunks so that you could blackmail them.' She wanted the negative back for the Satan Lure photo, but digitals don't have negatives."

"If she didn't want to pose for the picture, why did she?"

"Once they had started to get... well... intimate... Father Avery explained that if she was *not* willing to tempt the devil, then she *was* willing to let the devil tempt her. Was she strong enough to stand face to face with Satan? It would have been unfair to let her join without proving her commitment. So she posed. She was the only one allowed in his room for a whole week after that. That picture was taken at her house. It's a really nice place in Tonopah. She had the accident in Beatty. He felt terrible that she stopped breathing when he tried to quiet her."

"I know. Her death was a horrible accident."

"Yes, she wouldn't stop fighting. She was trying to hit us and he grabbed her from behind... he put his arm around her neck and she suddenly collapsed. She would have been the First Sister, sitting at the head of the table."

"So you were present when Father Avery subdued Aleta too much and had the accident."

"Yes, I tried to comfort him, but it was too much. We needed to protect him so we threw her body in a ditch somewhere around Pahrump. And then Father Avery dropped me off down here to get my medical checkup and that's all I know."

"Well, Diedra, you've passed the first part of the test. We're going to take you to see this fella... do you know him?" She showed her the driver's license photograph of Avery.

Diedra squealed. "Oh... Isn't he handsome?"

"Yes," said Beryl, smiling broadly. "He certainly is. First, let's call Dr. Lassiter. We'll let him schedule whatever he needs to do, and then you can get your things and come back to the motel with us. After you get the surgery you need, we'll be ready for Part Two... a trip to Tonopah."

"Will you stay with me?"

"I won't, but Brother Akara will. Not here, though. Since you'd be leaving right away, it would probably be better if you stayed with him in our motel. Let's get you some medical care as soon as possible."

Dr. Lassiter arranged that Diedra would be admitted to the hospital Sunday night and have the hysterectomy Monday morning. Since she had no insurance, Akara used his debit card to pay in advance for the procedure. If everything went well, she'd probably be released on Tuesday and would be back to normal within a week.

Beryl made plans to meet Liam in Tonopah and to speak personally to his client. After that, they would set up a meeting with the Novalis Agency, a well-respected private investigation firm in downtown Las

Vegas to interview their candidates for the female operative who could infiltrate the group.

The single instruction she left with Akara was to be absolutely certain that Diedra had no telephone privileges at the hospital and that she made no phone calls when she was with him in the motel.

Akara secured Diedra's solemn promise not to use the phone until after she had returned to Tonopah. He agreed to help her prepare to reunite with Avery Christian. The stores were open so he took her shopping for clothing and got her an appointment with a hairdresser on Tuesday.

After dinner, as Diedra lay on the big bed in their double room, surrounded by boxes and garments, Akara went to the bathroom; and even though he told her not to call anyone, she was too excited and giddy to follow such an unreasonable order. She could see no harm in telling an old and trusted friend, Father Avery's cousin Eugenia, the good news about Father's angels, patience being rewarded, and a blessed reunion soon to come in Nevada. She picked up the phone and made a quick call.

Liam MacDonald, eager to see the video recording of Diedra Swanson, was waiting for Beryl at his home in Tonopah. It was late when she arrived.

He whistled as she played the tape. "So this is a sex cult. And the son of a bitch killed Aleta. This guy is evil." He looked again at the photograph of Avery Christian. "And he just takes every cent this poor woman has and sends her home, telling her to wait even though she needed medical treatment. I wonder if he's killed or abandoned other women."

"She's getting surgery Monday morning. This witness was expensive, but, as we say, 'Cheap at twice the price.' Before I forget!" Beryl announced, "you've got to transfer big bucks into Akara Chatree's account - he paid in advance for Diedra's surgeon and hospital costs - and also into my account."

"I'll take care of it. Never fear. Now, what's the plan?"

"Akara will have her up here in Tonopah by Wednesday or Thursday. I don't think she'll make a great witness, but she should be enough to do Niles some good. The best hope for him is to have an operative infiltrate the Sisters and learn from them when they are scheduled to run another blackmail scam - in what city and in what hotel. We can alert security at the hotel. I've seen these women and can identify them and Avery, too, when he checks in. They can then actually film him planting cameras in the rooms and tail the women as they lure the marks back to their rooms... or follow him if they go elsewhere. Most of the top ranked security officers are well trained in police interrogation. They'll be able to get the women to turn on each other, especially if they offer deals to plead to lesser charges.

"But as to Aleta's death, I'd still like to interview Niles. I need to hear his side of the story from him."

SUNDAY, MAY 19, 2013

At the Tonopah jail Beryl sat quietly while Liam explained to Niles Portmann the circumstances of his wife's death. "We'll have the witness up here on Wednesday. I'll talk to Sheriff Hornsby and the D.A.'s office if he thinks that's necessary. All you're guilty of now is making a stupid phone call. It's a crime to falsely call the police and make a charge against someone... even though that someone is yourself."

"That was the most stupid thing I've ever done in my whole life."

"I can readily imagine that," Liam said. "It's hard to believe an educated man could ever be so unrealistic."

"Blame it on my state of mind. I loved Aleta so much. That I lost her while I was away I blamed those rats who perjured themselves. I wanted to get even. I went about it stupidly.

"And then she turns up dead. I couldn't believe it. I loved her... so I not only screwed myself but I lost her. What was I going to do? I still don't understand why she had cactus needles in her behind. What kind of man was he? And she preferred him to me? Who were these evil people?

"So here I am. The people I loved betrayed me and the people I hated are still living it up, laughing at me... and runnin' foals to death."

Beryl suddenly felt sympathy for him. "For the record, they forced her to sit on a coil of barbed wire. They called it a Crown of Thorns. She was killed during a violent argument in which she refused to divorce you."

Niles Portmann looked up in disbelief. "Why did she say that?"

Beryl answered. "Obviously she loved you. When she thought you'd be up here for six years, she got involved with religion and then met him... and he is one persuasive character. You have to take into consideration her state of mind. She had one miscarriage after another and had to be depressed and confused about her failure to have children. She was ripe for this guy's picking. She thought she'd devote her life to helping others find Christ. But she told him that she couldn't give him your house. And then she found out that the house was what he wanted and that they were a bunch of sexual perverts and extortionists. She fought them, and he put her in a chokehold and accidentally killed her."

Niles needed a few minutes of blank staring to process this unexpected news. "Thanks for telling me that. I didn't know. What happens next?"

"We have to find more proof that he killed her. What we have is a witness that he can discredit because he dumped her and he can say, with a certain conviction, that she's just trying to get even. And if the other girls won't tell the truth - and why would they? - we have no unassailable proof. But we do have a plan that will get the proof we need."

"What can I do?"

"Just don't talk or write to anyone. Stay absolutely silent. Don't get any more brainstorms. This time play it smart and say and do nothing. Let us do our work without interference," Liam said with quiet firmness.

Niles nodded. "Thanks for calling in the P.I.s for me."

Outside, Liam asked what Beryl thought Avery Christian's next move would be.

"This guy is slippery," she said. "He says he's probably going to be in Las Vegas next week. I think I was pretty convincing when I gave him that story about investigating him for the father of a young woman who wanted to join his group. He wants to meet my client's daughter, which means that you and I have to find someone who fits the bill. Other than that he claims that he likes to get a 'controlled' tan before he gets blasted with sun on his boat. That's all I know. His boat is called 'Darien.' I don't know where he keeps it, but with seven women on his hands, he's probably got a beach house of some kind."

"The Novalis Agency in Las Vegas has a few candidates for the job. I'll make the contractual arrangements with Novalis for the operative's engagement."

"When are the interviews supposed to take place?"

"Tomorrow morning at your motel. I'll get one of my friends who has a small plane to fly me down."

"Then I'll drive back now and you can call me when you arrive and either Akara or I will pick you up at the airport."

Diedra Swanson's good friend and confidante, Eugenia Pulaski, Avery Christian–Jebel Kitchener's cousin, had solemnly promised to keep their brief conversation secret. But then she did what such good friends and confidantes invariably do. She immediately tried to contact Avery Christian to tell him the news. Unfortunately, she did not have his current disposable phone number. To get it, she had to contact someone she did not particularly enjoy speaking to: Margaret Cromwell. Reluctantly, she called the Cromwell residence; but she was told that Madam was indisposed for the remainder of the afternoon and evening.

Eugenia Pulaski said that she'd call back in the morning.

By 4 p.m. Liam MacDonald had replenished Akara's and Beryl's credit card accounts. He made a copy of the video and sat and watched it with his wife.

"Hard to believe," Luella said, "that people could get so desperate they'd say or they'd believe such incredible lies. She gave that man every sent she had. It would have been bad if he had merely swindled her; but in the cause of his greed, he stole the money she needed for surgery. And then, pretending to be a man of God, he tampered with her faith by having her pray for a cure. Jeopardizing a person's faith in God is the biggest sin of all."

The plan remained intact. On Wednesday morning, Akara would drive Diedra to Tonopah from Las Vegas. Diedra would become a house guest of Liam and his wife Luella who had promised to watch over her personally to be certain that she did not contact anyone. By then, Beryl would have the Novalis operative prepped for a meeting with Avery Christian at whichever location he chose.

Liam would sign the contract with the agency once Beryl and the Novalis operative agreed to the nature and terms of the assignment.

On the long drive back to North Las Vegas, Beryl talked at length to Martin and George.

They thought the investigation was moving along nicely; but they did not know Avery Christian. Beryl felt it necessary to remind them of this. He was more clever and powerful than they imagined.

After getting the needed transfusions into her credit card account, Beryl decided that it was time she bought a few new outfits to wear to the audition and for the occasion of presenting the "client's daughter" to Avery. On Sunday morning, she went to a mall and bought two new suits - one cream and one blue - and the shoes and bags that went with them. She spent twice as much as she ordinarily would, but something told her that Avery's attention to garments demanded a greater degree of refinement in her choice of clothing.

She had just finished dressing in the cream colored suit when Liam called from the airport. She picked him up and the two of them went directly to the Novalis Agency's office.

Four young operatives were presented. Two were, in her opinion, too masculine and would not have attracted the kind of "quickie" type of encounter a man attending a convention naturally preferred. The third and fourth candidates agreed to be tested extemporaneously.

"He believes that you've spent time in an ashram. Do you know what that is?" she asked.

"One girl did not know what the term specifically meant; the other had spent time in Kerela, India. She had been learning Vajra Mushti, an Indian Martial art, but she learned enough of the "lingo" to be persuasive in her accounts. Beryl chose this operative, Sally Snyder, and asked that she be provided with fake credentials from Pennsylvania in the name of Sally Bridges. The contracts were signed.

Leaving Liam at the Novalis Agency, Beryl took Sally to her motel room to brief her on Avery's peculiarities and to the general background she'd need to possess as the daughter of the fictional Norton Bridges. She played the video for Sally. "He's ruthless," she said. Sally agreed.

Avery Christian called Beryl at 9 p.m. "I'm up here in St. George," he said. "Is the candidate with you?"

"Yes, she is. But she's in the ladies' room right now."

"That's fine. I'll go down to an internet cafe here in the shopping center near my house and video call you on your laptop. Before I schedule an appointment, I'd like to see what kind of personality she has. I must consider the peaceful integration of a new Sister."

"Wonderful. When she comes out, I'll tell her. We'll await your call."

Even though she disconnected her phone, she whispered to Sally. "He says he's in St. George but he could be in the room next door. He says he's going to an internet cafe. He really believes that I believe that.

"Well, when he calls again, you'll have to talk to him. Remember, he loves Shakespeare and is a kind of shape-shifter. You'll see him as a person of great boyish charm. And part of him is exactly that. It's the other part we have to worry about."

Fifteen minutes later Avery called again. Beryl answered. Avery asked, "Is she still interested in becoming a member of our religious community?"

"Well, she wants to meet you first. She doesn't seem to be the type who will jump into the great unknown."

Sally walked across the room and called, "Are you speaking to Mr. Christian? That's sounds like *Mutiny on the Bounty!*"

Beryl sighed. "It's The Reverend Mr. Christian... or Pastor Christian."

Sally said, "I'll only be a minute." She shut the bathroom door and returned to the bed.

Beryl lowered her voice. "She could use a little discipline. She has a few peculiar ideas, but I don't think she'll give the other women any trouble. She's sort of easy-going. I can see what her father means by 'needing a strong male hand.'"

"How long will you be down there?"

"As soon as I'm finished I'll go back to Philadelphia."

"I'd like to meet her but I can't get away. Can you come here?"

"No... I'm afraid I've already spent too much time away from my office."

"How about meeting me at Furnace Creek Lodge for lunch? That should only be an hour's drive for you."

"Let me talk to her and I'll call you back."

"Put her on the phone now. I'll say hello to her."

"She's in the bathroom... hold on... I'll get her." Beryl called, "Sally!" Sally Snyder got up, opened the bathroom door, and flushed the toilet. "Miss Bridges," Beryl playfully called, "you are wanted on the telephone."

Sally sat in front of the screen. "Hi," she said. "I'm supposed to call you The Reverend Mr. Christian. So how are you, The Reverend Mr. Christian?"

"I'm fine and getting finer now that I see how pretty you are. Can't you tell Miss Tilson to bring you up to me here in Saint George... or would you prefer to have lunch with me tomorrow in Death Valley? We could meet at Furnace Creek Lodge. The food is quite good."

"I'd prefer Death Valley. What time?"

"How's one o'clock?"

"Cool." She turned to Beryl to ask if the lunch date suited her schedule. Beryl nodded and Sally concluded the conversation. "All right," she said, "tomorrow, Monday the 20th, at 1 p.m. at Furnace Creek Lodge in Death Valley. See you then. Ciao."

Sally went home to pack and Beryl watched television until she fell asleep. At eleven o'clock Sally returned and five minutes later Akara called Beryl.

"Diedra got checked into the hospital," he said. "They run some tests before surgery so that's what they were doing when I left. I explained that she wasn't to have telephone privileges. I said that there was a lot of controversy in her family about the surgery so it would be best if she didn't get upset by squabbling with anyone now that the surgery is officially scheduled. The nurse said she'd be getting a sedative and there were no calls permitted after 8 p.m. anyway."

"Good. We've contracted with a new operative. A very pretty girl. Sally Snyder, but she'll be called Sally Bridges. She could use some pointers about Shakespeare - but before I forget, Liam put thirty thousand dollars into your account. He replenished mine, too.

"Tomorrow, Sally and I will be driving up to Death Valley to have lunch with Avery. We just talked to him. He said he was in St. George and would drive down to meet us. For all we know he's here in Vegas or at Cazarina, near Pahrump, Nevada, which is close to the entrance to Death Valley. He lies so sweetly. Well, at least he wants to interview Sally in person."

"Can you put Sally on the phone. I'll talk to her about the Bard."

Beryl handed her phone to Sally. "Talk drama with the good Dr. Chatree. He's young and handsome, and I need to get back to sleep."

They talked another hour and then, fearing that she was disturbing Beryl, Sally ended the call and put the phone into the charger.

Things were going smoothly. Beryl awakened long enough to try to think of a way to snare Avery Christian. As Sally finally got into bed, Beryl twisted her voice into a spooky whine and said aloud, "'The play's the thing wherein I'll catch the conscience of the king.'"

In the other bed, Sally Synder-Bridges replied in a cackling voice, "I thought you said Avery doesn't have a conscience."

Both women giggled.

MONDAY, MAY 20, 2013

"We play at paste till qualified for pearl," noted Emily Dickinson. The observation also applies to instructions about Zen's attitude towards life. We begin with parables that seem, to the beginner, to be such pretty little jewels. Later, when we deepen our understanding, we see them as the glass substitutes used to acquire the "gem-tactics" needed for handling real pearls.

Early on we learn about the monk who, while fleeing from a tiger, clings to a loose sapling on a cliff's side and sees death whether he goes up or down. Yet, he picks a wild strawberry and savors its sweetness. Yes, we say, we should all live in the "now" moment. But once we grow in Zen, the story loses its charm. No longer is the easy acceptance of an unfortunate fate so admirable. Now we call out to the monk, "Instead of picking a strawberry, scrape out a foothold for yourself! The tiger will pass." We know that if we do not survive, we cannot prevail. There are degrees of advancement in Zen's regimen; and we have to be alive in order to experience them.

To grow in Zen is to cease acquiescing to hardship. The man of Zen plans; repairs and prepares; knows the difference between feeding and starving, warmth and cold, safety and peril. What he does not do is desire or tolerate excess. There is no place for conspicuous consumption or honorific waste in the natural life.

Appreciating the natural essence of a person, place, or thing and valuing its most unadorned expression, the elegance of simplicity, is the way of Zen. By paring away embellishments, the evidence of rampant desire, the essential core is revealed. We value a spoon because it can lift a liquid to our mouth. When we additionally require that it be made of sterling silver, we have left Zen's precincts. We love someone who cares for us for caring to care. The moment we place burdening conditions on our love, requiring that the person also be fashionably dressed, perfect in speech, significant in society, and a reliable source of funds, we have missed Zen's boat.

Avery Christian knew only an endless beginning. He was blessed with a pleasing form and a fondness for the written word. He had been a beautiful child who grew up where the only people he knew fawned over him for no other reason but that heaven had dropped a bright and innocent soul into their shadowy world. Nothing threatened him. He needed no scraped-out footholds.

What was he to think, he wondered, when his cousin told him about the two angels, a young man and a woman, who Diedra Swanson claimed he had sent to help her? She said that he had commanded his angels to pay for her surgery, to buy her clothes, and to bring her to a meeting place in Nevada. The mysterious female angel had left quickly and Diedra had given no information about her. Could that woman have been Beryl? All he knew was that Beryl's trail began in St. George when she questioned his mother and that the man associated with that visit was an elderly gentleman named MacDonald. She then went to La Casa Serena. Could her son be that mysterious young man?

Diedra had regarded the angels as mere messengers. She wanted to speak only about Avery since she believed that it was he who had helped her, not they. It was his money that provided for her, not theirs. Avery wondered why anyone wouldn't take credit for such charity? Did Beryl do this out of love for him? As an act of service? That, he allowed, was certainly possible.

But then, it may not have been Beryl at all. Perhaps it was some other devotee, relatives of the Sister who had succeeded Diedra. He called his cousin and asked her to trace back the source of the phone call Diedra had made. She had said she was calling from a motel. He needed to know to whom the room had been registered.

He decided to put his suspicions aside and to let the events play out. He liked Beryl and if she were legitimate, he'd use her as his administrative assistant. But if she were not legitimate and somehow intended to damage his ministry, he'd teach her a lesson she would not soon forget. He knew that there were deceivers in the world. They were the minions of jealous competitors.

The prospective Seventh Sister, Sally Bridges, was the sexy, brazen type who would do well. He knew women, and he'd have her kissing his feet in less than a week. It would be good to turn her if she were legitimate. But it would be better to turn her if she were a phony. There always was a challenge, he thought, in forcing a woman to do what, in her heart of hearts, she really wanted to do.

But they both did not have to be guilty. It was entirely possible, for example, that Sally was genuine and that Beryl might have seized upon the opportunity that Sally's quest presented as a way to worm herself into the group for some nefarious purpose. Maybe she was anti-religious. Maybe she represented a rival religious group. It also could be that Beryl was innocent and Sally was the worm in the apple. So very many things were possible.

Late Monday morning Beryl and Sally Snyder drove to Death Valley. They arrived a few minutes early, and not seeing the Escalade there, they parked and went into the gift shop. Sally bought a couple of silver and obsidian rings. When they left the shop, Avery was parking the big black car. He was alone.

As they ate lunch, Avery casually tested Beryl about the information he had received from Akara about her marital history. "Tell me about your husband," he asked.

"Which one?" she replied, easily repeating the lie. "I've had two. My first was a student from Thailand who turned me onto Buddhism and returned to Bangkok to live his own life shortly after Akara was born. His name was Chatree. My second husband was a Navy man from Phoenix named Tilson."

"I was wondering about that," Avery said, clearly relieved. To be sure, he asked one final question: "Was Akara with you when you met my mother?"

"No, he had just finished his school finals and met up with me in Las Vegas."

"He's a handsome boy," Avery said.

"Yes, your mother and I shared stories about our handsome sons."

Avery giggled. "I'd like to have been a fly on the wall for that discussion," he said.

Beryl shook her head and smiled, thinking that she had never met anyone who was quite as weirdly adorable as Avery Christian.

When they had finished lunch, he asked Sally to ride with him to a special place while Beryl returned to Las Vegas alone.

La Casa Serena had gone through many seasons of profit and of loss in Pahrump. When the Nuclear Test Site was in its atomic bomb heyday, the brothel-restaurant-motel-spa made money. The owner had a special home built for his family, higher on the mountain, away from the music and noise of the saloon part of the complex. When the test ban kicked in, it went through years of decline, of having the family moved away to places nearer to schools and churches and normal life. The business struggled, trying to make income equal expenses. The old family house was sold to Margaret Cromwell who then rented it to her son Avery for a single dollar a year.

But then, after the Nuclear Waste Repository began its long construction period, business was good again. The owner and manager of La Casa Serena was now Florian Kitchener, a cousin of Jebel Kitchener, a.k.a. Avery Christian, who had no family and preferred to live in a small and separate cabin.

Margaret Cromwell had foreseen the large cabin's use as a kind of private spa. A mere quarter-mile away was a swimming pool and veranda with gaily-colored umbrella-tables and a waiter who served them from both restaurant and bar. It would also function as a training place for new Sisters and also as a recovery place. Margaret Cromwell had assured her son that a Sister's essential quality was a masochistic personality. Beauty could be easily manufactured. A fat candidate could be slimmed. One whose teeth were crooked or missing could have dental repairs. A flat chested candidate could undergo breast augmentation. Pocked skin could be made smooth with laser treatments. Plastic surgery could correct many unfortunate facial features. These were all easy fixes, but no amount of medical intervention could cause a debased sense of self-worth to exalt in sexual slavery or allow an intelligent mind to accept as factual ludicrous religious claims. No, only a masochistic personality could be made to participate enthusiastically in criminal activity and would conflate orgasmic ecstasy with torture.

While Avery headed to La Casa Serena, he wanted to give Sally a preliminary test before he revealed the location of the cabin to her. Trying to speak casually, he asked, "What was your Guru's name and what kind of ashram did he have?"

"Shivadas. Guru Shivadas. I guess the ashram was the standard type. I've only been to one."

"Which Path did he follow?"

"What do you mean?"

"Left or Right."

"Left. Strictly vama-marga."

Avery was encouraged by her answer. Still, he continued, "Did he give you a *mala*?"

"No. We didn't use them."

"Not use a *mala*?" Perhaps he had caught Sally in a lie. "What dietary restrictions did you observe if you didn't use a *mala*?"

"What would beads have to do with diets? A mala," she patronizingly explained, "is a long strand of prayer beads. We did wear necklaces, but they were metal and wide. They went all the way out to the shoulder line and had dangling junk on them that teased our nipples."

Avery reached across to Sally's leg and squeezed it. "Good girl," he said, and he headed for La Casa Serena.

Avery put the Escalade in the little parking space near the cabin. "My cousin Florian owns the business but my mother and I own this cabin-house. The Sisters and I come here to relax; and naturally, it's a great place to train in the techniques of our ministry. I'll let the Sisters explain the unusual but really commonsensical way we have of raising money."

He took Sally immediately to the pool area where the six Sisters were swimming or sitting at umbrella-tables.

Avery introduced her to Annie who led her to a separate table as Avery, after handing each woman a bottle of iced tea, left to go to his own room to change into a bathing suit.

"Everything," Annie began her introductory spiel, "depends on the sacrifices a person is willing to make to serve God. We fund a dozen different shelters... three orphanages, two centers for battered women, four soup kitchens to feed the hungry, and three 'Pathfinding' schools for wayward kids, kids who have lost their way and need to be helped to find the path back to God. We teach trades and for the really smart kids, math and science since these are the subjects they need most when they return to mainstream schools." Annie spoke with conviction although she had never seen any of these non-existent charitable schools and shelters. She had seen a variety of photoshopped photographs of Avery apparently involved in the hands-on, nitty gritty, humble work for which he was justly proud; and he often issued an addendum to an admonishment: perhaps the sister needed to learn obedience at one of these labor intensive jobs.

She continued, "The question is this: should we beg for the money to run these charities from hard working Christian folks, or does it make more sense to use the money that sinners would otherwise squander on roulette wheels, craps tables, bars, strip tease dancers, drugs, and whores? Which makes more sense to you?"

Sally nodded. "Naturally, it makes more sense to use the sinners' money."

"Then," Annie said, "I have to ask you how great is your love of God and your devotion to Father Avery? How much would you be willing to sacrifice to feed the hungry, teach the ignorant, and shelter the abused?"

"I don't know... a lot, I guess."

"Let me ask you this. Have you ever been in a relationship where you didn't feel like having sex but you let the man... or woman... do what he or she wanted because you didn't want to suffer through something as silly as an argument?"

"Yeah, sure. Everybody who's in a relationship has many nights like that."

"And you gained nothing from that night except the avoidance of an argument. Suppose for a similar inconvenience, you could gain a lot of money, money that you would put to use to serve God and the good souls who are in trouble and need good Christian help? Would you submit to a man or woman's advances if you knew that that person was a sinner... a follower of Satan... and you could take his or her money and put it to good use instead of letting him squander it on dice, booze, drugs, and whores? And also - and this is important - by diverting his money to good causes, you might even be helping him to redeem his own soul?

"Nobody's going to ask you to stand in the subway every night and sell roses for a dollar to raise a little money for charity. I'm not going to suggest that you would indulge in a sexual encounter for the enjoyment of it. That is too outrageous even to consider. But you would enjoy the wonderful spiritual pleasure of knowing that what you were doing was truly God's work. Such a sacrifice of your time and body would be made only two or three times a month. Is that too much to ask?

"So you have to answer this question: Are you willing to offer a sacrifice of your body and your time on two or three nights in a month in order to do the Lord's work? Be honest with yourself. There is no shame in answering that you would prefer to beg religious persons to give you money to support your Christian charities, or to manufacture and then sell trinkets or pot holders to support your ministry, or even to try to con money out of poor, hard-working Christian folks in order to help those who are even poorer."

"Yes... now that you put it that way, it does make a whole lot of sense. I'd be willing to do that... as you say... two or three times a month."

"I shouldn't tell you this... but girl... Father Avery will buy you clothing from the finest shops on Rodeo Drive... the idea being that a smartly dressed lady will attract sinners with money."

Sally laughed. "Rodeo Drive? I'm convinced. Where do I sign up?"

"Tomorrow we'll give you a test... what the prohibition era moonshiners called, 'a dry run.' You look prosperous now in those clothes... like a young business woman... a sales rep from whatever industry you're familiar with. Make sure you hang them up properly so that you can wear them for the test."

"What does the test consist of?" Sally asked.

"You'll go into the lounge and sit at the bar and Father will watch you to see how long it takes you to get a man to buy you a drink and invite you to go back to his room. Father Avery will have your cellphone number so leave your phone on. As soon as he sees you go into the motel room with the man, he'll call you about some phony emergency that has come up. You'll have to act the part of an annoyed 'summoned employee.' Then, you can give your regrets to the mark and promise to see him later as you leave to attend to business.

"But right now, while the sun is still so strong, why don't you take a nice swim and get a massage. I'll show you the bedroom you can share with another sister. We don't watch TV, so after dinner, you can either sit outside and enjoy the evening air or you can stay in your room and rest."

So far, Sally thought, everything at La Casa Serena was going smoothly.

TUESDAY, MAY 21, 2013

On Monday, Avery Christian had had all the sun exposure that he had allotted for the early days of his controlled tan. On Tuesday, wearing street clothing, he sat at a table, drinking gin and tonic, as he watched Sally enter the lounge and sit at the bar. He checked his watch.

After no more than two minutes a prosperous-looking man approached her. He watched her laugh at the man's amusing anecdotes. He watched her seem to be an attractive but ordinary working woman. She accepted the man's business card and then looked through her purse and apparently was distressed to see that she hadn't a card of her own in her purse.

The man wanted to dance and Sally seemed to charm him as he selected a song at the juke box. A Texas line dance played and she gamboled in a natural way and made no suggestive movements. They returned to the juke box and he selected a sexy bossanova. This time he held her tightly and whispered something in her ear. She grinned sheepishly and shook her head negatively. In another few moments, he whispered again, and she finally seemed to blush when she said, "Ok." Avery could read her lips. She got her purse at the bar and left with him. Exactly twenty-five minutes had passed since she first entered the bar. "Gosh darn it!" he murmured. "She's really good!"

Avery went to Annie's room and sat with her while he called Sally's cellphone and pretended to be her boss. Sally had just finished removing her jewelry. She pretended to recognize the caller's identity. "Hi Boss, what can I do you for?"

"We have a problem," he said. "Mrs.Tannaker says that they didn't receive their merchandise."

Sally protested, "The order was phoned in last week and the guys in Shipping said that it went out immediately. Check with Sam O'Malley in Sales. He was there and heard them say so."

"O'Malley doesn't know squat," Avery said. "Mrs. Tannaker is on her way."

"Here?" she said incredulously. "She's coming here to Cazarina? Now? Oh my God! Yes. Yes! But if other people did their jobs the way they're paid to do them, we wouldn't have this problem!"

He told her to remember how valuable a customer Mrs. Tannaker was. She looked out the motel window and saw one of the Sisters park a Lincoln sedan in the parking area. "Uh, Oh! She just pulled into the parking lot!" she hissed as she disconnected the call. "Bruce," she said to her companion, "I gotta go. But I'll try to be back here tomorrow. You're a really nice guy! I had fun today."

"Great!" said Bruce Turner, her unsuspecting audition partner. "Me, too."

When Avery discussed the events of the completed test, he included Sally's clever rejoinder to his fake customer's complaint.

Annie asked, "If Sally's from the east coast how did she know that this place is called 'Cazarina' by the locals?"

As soon as Sally returned from the motel section of the spa, he asked her to come into his room.

"How did I do?" she asked.

"Fine. But I have one question. How did you happen to know La Casa Serena's nickname? You called it 'Cazarina.'"

She shrugged. "That's what the john called it. Why? Is that some shibboleth? Or some sacred name that only high priests can use?" She affected anger. "I thought you'd be happy with my test results. Instead, I get the third degree. This business of analyzing every word I say, trying to determine where I learned it as if you're playing some sort of 'clue' game, trying to catch me in a lie... like that 'mala' business. A dietary 'mala'! Really? Well, this constant suspicion can get old real fast."

"I'm sorry," Avery said contritely. "I was just wondering. Don't be mad at me. I was just funnin' with ya'."

Sally lay in her bed up in the cabin's loft and listened to the faint voices that were coming from the main room downstairs. She had at first thought she was hearing typical nonsense talk, until she heard "P.I." distinctly pronounced. She stiffened and listened intently to the voices. Annie was saying, "I think she's too young to have a son that old. He didn't look like any college boy to me. How old did he look to you?"

The other voice replied, "I'm such a lousy judge of age. I wouldn't even hazard a guess. But what about Sally! Wasn't she terrific! Father is so happy with her."

Annie's tone changed to obvious resentment. "She's smart and you know how much he likes smart women. I don't think he should trust her at all. Or the other one! Keep your eyes open in case she starts to snoop around. When are we leaving?"

"After dinner, so we better get ready."

"St. George or someplace else?" Annie asked.

"I'm not sure. I don't think Father has made his mind up yet about where we're going."

Sally carefully got out of bed and grabbed a towel and some shampoo and pretended she wanted to bathe. She encountered Annie at the top of the stairs. Sally asked, "Anybody in the bathroom? I forgot to ask if there was a bathing schedule."

"Yes, I was just going to use it," Annie said. "There's no schedule. It's first come, first serve." She assumed the attitude of a superior. "When you do use the bathroom, just don't take more time and hot water than you need."

"Ok," Sally replied and returned to her bed. Annie did not sleep in the general loft area. She had her own room which she kept locked.

What, Sally wondered, did she keep in the room that was so worthy of being protected?

Avery Christian felt reasonably certain that Beryl and Sally were not threats to him. Yet it was always wise, he knew, to err on the side of caution.

None of the Sisters was permitted to have a cellphone or even to discuss ministry affairs with each other. As soon as the celebration for Sally's expeditious snare of a potential sinner was finished, he removed her cellphone from her purse and looked through it. The phone was part of the Bridges identity package prepared by Novalis and, as such, contained none of her old contact numbers or photographs. He felt sure she was legitimate... yet... yet... the nagging duty to be certain persisted.

Sally knocked briskly on his door and called his name. He immediately was afraid that she had come to quit - and he could not let her do that now that she knew the details of the ministry's operation. Her phone was on the bed beside him. He made no attempt to hide it. Warily he asked her to come in.

She entered and glanced around the room, seeing a locked box the size of a shoe box that she had often seen Annie carry and lock in her room. She immediately stated her problem. "I didn't come here anticipating the test procedure. I have personal items back in my hotel room; and if I don't go and pick them up, Beryl will worry. She doesn't know where I am. So can you take me back to Vegas so that I can get my things."

"Sure," he said, relieved. "With pleasure." He saw her glance at her iPhone. "It's a safety precaution," he said. "We don't let any of the new members keep their cellphones. I hope you can understand that."

"Sure," she said. "And I hope you can understand that I'd like to live a normal life. I lost an earring stud and I think it's probably on the dance floor. Would you mind if I did a quick run over there before they sweep the floor and ruin my life forever?"

Avery laughed. "I don't want your life even inconvenienced a tiny bit. Go look for your earring. I'll get the Escalade gassed up."

As Sally entered the cocktail lounge she spotted Bruce Turner. "I had to stay over to solve my boss's problem. I'll be leaving in a minute, but can I use your phone for just one little second?"

She called Beryl who had just gone into the bathroom. Akara answered. He noticed that the caller I.D. was Bruce Turner. A whispered female voice said, "I'm at La Casa Serena - Cazarina. He's taking me into Las Vegas now so that I can pick up my things. Tonight we may be moving out. I don't know where. It may be to St. George. I can't talk. He's got my phone." The call was disconnected.

"I think that was Sally on the phone." He repeated what she had said.

Sam Nichols, Sally's boss at Novalis, was also sitting in Beryl's room. Beryl came out of the bathroom. Akara said, "That was Sally. They may be moving out tonight. She doesn't know where. But they're on their way here, now. Sally will pick up her toiletries and clothing. She said, 'He took my phone,' by which she meant Avery."

Nichols asked, "Did she seem in any way scared or concerned?"

"In that brief conversation, she sounded ok. But I wouldn't say she wasn't concerned. It's the same old story of the singing horse. It's not how well it sings, but that it sings at all. That she used the occasion to stress that Avery took her phone says more than her tone of voice. I don't know how her safety is influenced by the move to another facility."

Nichols made a phone call. When he concluded it, he said, "Well, they seem to be cleaning up and getting ready to vacate the Cabin, even as we speak. I know he told Sally that he was in St. George when he called to arrange the lunch date, but I've been having the place watched for days ever since Wagner told me that they were using it."

"George Wagner?" Akara asked ingenuously. How did he know about it?"

"Beryl told him and he told me. We're on the same team, Son."

"If you knew they were there," Akara said, "why didn't you put a GPS transmitter in the Escalade? Now we don't know where she's gonna be."

"I didn't have men stationed out there. We periodically checked by phone calls to the desk. Sure... in retrospect..."

Beryl quickly changed the subject. "Have you any specifics regarding the Sisters' operation? How did they snare the mark?"

"I can't assign specific strategies to this Gethsemane group," Nichols replied, "but I figure they're more of the same scams we've already come across here and in other cities where conventions are held. He hides video cameras in a girl's room and has a lot of frames to pick from for straightforward blackmail shots. Some blackmail scams involve assault and battery charges. If the guy likes to play rough, the pimp beats the girl up right away and then has her complain to hotel security so fast that the bruises are still coming out while she's sitting there crying, pretending to be a housewife on a holiday."

Beryl interjected, "I saw a nylon stocking filled with balls - tennis balls mostly - that I figured was the kind of battering ram that did the most superficial damage."

"That's right. The balls don't do any deep tissue damage, but they sure look like they just about killed her."

"How would he get the blackmail shots if the Sister didn't get the mark to go back to her room where the hidden cameras were?" Akara asked.

"He'd be disguised as maybe a room service waiter and knock on the door. When he got in, he'd say something and the girl would act as though the mark had set *her* up when he insisted that they go someplace else. She'd use a stun gun or Mace on the mark and then pretend she was going to use it on Avery - assuming he was the guy with the camera. She'd be sure to get the guy's identification - or the woman's because they go after them, too - so that she could let him or her know that she was being blackmailed because of their encounter and that because she couldn't pay, he'd have to come up with the money, and so on."

"And how do they get the blackmail payment?"

"All kinds of ways. They make the mark buy chips and then they cash them in. It's never noticeable. A man and six or seven women can cash in thousands of chips in a night and never be noticed. Where gambling is not legal, I've known of a banker who got photographed in one of these operations. It was arranged that one of the girls came right into the bank and obtained a loan for $30,000 and then the next day the banker had to mark the loan as 'paid in full' and pay the money back to the bank. I've known of the payments being made on ships - in international waters. The mark has to play poker with one of the women and he has to lose the appropriate amount to her. They do that also with private games played in hotel rooms in Indian casinos. One of girls... one he's never seen before... opens a fresh deck of cards and keeps the deck afterwards... with the mark's fingerprints all over the cards. They also secretly video the card game. They tell him in advance how much he has to lose."

Akara laughed. "What a racket! But how does the blackmailer determine how much the vic's good for? I mean... if he asks for too much, the mark could confess or kill himself."

"You're the internet guy. How long would it take you to determine how much I was good for if you got my business card?"

"*Moi?* Would you like me to try right now?"

"No!"

"Ok. If you gave me twenty minutes and if you kept your personal data the way that most people keep them, I'd know your net worth down to the penny. But the vic might have concealed his assets. Even the IRS has to look hard to uncover certain income sources."

"Don't tell me that you can just hack into the IRS's files," Nichols scoffed.

"I don't have to hack into their files. Before the IRS gets your tax returns, a copy of them exists in your CPA's local office computer. And those files, I assure you, are no trouble to access. But a more interesting question is: what do they do if, say, time is of the essence, and the guy's financial information is well hidden?"

"Then, believe it or not, the blackmailer just looks at the man's shoes. Every one of these guys I've come across has been a shoe expert. Shoes are dead-giveaways. You don't rent or borrow shoes and you can't conceal their quality or lack of it. Some of these crooks can look at shoes and tell you where the mark's from... what country. But all of them know the shoes' value."

Akara grinned and shook his head. "And I guess you can buy a new suit, shirt, tie, and shoes and get a manicure yesterday and you'll look prosperous and pampered... but your shoes will be unworn... a tip off. But if you've worn your high-quality shoes normally, that 'lived-in' look will say that you're at home with your expensive stuff. I guess," he agreed, "shoes really are a good indicator of a man's ability to pay."

Nichols stood up and pointed at the door. "You and I," he said to Akara, "have got to get out of sight. Let's go down to the coffee shop and you can tell me more about your adventures in CPA files."

When Avery and Sally parked at the motel, it was not necessary for him to insist on accompanying her to the room she had shared with Beryl. As she got out of the car she teased him, "Let's go see that pretty P.I. who seems to have caught your eye."

"No, no no!" Avery protested and laughed. "I just have a weak spot for smart gals... like yourself." He got out of the car and took Sally's arm as they walked.

At the room, Sally had no key-card and had to knock on the door.

Beryl greeted them with surprise. "Sally! Avery!"

"Well, Howdy!" Sally said. "We came to pick up my stuff."

Beryl looked at Avery. "I guess you've got a new Sister!"

"Oh, yes," he said, "and she's perfect. The Sisters and I love her already."

"I'm jealous!" Beryl said, teasing him.

"I just came to collect my things," Sally said. "Look... would you call my dad and tell him I'll speak to him later? I really don't want to talk to him. Just tell him I'm considering *another* Christian group beside the one you were checking out. I don't want him to start nosing around the Sisters of Gethsemane. Tell him everything is cool." She stuffed her garments and make-up into her overnight bag and then remembered her shampoo. She went into the shower stall and grabbed her shampoo, creme rinse, and body wash.

As they left Beryl called, "I can't keep your father happy with excuses. You'll have to call him… and sooner than later!"

When they returned to the cabin, Avery called Eugenia and asked her to review the conversation she had had with Diedra. Eugenia repeated that other than saying the male angel was young, Diedra had given no physical description of them. "I called the motel she called from and tried to find out who was registered in the room, but there was no way they would give me the information. Diedra thought you had paid for everything… the surgery… the clothes… the gold necklace. She couldn't wait until she saw you again, but she didn't say where she expected that to be… she just said Nevada."

Avery could not remember whether Diedra had ever been to the spa. He asked Annie who assured him that while she may have heard the Sisters discuss the place, she had never been there. "She was at the rented place in Beatty, and she couldn't have known about the place in Boulder City since you got it after she left the group."

"Somebody's on our trail," Avery said. "First my mother is interviewed, and then a couple of angels show up at Diedra's house. Let's not invite trouble to follow us here to Pahrump. I had considered moving out tonight, but now I've decided it's definite. Tell the girls to get ready. We'll leave after dinner."

At dinner Sally sat with Avery, Annie, and Loralee, the girl from North Las Vegas who had replaced Diedra.

She feigned hunger and tried to read the menu with appropriate excitement. The discussion about various dishes was abruptly ended when Annie asked, "What was the occupation of the man you met at the bar?"

"He was an electrical engineer."

"Did you get his name?" Annie asked.

She answered in an emotionless factual way. "Yes. I got his name and his business card. The card is in a side pocket in my purse which is back in my room. Would you like me to go and get it for you?"

"Yes," Annie said, surprising Sally. "And perhaps Loralee will walk you back so that you don't get lost on the way."

Sally stood and pushed her chair back to the table. "If the waiter comes," she said to Annie, "you can order for me. I'll have the sirloin, medium rare, a baked potato with sour cream and chives, and green beans. Can you keep the order straight? Would you like me to repeat it?" She turned to Loralee. "Come on. The Q&A may last into the wee hours."

Avery was smiling. Sally and Annie were in a verbal boxing match, and Sally had just won the round.

By nine o'clock the Escalade pulled into the garage of Jebel Kitchener's house in St. George.

There were only four bedrooms in the house, and Avery-Jebel used the master's bedroom.

At a farmer's roadside market he had bought a variety of fresh vegetables, several cucumbers among them. He was tired and as the women unpacked the car, he diagonally sliced one of the cucumbers and retired to his bedroom to lie upon his bed with the slices on his eyes, cheeks, neck and mouth. No one was permitted to disturb him.

WEDNESDAY, MAY 22, 2013

Since Diedra was scheduled for several early examinations and consultations, Akara left the hospital in Las Vegas and came to the motel to have breakfast with Beryl. Nichols would also be joining them.

"We can't lose sight of the objective," Nichols said, "which is to prove Niles Portmann's innocence. At the same time, I've got Sally to worry about. Without a phone connection, she could be in trouble or she could be involved in an operation without being able to tell us where and when it was taking place. I'm seventy-one, which is a little too old to play her father or else I would consider bursting in to extricate her from the group - if, of course, I knew where the hell she was.

"We've got a problem involving law-enforcement. Avery's mother is an old whorehouse madam, and I don't think I have to tell you the kind of bureaucratic muscle that old tomato has. She knows politicians and cops in half a dozen states. And they all do her favors."

Beryl nodded. "Yes, we ought to stay with people we know. We could call George in. He could pass for her father. I mean... if I can pass Akara off as my son, Sally can call George, 'Dad.' I think we can safely wait a day or so. She'll need time to learn their routine. But it's your decision. How do you want to proceed?"

"These crooks are operating under the aegis of religion; and if they're legally registered, messing with them is gonna put us all in a world of pain if we're unable to prove our assertions. Akara has got to take charge of our principal witness. So he's tied up with Diedra Swanson. He'll have to baby-sit her here and then in Tonopah. The Sisters don't use conventional communications, so it's tough to spy on them. But an in-person inspection of the house in St. George will settle the question of whether or not they're in Utah."

"I can go up to St. George tomorrow and check-out the house up there. I'll cook up a story about Sally's father being upset by something he's heard about the group. If George agrees to play the part of the irate father, I can say I came to warn them. Just tell me what you want done."

"Without law enforcement, we're on the short side of personnel numbers. So, sure, we could use Wagner. Let me get him on the horn. I wanna discuss the situation with him."

George answered on the office phone. Sam Nichols explained the situation and asked, "Would you be available to go to St. George to play the part of Sally's father... the man who's supposed to be your client? We might have to extricate her from something unpleasant."

George agreed to play the part. "I think they all sound like a bunch of dangerous lunatics," he said. "And I guess you can't risk asking local law enforcement for help in any of the places they go."

"That just about covers it. Beside a natural reluctance to interfere with religious organizations, the police might also be influenced internally. Avery's mother has friends in high places."

George was worried. "I'm concerned that Beryl has been in too many places that are associated with him. She's been to Tonopah, his mother's house in St. George - which was an unnecessary exposure, but that's another story - and his place in La Casa Serena. She'll be the first target they aim for if trouble comes."

Sam Nichols apologized for Liam. "I know he got too frazzled when he met the old lady. He blew the interview, and Beryl had to step in. But he and his wife will be watching Diedra soon and things will quiet down."

George agreed that it was time to locate Sally. "We don't have to intrude. If all seems well, we can give her a chance to work things out. But we have to realize that they could be anyplace. I checked and old lady Cromwell owns real estate all over the Southwest and the Gulf. I can fly to St. George tomorrow and Beryl can meet me at the airport. If events indicate that it's necessary, I'll make a solo entry as Sally's father. *Solo*," he repeated. "I want Beryl's profile lowered. She's too exposed."

"Ok," Nichols agreed. "And listen, if you don't want the hassle of carrying a piece on the plane, I'll let you use a Colt .38 Mustang of mine.

Beryl said you like that weapon. She can bring it with her along with some identity documents."

Avery was restless. That there was conflict between Sally and Annie amused him on one hand, but on the other gave him an uncomfortable feeling of not being in control of the women. He knew and trusted Annie, but he still wasn't sure about Sally's sincerity. Thinking that he needed to interact with her more closely, he opened a deck of cards and tried to teach her how to play poker with the panache of a professional card sharp. They laughed at the difficulty of trying to teach a game when the hands were fairly dealt and the tedious explanations when the hands were arranged. "Let's do something else after lunch," he said. "A little Shakespeare!"

Annie picked up the deck of cards and put it in her pocket. On the pretext of going to the grocery store, she dressed in ordinary clothing and drove directly to the Cromwell house.

Margaret Cromwell, sipping tea without benefit of wig and makeup, tightened her bathrobe and the kerchief she had around her head and asked Annie to join her in the breakfast nook. She had just awakened and phlegm was still clogging her throat. "What can I do for you?" she asked, coughing and spitting into a tissue.

"The new girl, Sally Bridges," Annie began, "may be a phony. She says she's from back east... in Philadelphia... but she doesn't sound like an easterner. She may have conned that P.I. who was here a few days ago, or she may be in cahoots with her. Or they may both be legit. I just don't know. I'm relying on instinct and I have a bad feeling about her." She put the deck of cards on the table. "Could you have Sally's prints run so that we can see if she is who she says she is? But please, don't let Father Avery know I asked for your help."

"I already had the P.I.'s prints run from the business card she gave me. Tilson's name and occupation are legit. But who knows what her purpose is? You're right to check the new one out. I'll have these prints run for you. Do not worry. Worry puts lines on your face."

THURSDAY, MAY 23, 2013

After lunch Avery gave Sally a copy of Romeo and Juliet. "Let's make our own entertainment!" he exclaimed. "We'll do that balcony scene. Act two, Scene two."

He positioned Sally on the staircase and took his position at the base of the stairs. The Sisters were summoned to sit on the floor and be the audience.

Avery knew Romeo's lines and, without consulting a script, he competently recited them; and Sally, even though she had to read her lines, took the challenge seriously and played her part surprisingly well. Avery was giddy when the scene concluded. He hugged Sally and made her promise to memorize the lines of several important scenes. "We can even get costumes!" he gushed. "It'll be perfect! And then we can do," he began to sing, "Lay-dee... Mac... Beh-eth!"

Annie had maintained a grim expression throughout the performance. At the suggestion of even more Shakespeare, she sniffed the air and invented a chore that she had to do in the kitchen. Sally whispered in Avery's ear, "If you let her play Lady MacBeth, for God's sake don't give her a real knife!"

Avery laughed. "You could be Lady MacBeth, and we could let her play Duncan!" Sally, not entirely sure of Duncan's part in the play, correctly surmised that Duncan was stabbed in the story. She laughed malevolently with him. It was their little secret.

"Let's go shopping for copies of the play!" Avery whispered. "There are other roles for the girls to play. We can get those versions that explain all the funny words."

Like two childhood conspirators, Avery and Sally drove to a bookstore in a downtown mall.

In Las Vegas, Akara prepared to drive Diedra to Tonopah where she'd be staying with Liam and Luella MacDonald. Beryl stood out on the balcony and enjoyed the spring sun and then went inside to take a seemingly endless hot bath. She did not have to leave for St. George until the afternoon.

George had to change planes in Chicago. He would not be arriving in St. George until 5:30 p.m.

At noon, Sam Nichols gave Beryl a Norton Bridges identity packet he had prepared for George. It contained a fake driver's license and other credit cards, and a few wallet-sized photographs of Sally that George would be expected to have if, in a worst case scenario, he had to pretend to be retrieving his daughter. Beryl would hand-carry the packet, along with the Colt, to give to George at the airport.

"Give me some personal details about Sally," Beryl asked, "that I can pass along to George. You know... was she ever a cheer leader? Did she ever study to be a ballerina? Can she play the piano? Avery might buy into the paternal angst and sit George down to have a heart-to-heart talk about his daughter's missionary career."

They also discussed a variety of scenarios and the strategies and tactics they'd use to gain their objectives. The main problem was location. The Sisters did not have to be in St. George. Nichols knew how many properties Margaret Cromwell owned.

There was also the possibility that he had taken Sally on his boat, *Darien*.

When the meeting ended the previous day, Beryl had thought that even though she would be functioning in a back-up position - appearing only if it seemed necessary to inject George into the problem - she still should be seen in a fresh suit of clothes. She therefore wore the second suit she had purchased, the blue silk and linen one that the salesgirl insisted took ten years off her age.

Dressed and feeling very good, indeed, she went into the parking lot and drove her rented black Ford Fusion onto the highway that led to St. George. It was a two hour trip. She had plenty of time.

At the Kitchener house, Margaret Cromwell's houseboy knocked on the door with a message for Annie. "She told me to tell you that you should come down and pick out chicken and some other stuff she brought home from a lunch she just went to."

Annie did not bother even to ask Avery if she should go. It was taken for granted that when Margaret Cromwell summoned one of the Sisters for any reason whatsoever, the Sister would go.

Inside her flower decked breakfast nook, Margaret waited to deliver the news that Sally Bridges was actually Sally Snyder, a licensed private investigator from Las Vegas.

Annie smirked when she heard the truth. "I knew she was trouble. You can always spot a phony."

"Where is she now?" Margaret asked.

"In Father's bedroom, rehearsing *Romeo and Juliet*."

"She's got to be neutralized. Avery will know what he must do and you must do all that you can to help him. Keep the girls in line. The sad thing is that what Snyder knows, that Tilson woman might know, too. You've got to get her up here to find out what she knows."

"She'd suspect any pleasant call I made by way of inviting her to come. If they're working together, she'd have to think Sally's life was in jeopardy. She wouldn't fall for any stupid reason. If she doesn't really know what's going on, then she'll think she's finished with her assignment. After all, that bitch Sally may be using her. I know that we can't take chances; but I also don't want to do more 'correction' than is necessary."

"The Swanson woman is back in the picture. I don't think she poses any threat. Avery can keep her in line. I'm thinking about that Loralee who took her place. What kind of actress is she?"

"She won't win any awards, but she's competent."

"Get her to call Tilson and pretend that she and Sally are being abused and are trying to leave the group and that they're being imprisoned in St. George. She can say that because you came down here when I sent for you, she had to go to the store in your place. So she finally got to a phone and is trying to get some help for herself and Sally. Tell her to tell the Tilson woman that Avery requested a friend of his to run Sally's prints through IAFIS. Sally's scared out of her mind because his friend is gonna come this evening with the results. She should beg Tilson to get to the Kitchener house as soon as possible. She should say that Sally's life isn't worth a nickel if Avery finds out she's a P.I. or a cop."

"What should I do about telling Father Avery? He'll be mad at me for going behind his back."

"Then let's not upset him by telling him about your participation. In my desk in the library, I have a laptop computer and a printer. Let's go over there now and I'll write a note you can give to Avery. I'll say that someone noticed her at Cazarina and I asked him to verify her identity using her fingerprints from a glass she used. He called me with the results and I summoned you to give the results to Avery and to tell him not to trust Tilson. How's that?"

"My goodness! It's no wonder you are so successful. You think of everything!"

"But before you give him the letter, have Loralee make the call to Tilson. My son can sometimes act irrationally. Say that I ordered you to do this and you were not to disturb him while he was with Sally... as per his own orders." She opened a drawer and removed a cellphone. "Let Loralee make the call on this."

It was 4 p.m. and Beryl had another thirty miles to go. She became anxious and started to hurry, telling herself that it was impossible to estimate the amount of time it would take to park and find George.

Her iPhone played its little "Ding, Dong. The witch is dead" ringtone. The caller was not identified, and while she thought the call was probably a nonsense call, she answered it. A hushed and seemingly frightened voice began to relate the ordeal that Sally Snyder was about to face.

A few seconds later, the call was disconnected. Beryl changed the highway exit she had planned to take to the airport to one that would deliver her to the Kitchener house. If Sally and the caller were being restrained, they'd have plastic zip ties on their wrists. Beryl reached into her purse for a small folder that contained lock picks and a small screwdriver for reversing the lock of zip ties. She pushed it down into her bra. Then she called Sam Nichols of Novalis. After she related the strange phone call she had received from Loralee, she said, "Call Akara and Liam and tell them that the gang may be here in St. George. I'm on my way to the Kitchener house right now. I'll get word to you as soon as I can. Also, see if you can contact George. I'm exiting the freeway now."

Avery Christian and Sally were still in the master bedroom when Beryl arrived at the house. Annie answered the door bell and was shocked to see Beryl standing there. She had not known that Beryl was on the highway when she answered the phone. Instantly she blamed Loralee for not learning where Beryl was when she took the call. She stammered, "What brings you here? I thought your job was done?" She did not open the door any wider or step aside to let Beryl enter the house.

"May I come in?" Beryl asked.

"Oh, of course," she said, stepping back. "I'm so surprised to see you, that's all."

"Where's Father Avery?" Beryl asked. "I've come mainly to speak to him. There's been a glitch, I'm afraid, about Sally Bridges' participation. Her father in on his way here. I need to talk to Father Avery right away."

One of the sisters was already half way up the stairs. "I'll get him!" she cried. "He wanted to be given enough time to dress for dinner." Before Annie could think of a way to contradict her, she was knocking on his bedroom door.

The women did not speak as they waited to hear what would happen next. The Sister whispered something inaudible and then Avery yelped, "She's here? Beryl's here?" He told Sally to put her shoes on and come downstairs.

And then Avery Christian, wearing a shiny blue silk shirt that was open to just above the waist, came down the stairs with Sally following him. "Beryl!" he shouted. "You've come just in time!"

Sally hugged Beryl. "The Reverend Mr. Christian is as talented as he is handsome. He's a lot of fun, too." Beryl could smell marijuana in her hair. The warning call, she could see, had been a hoax.

"Thank you, Miss Bridges," Avery said, pulling her away from Beryl. "But would you excuse me for a moment while I intoxicate my favorite Inspector Javert? She likes my cologne." He grabbed Beryl and forced her face into his neckline and began to whisper in her ear, "Look at you! You look like a million bucks in that suit. I want to take it off and hang it in my closet."

Beryl pulled away from him. "I told you he was irresistible," she said to Sally.

Avery pointed to the couch. "You are in for a treat! You must sit right down and watch this scene."

"I need to talk to you," Beryl said. "It's important."

"Nothing is more important than Shakespeare. Sit! You must be quiet and listen. You will be amazed."

Annie interrupted in a loud voice. "If you've been rehearsing upstairs, your throat could probably use a cold drink before you recite your lines again. Who wants iced tea? I just made a pitcher of wonderful tea from Sri Lanka. It's sweetened with honey." Everyone wanted tea.

Annie went into the kitchen and took a vial of chloral hydrate from the cabinet. She took nine cut-glass tumblers and squirted more than enough chloral hydrate into two of them to put the person who drank

165

from the glass to sleep for an entire day. She put ice cubes in each glass, filled the glasses with iced tea, and placed them on a tray which she carried into the living room. One by one, she distributed the glasses, making sure that Beryl and Sally received the drugged tea.

Sally, who's voice had become slightly strained, drank half of her drink immediately. Beryl, trusting no one, pretended to take a sip and then placed her glass on one of the coasters Loralee had put on the coffee table.

A Sister, whose name Beryl did not know, played a little Renaissance tune on a mandolin as Sally and Avery took their places.

Romeo and Juliet had delivered several memorable passages before Juliet's speech began to slur. She began to blink her eyes continuously. The slurring increased and Avery's expression registered alarm. Finally, when Sally tried to say, *I would not for the world they saw thee here*, she could not pronounce "world" although she tried repeatedly to say the word.

Recognizing the drugged speech, he glared at Annie. As Sally continued to try to recite the words, muttering in mangled syllables, "they saw thee here," her hand reached out to grab the bannister and she tumbled down the carpeted stairs.

Avery was at her side immediately. He looked at Annie. "What did you put in her drink?"

"Here!" she said, producing the letter his mother had sent. "Madame told me to give this to you but to wait a bit to do it. She didn't give me a specific time. I was following her orders."

Avery opened the letter and read it. He gasped and crumpled the paper in his fist. Since Sally was already unconscious, he turned to Beryl, "What does this mean? What have you done?"

"What are you reading?" she asked.

"My mother had Sally's prints run. Sally Bridges is really Sally Snyder, a private investigator from Las Vegas. And you knew who she was." He brought his fist up to his mouth and bit his knuckles. He stifled a wail and gasped again. "Why have you done this to me? You came into my home. You ate my food. We sat together and laughed together and you smiled at me. And all the time you were intending to destroy me, just gaining my trust and my love so that you could get close enough to destroy me. Why? What did I do to you to make you hate me so much?"

Beryl looked at him as he knelt on the floor beside Sally's seemingly lifeless body. She did not know what chemical was now flowing through Sally's veins. She wanted to defend herself by countering with examples of his own callous acts, but that kind of response would have to wait. She needed to say something... anything... that would help to save Sally's life and her own. "If what your mother learned is true - and I have no reason to doubt it - all I can say is that Sally was presented to me as Sally Bridges. I was supposed to pick her father up at the airport at 5:30. I came to warn you that he was on his way and to tell you that I'd be available to help calm him if you needed me."

"No she didn't!" Annie shouted. "We called Beryl on the phone and set a trap for her. Madame told us to. And she was right because Beryl fell right into the trap. That's why she's here. We told her you were going to hurt Sally."

Avery put the note on the floor and pressed it smooth so that he could read it again. "My mother says not to risk trusting you any more. Your credit is no longer good. This is why we don't accept checks." Avery dropped the note and put both hands around Sally's neck. He looked at Annie. "Cuff her," he said, "and if she makes the slightest move to prevent you from cuffing her, I'll squeeze the life out of Desdemona."

Annie had several zip ties in her apron pocket. Beryl held her hands out in front of her. Annie put Beryl's hands through the loops and tightened the tie.

Avery looked at his watch and went into the kitchen. When he returned he brought a syringe that contained a clear liquid and sat on the floor beside Beryl. Holding the needle against her skin, he asked, "Who is supposed to come here?"

"Norton Bridges."

"To this house? Who gave him the address?"

"Whoever it was who told him your name was Jebel Kitchener. I guess Sally did. All I know is that I was supposed to pick him up and bring him to this address. He evidently heard something he didn't like about the Sisters and is coming to take Sally back. That's what I wanted to talk to you about."

"She came because I called her!" Loralee sneered.

"When did you call her? How long have you known about this?" Avery asked Loralee.

"Not until this afternoon. I called her at exactly four o'clock."

Beryl spoke softly. "Think about this, Avery. My car is out front. It's five o'clock. I got here at 4:30. Could I have driven here from Las Vegas in half an hour? Could Norton Bridges fly here from Philadelphia in an hour?"

"Oh," he whined. "I don't know what to think. You're all so jealous and... perfidious! Yes... perfidious!" He turned to the Sisters. "See if her car is outside."

Annie had seen the car when she answered the door. "Of course it's there!" she snapped. "Did you think she arrived by parachute?" she asked sarcastically, insulting Avery.

He suddenly stood up and jabbed the needle into her arm. "Don't you ever speak to me like that again!" He held her arm, keeping the needle inside the muscle, but he did not depress the plunger.

"I'm sorry, Father," she pleaded. "I was worried about you. I forgot myself. Forgive me."

He released her and withdrew the needle. Then he turned and backhanded her so hard that she fell to the floor. "I'm so sorry," she cried, holding a tissue up to her eyes.

One of the sisters looked out the front window. "There's a black car parked at the curb."

He knelt again beside Sally, dimpling the skin on her neck as he pressed the needle point against it. "Get her car keys!" he shouted at the Sister who stood at the window.

Avery watched as she withdrew Beryl's keys from her purse. "Drive her car to the parking lot where the pizza place is and leave it there!" he ordered. "And get back here right away!"

He kicked Annie's back and threw Beryl's purse at her. "Get the Cadillac loaded! We're leaving."

The Sisters scurried to load food, beverages, and luggage into the Escalade. "We've just filled the gas tank," Annie softly announced, trying to say something that would please him. She asked, "Should I strip the beds and bring the linens with us so that we can wash them wherever we're going?"

"Yes," he said. "It's better to leave the beds bare than it is to leave them with dirty sheets." He handed the syringe to one of the Sisters. "If the old one makes a move, stick the needle into Juliet and give her the whole shot." Then he wailed, "I am so disappointed! Why does everything have to get all wormy and rotten? Why can't people be honest and true?" He sobbed a few times then wiped his eyes with his shirtsleeve. "Put a zip tie on Sally's wrists. She may be faking a reaction to the drug. Who can tell what is genuine anymore? Everything is a lie... a jealous lie!" He picked Sally up, carried her into the garage, and carefully loaded her into the Escalade's rear seat.

He returned to the living room, took the syringe from the Sister, and jabbed it into Beryl's thigh. "It's morphine," he said. "You'll sleep now and I won't have to listen to your lies anymore!"

Beryl knew that she had only a few minutes to speak rationally to him. "Avery, think about what you're doing. There's no need for violence."

"Sally's a spy! Don't tell me that you didn't know that. If you don't stop lying to me, I'll cut out both of your tongues! Who hired the two of you?"

"I don't know who she's working for, but my client is Niles Portmann."

"Portmann? Aleta's husband? How can he hire you? How can he pay you? I thought he was broke."

"Through his attorney, Liam MacDonald."

"That old guy who went to my mother's house?"

"Yes. You know that Niles didn't murder his wife. You know that she wasn't murdered at all. Her death was an accident. I've been able to establish that! You intended only to subdue her when she went berserk. Law enforcement personnel deal with this problem every day. They use the chokehold to get a violent person under control and the action sometimes results in an accidental, defensible death. You're a smart man. What happened to Aleta was an accident. But if you hurt Sally now, you can't claim you were acting to defend yourself. Please, Avery... don't make things worse!"

A flicker of doubt showed in his expression. He had not been prepared to have Aleta's death considered a defensible accident. He looked again at his mother's note. "I can trust my mamma," he said. "I don't know if I can trust you... not anymore." He took out his disposable phone and removed a business card from his wallet.

He walked into the next room and spoke softly. The only words that Beryl could determine were his final words, "Yes, get it ready as soon as possible."

George Wagner checked his watch. It was still beating its Seiko quick-tick. And the hands indicated that it was 6 p.m. Beryl was nowhere to be found. He called Sam Nichols.

"I'm on another line about this case... just hold on, George." In another minute he brought George up to date. "I called before but hung up when my call went to voicemail. I figured you were landing."

"What's happening?"

"My news is nearly two hours old. Sally's cover's been blown. Beryl went to help her. Her phone's off. I didn't know whether she had it off because she didn't want that Ding Dong thing to give her position away if she had it on. What do you want to do?"

"I'll take a cab out to the Kitchener place. Beryl's got the black Ford with her. I'll let you know what I find out. Did you give her the Colt?"

"Yes."

"Then it's in the glove compartment of the rental. At least that's where it probably started out. Ok. 10-4." He disconnected the call and summoned a cab.

No one at the Kitchener house answered the bell or George's knock. He looked in one of the small garage door windows. The garage was empty. Twenty minutes before George arrived, the black Escalade had reached the highway and was heading southwest.

George called Nichols and reported that the house was deserted. "Where do you suggest we meet? I doubt that he'd be heading for Las Vegas."

"Maybe we can get more out of Diedra. Why don't we meet in Las Vegas? We can head up to Cazarina if that becomes necessary."

"Ok. I'll call the small craft commercial airport and see if I can hire a plane to take me down. Meanwhile, can you call the Utah Highway Patrol and put an alert out for Beryl's rental? I don't know which rental car agency she used."

"I do. Consider it done."

Beryl and Sally slept in propped-up positions. Two sisters sat beside them and, while Avery slept on the middle row of seats, Sister Annie sat with him in order to hold his head in her lap and another sister sat on the floor rubbing his feet. A locked box kept inside an ordinary shopping bag was under the front seat right by Annie's feet. All of the available floor space was filled with luggage. The other two Sisters sat in the driver's and passenger's seats.

During the drive, Sally stirred and Annie awakened Avery to ask if the two women should be given another shot. "How much farther is it?" he asked.

"We're coming now to Las Vegas. We need something to eat and we can refill the tank as long as we're here."

"All right. Get me three different sandwiches so that I can choose. Give each of the women another half-shot of morphine." Annie held his head up so that she could replace her lap with a pillow. Sally pushed herself up far enough to look over the seat back. She saw the mysterious locked box under the passenger's seat. As soon as Avery rested his head and wriggled into a more comfortable position, he fell back to sleep. The Sister who was driving pulled into a gas station as another sister administered the injections and Annie got out to fill the gas tank and go to a nearby sandwich shop.

Beryl and Sally awakened as they were being pulled from the car inside a garage. "Where are we?" Beryl muttered, looking at Avery.

"By the sea, by the sea, by the beautiful sea," he sang, teasing her.

She looked at Annie's gingham dress. "Red, Dead, or Galilee?"

"My God. Even junked up you still keep your wits. Why do I let you perplex me?"

Sally groaned. "My wrist is hurting bad."

"I dislike complainers," Avery said, reaching out to pinch her breasts. "Get inside the house."

Beryl pleaded, "Avery, please let the girl go. For God's sake. You've got enough women in your life."

"She needs to be trained to obey and to remain loyal. That's an art. I'm an artist."

"I know."

"Sally needs her nipples pierced." He snapped his fingers and several Sisters carried Sally into a bedroom, removed her dress, and tied her hands to the headboard and her feet to the footboard. A ball gag was inserted into her mouth and buckled at the back of her head. Another Sister hurried to unpack a suitcase. On a tray she placed alcohol, surgical gloves, a strange kind of locking pliers, and a threaded needle that was intended to pull through the ball of a horseshoe-shaped bar.

Avery pulled Beryl to her feet. "You should watch the procedure. We're very professional." Beryl's expression was grim and sympathetic as she looked at Sally whose eyes desperately pleaded for help. One sister used the pliers to pull and stretch the nipple outwards, while the other pierced it and pulled the bar through. Sally's scream was a throat-wrenching grunt.

Avery looked at a Sister who wore a green gingham dress. "Stay here and apply red wine with sterile cotton. We don't want the wounds to get infected." He turned to Beryl. "Go back to the kitchen, and remember... if you make the slightest hostile movement, the Sisters will show Sally the Wrath of God."

He turned to speak to the two women who were dabbing burgundy wine on Sally's breasts. "I prefer to die a martyr, than to think you would be disloyal to me and, in your weakness, fail to obey a command. If Beryl escapes or attempts to use me to force you to free the young one, kill the young one. There's acid in the cleaning supply closet."

Beryl walked ahead of him into the kitchen. "This will not end well for anyone."

"It doesn't have to end badly. You like me. I like you. You need a change - whether or not you think that that's just a line I use. I can show you excitement you never dreamed of."

"All your women like you. You're charming... very charming."

"Are you being hostile?"

"No, my dear. How could telling a charming man that he's charming be hostile?"

"Tell me," he said, "if you were going to cast me in a play, which character would you pick for me to perform?"

Beryl, knowing that men always played female roles in Shakespeare's time, did not hesitate. "Portia," she said.

"You are a bitch," Avery said, pulling out a kitchen chair for her to sit on.

"Could I please have some water?" she asked.

Avery snapped his fingers and Annie opened the refrigerator and removed a bottle of water. Hearing the Sisters laugh at the front of the house, she opened the bottle and placed it on the table in front of Beryl, and then she went to join the others. Avery's eyes registered a furious expression. "Release her hands! As long as you've got Sally, she won't dare do anything."

Annie opened her suitcase and removed a pair of sharp electrical pliers and cut through the plastic zip tie. She threw the cut ties into a plastic trash bag and returned the pliers to her suitcase. Then she bowed her head and stood before Avery. "You may go," he said. She curtsied slightly and left the room to join the Sisters in the front of the house.

Avery stood in the kitchen doorway and listened to their remarks. The Sisters were chattering about seeing the house for the first time. They giggled and spoke about being able to smell the fresh-water lake from the front door of the house. The house was at least a mile from the marina and the dam, but the women imagined that during the night, when all was quiet, they'd be able to hear the dynamos of Hoover Dam.

They returned to the kitchen. Avery let them pass as they went to look inside the kitchen cabinets. "Oh, look at these beautiful pots!" Loralee squealed. They gathered around to admire the polished cookware.

"No talking!" Avery commanded. "You know you're not supposed to chatter amongst yourselves. Are you scheming about something?" His voice was unmistakably threatening.

Instantly the Sisters stopped talking and did not look at each other. Instead they assumed guilty expressions and bowed, staring at the floor. Avery walked into another room and returned carrying a leather belt. "Line up!" he said.

Beryl was astonished to see the women obediently form a line. Annie was first. He grabbed her by the hair, forced her down onto the floor and dragged her into the room he had gone into to get the belt. There was silence and then some groaning and then Beryl could hear him hitting her with the belt, but Annie made no noise. It took another hour before Avery returned to the kitchen, and during the entire time he was gone, the women had not moved. Beryl said nothing, fearing that if she spoke she would antagonize Avery further. Intermittently she fell asleep only to awaken with a fearful jolt.

Annie returned to the kitchen, smiling. She hummed a song, a hymn of some kind Beryl thought, as she watched her toss some linens into the washing machine at the end of the kitchen. But she did not turn the machine on. Instead, she filled a kettle with water and put it on the stove. As she turned the knob, the burner clicked and the gas ignited. She then began to set the table. There were no marks on her face or arms, but what was under her gingham dress could not be seen.

Avery came out of the room. Annie asked, "Do you want me cut your sandwiches into sections?"

Avery snapped, "Yes... and don't let anything fall out of the bread!" He turned to the third Sister. "Take care of the tea." He offered Beryl her choice of sandwich but she was too sleepy to eat. He nibbled on a quarter of one of his sandwiches and then ordered Annie to wrap the other pieces and put them in the refrigerator.

Then he stood up and ferociously grabbed the hair of the second woman in line, swung her to the floor, and similarly dragged her into the room. Again, there were sounds of thuds and groans and finally the sound of whipping. The kettle boiled and the third Sister turned the burner off and continued preparing tea. In the bedroom the whipping sounds stopped. For a few minutes they heard nothing and then they heard a buzzing, electrical sound and some yelping. The tea was still warm when the bedroom door opened and the second Sister, her pleasurable ordeal over, returned to the kitchen, smiling as she tossed urine soaked sheets into the washing machine.

Avery entered the kitchen. "I'll deal with you later," he said to the women who were still standing, waiting their turn.

"I'm going to shower," he said to Beryl. He turned to Annie. "Make sure the one in the bedroom is taken care of. Remember! If anyone attacks me in any way, kill the girl." Annie curtsied and nodded. "And you, Shylock the Gumshoe," he said to Beryl, "you can come with me."

Beryl got up and followed Avery into the bedroom. "I'm really tired," he said. "You at least got to sit up comfortably. I'm stiff all over. Let's shower, eat, and then take a nice nap. You can bathe me."

"As you wish," she replied, barely able to keep her eyes open, and confident that he was sexually exhausted.

"My boat won't be ready until tomorrow morning. Maybe later we can dress and go out for midnight cocktails. I belong to a country club down here. Hang your suit in the closet so that the wrinkles get out of it." She removed her new suit and hung it carefully on a hanger among his garments in the closet. Then she carefully removed her bra so that the lock pick and zip tie opener remained hidden and put her bra, underpants, and pantyhose in a dresser drawer. "Can you do your own hair?" he asked.

"Yes. It was cut into the natural wave... which isn't much of a wave, but it still looks presentable when I comb and blow dry it." It amazed her to think of this seemingly commonplace question and answer taking place at such a moment in time.

She forced herself to stay awake as she bathed a grown man who acted as though he were a child. He held a cloth up to his eyes so that no shampoo would get into them. When she lifted his arm to wash his armpit, he held his arm up until she pulled it down. When she was finished washing his torso, he turned around and spread the cheeks of his behind. Normally she would have joked and asked if he thought she intended to do a strip search on him; but she knew that in some strange way he had reverted to being a child... a child who was pushing forty. An ugly thought occurred to her. "Am I substituting for Margaret Cromwell?" She nearly laughed aloud.

He made no attempt to bathe her. Instead, when she finished washing him down to his knees, he leaned back against the shower wall, and held up his right foot for her to wash... particularly between the toes... and then he switched feet. When he was finished being bathed, he opened the shower door and left. Beryl turned off the water and staggered out of the shower stall. She tried to shake off the effects of the morphine injection but the most she could do was strain for a few minutes to focus her eyes and collect a few thoughts. She saw a man's shirt hanging on a hook on the bathroom door. She put it on and went into the bedroom.

She tried to stay awake to look for clues... details... something that would help in the case's eventual solution. Avery Christian was already asleep. She momentarily studied the man who lay on the bed naked, in the innocence of a work of art. His wet curls clung to his forehead and his expression was serene. "He looks like a Greek god," she muttered, "but not like the statue of a god." There was no marble stiffness to his body. "No," she said, "like a living one." She laughed to herself. Nothing about this man made sense except, she thought, that he was absolutely insane... not legally so... but in the way that is even more dangerous: the totally conscious man who has no empathy for other living beings. But yet... she recalled... he called her a bitch when she suggested that he play Portia's character. And he did call her "Shylock the Gumshoe" which meant that he was cognizant of mercy even if he did not subscribe to its demands on conscience.

The residual effects of the morphine injection, like embers in the presence of oxygen, flared up to consume her will to stay awake. She flopped on the bed and before her head even touched the pillow, she, too, had begun to sleep.

As Nichols met George at the North Las Vegas airport, he told him disconcerting news. "Liam got a bit rammy when he learned that we had lost track of Beryl and Sally. He talked to Sheriff Hornsby and told him some of our problems. I'm not sure what all he told him, but the police know the girls may have been kidnapped."

"The sheriff has a right to know. I'm an ex-cop. I can't work outside the law. I mean... it wasn't the feds he told." George thought again. "Tell me that it wasn't the feds he told!"

"No, just the sheriff. But if I know Hornsby he'll stay at his desk until he gets more information or a resolution. He'll want to know where the girls have been taken. He asked Liam to stand down and do absolutely nothing until he could try to find out where the group was."

George understood the order. "He doesn't want the situation to be made fluid by our interference. He'll want to get a picture with as little change in it as possible. I'll start bitchin' if he thinks his request is carved in stone and is good in perpetuity." He changed the subject. "How's that Swanson woman doing?"

"Diedra? She's fine. Liam's wife's been watchin' her like a hawk."

In Tonopah, Liam and Akara convened on the veranda. Akara complained first. "I don't see why I am suddenly forbidden to do something that cannot possibly alter anything. I just want to do searches to locate property. That can't affect anything."

"Son," Liam said, "when the sheriff tells you to do nothing, what you do is nothing. I don't like it any better than you. But when you consider the forensic resources law-enforcement has at its disposal, they're just not the kind of people you want to piss-off."

George called and spoke to Akara. "I've just landed in North Las Vegas. I'm with Sam Nichols. Since nobody's at the Kitchener house in St. George, the gang might be anywhere. Hold on," he said, "Nichols just got a call."

Sam Nichols had just learned that Beryl's rented Ford Fusion was located at a small shopping center in St. George. George frowned at the news. Akara had heard Nichols remarks. "Well," said George, "the St. George police found Beryl's car in a shopping center. What does that tell you?"

"That she's in trouble. If she weren't, they'd have left her car outside his house."

"That's right. So, since we don't know where she is - and she could be in Tonopah or St. George for all we know - why don't the two of you stay put. We'll keep in touch. Meanwhile the sheriff is trying to outline the problem."

"I don't know why I can't research tax records to see where he might want to go."

Liam's phone rang. He put the call on speakerphone. The sheriff wanted to know if these Sisters had any identifying marks... some organizational or cult tattooing or scarring... in case they had to send out the description in the event they came across other abandoned or murdered women."

"Yes!" Akara said. "They have jewelry - a gold chain with a gold disk that had a logo on it... a Cross surrounded by a Crown of Thorns. No tattoos, but there's that Crown of Thorns thing... genital and upper inside thigh scarring from cactus spines or barbed wire."

"I know what you're talking about," Sheriff Hornsby said. He made a note about the logo.

"Listen, Alex," Liam said, "Akara here would like to start looking for the girls. I think we ought to let him. I mean... as long as they're not in Utah... they could be anyplace. We could use all the help–"

"Is that the kid with the private investigator?" he asked.

"Yeah. He's concerned and so I am. It wouldn't hurt to let him see what he can find out."

"Ask him to wait an hour or so. Liam, I have law enforcement connections in every state they could possibly go, and for that matter, the FBI's resources are available. Nobody likes civilian interference. The most likely place for the Sisters to have gone is Pahrump. I know you said that Novalis checked and they're not there. But I got a call from a federal agent questioning me about some Tennessee connection that I don't know anything about. He asked me to sit tight and I said I would. I don't want to act until they tell me it's ok. I'll be hearing back from them shortly and then I expect that you can let the kid start looking through government records and I'll start alerting neighboring states. So tell him just to wait and guard the witness. That's the most important thing you both can do. Keep the witness incommunicado."

Akara got back on the phone with George. "I've been asked to wait by the sheriff who got asked to wait by the feds."

George had the feeling that things were already spinning out of his and Novalis' control. "I don't want this to devolve into some keystone cops mess," he said. "Get that iPad thing of yours that you connect to your equipment in Philly and look up the property tax rolls for Orange County."

"Why Orange County?"

"Didn't Beryl say the boat was named 'Darien'?"

"Yes."

"Balboa discovered the Pacific at Darien."

"Like in Panama?"

"No. Like in Balboa Island off Newport Beach. It's a long shot. But he's got to put a boat someplace near water. So try the waters off

Southern California. They could drive there from St. George in one trip. Look up Margaret Cromwell; Lamont Marlowe; Jebel Kitchener; and Avery Christian. See if you can find anything owned by them in Orange County."

Nichols went with George to Beryl's motel. George got a room that was conveniently next to hers and stretched out on the bed. "I think better horizontally," he said to Nichols. "We'll hear back from our Computer Whiz Kid shortly.

In half an hour Akara called. "The Margaret Cromwells were too young and the Lamont Marlowe's were still alive. And nothing for Jebel Kitchener and Avery Christian. I hit a wall."

"We haven't heard anything yet from the sheriff," George said.

"Look, George, up to now," Akara said, "everything was going fine. But there are some new wrinkles, and I need to discuss them with you." He reviewed what he knew and didn't know about Beryl's activities since she had last spoken to George. "That's all I can tell you. I've been babysitting Diedra. What's going on?"

George considered Beryl's likely response. "Beryl probably figured that the only way to get this guy was to get one of the women to turn on him when she was charged with extortion and faced jail time. These gals think their motives are 'pure in the eyes of God.' They're probably proud of what they're doing... but they're neurotic and will react if they think they're being betrayed."

"Yes, that was her plan. Religious or not, 'These women,' Beryl had said, 'would brag or betray.' But she didn't know which hotel they'd hit next, and she knew she'd never get the police to cooperate until the crime had occurred. When she knew which specific hotel he'd be targeting, she'd alert hotel security and they'd take it from there."

"Right." George thought more and asked, "Who knew about her mission?"

"Actually, Liam and I and I guess the Novalis people are the only ones who knew about it. But they may have told others. I don't know what Hornsby knows."

"Where's the last place they know she was?" George asked.

"On her way into St. George, Utah, this afternoon at around 4 p.m."

George changed the topic. "Kidnapping a person requires planning and that requires a little time and preparation. A key item in this mess is that they left St. George in a big hurry. Beryl didn't get lost on the highway going into town. She made it to her destination. Within ninety minutes or so of the time she got their call, they were packed up and gone. They were tipped-off about something. What about this woman you babysat? She knew all about him and his past operations you said."

"Yes, but she's not very clear in her head. You'll see her in the morning. She's like... neurotic or in an early stage of dementia."

"Did you ever leave her alone?"

"I didn't go with her into surgery, if that's what you mean. I spent the day in the hospital with her after surgery."

"You said you babysat her in the motel room that you and Beryl rented. Did you leave her alone there?"

"No! I put up with her endless jabbering... all nonsense talk. Fashion... her childhood... her mean mother... her lousy husband. I ordered in and if we did go out, it was to a sandwich shop or to dress shops." He raised his voice. "I didn't leave her alone!"

"You showered with her? You held her hand while you pissed?"

"No... but I did leave the door open when I showered. And I was quick."

"Did you ever give her the opportunity to call somebody... like when you were on the can? Think! It's important," he said harshly.

"Well, no... I shut the goddamned door. But I didn't sit there and read *War and Peace!* Get a grip, George. There are limits!" George had never used this tone of voice before, and Akara did not appreciate being spoken to as though he were a stupid child or an incompetent adult. "Where do you want me to start drawing lines?"

George took a moment to compose himself. He was letting his fears for Beryl manifest themselves in angry responses. In a controlled calm voice, he said, "I apologize. I shouldn't have sounded so critical. Do you have your motel receipts?"

"Yes. They're in my carryon. I'll get them." He unzipped his bag and took out the receipts. "What do you want to know?"

"See if in the receipts there's a list of the calls you made. The local ones will probably not be there... it will just have a telephone use 'charge per call' so we won't be able to tell if she made a local call. But the out of town calls ought to be listed with the number."

Akara looked through the receipts and found the phone charges. "Ok. There's a call made to a number that I don't recognize. Area code 865."

George got out his iPhone. "It's Knoxville, Tennessee. If you didn't make the call, Diedra did. Can you get her in here?"

"Tennessee? Uh, oh. That's what the sheriff said the feds were interested in. Tennessee. I'll go bring her in here."

Akara went to knock on the door of the guest room in which Diedra was sleeping. He asked her to come back to his room. As she followed him she asked, "Why do you want to talk to me back here?"

Akara explained. "Because Father Avery called on the phone back here. Yes, we just got a call from Father Avery. He wants you to verify a call you made from the motel in Kingman. Area code 865."

Diedra spoke fearfully. "Why does he want to know?"

"He says whoever made that call did a wonderful thing and he wants to give credit where credit is due. He says that a few of the other girls want to take credit, but he thinks that only you have the brains and initiative." Akara suddenly felt dirty. This was the part of detective work that went against his grain.

"Oh, yes..." Diedra cooed. "I knew he wouldn't object if I made a quick call to someone we both know and love, his cousin Eugenia. I know you told me not to make any calls, but I thought this was important. I know he doesn't like to be lauded. He's so shy that way. I guess you can tell him I was just showing my love for him by disobeying you."

"Ah, you sweet lady. Two more things you have to verify for us. The full name of the person you called and exactly what you told her. He's glad you made the call, but he wants you to verify what you said."

"I called his cousin Eugenia Pulaski at her home. I told her about the two angels Father Avery sent. I said that the lady one had left but the man one stayed with me through the surgery and bought me clothing and was going to take me to Nevada to meet Father Avery. Then I heard you flush the toilet and didn't have time to say more."

"That's wonderful," Akara said. "You can go back to bed now."

As soon as she closed her bedroom door, he said to George, "Diedra lied to me. Ok. I'm sorry, George. I didn't–"

"Don't waste time apologizing. If Avery thinks Beryl's onto him, he won't linger in St. George or Pahrump, where he's known. You've got to find out where else he'd go. What else do you know about that boat 'Darien'?"

"He likes to sail - but it's not a sailboat, it's the motor kind. He likes to get a tan before he takes it out. He's concerned about his skin."

"If he doesn't have a tan now, then his boat has probably been in dry dock over the winter. It will need to be prepared for launching."

Akara asked, "Should I try the Gulf of Mexico? Texas? Louisiana? His mother used to have a brothel in New Orleans."

George asked, "Didn't Beryl say that he liked to get a *controlled* tan?"

"Yes. That's how he put it. She thought he meant poolside... a possibly private pool where he could get his tan all over and incrementally... safely."

"Then we're probably looking for a beach house with a pool... one that's near a marina where he keeps his boat. Think about it. He's got eight women with him, two of whom are quite possibly prisoners."

"If he's got a cabin cruiser he's not likely to take all eight women out with him at once. The logistics would be problematic. How's he gonna feed nine people and care for them? And he may not want any witnesses. As far as entertainment's concerned, he wouldn't need more than three or four. Half of them would have to stay home. The point is, for pleasure or for murder he's not gonna have a full boat. He'll be near a residence... not a motel. A residence."

"Yes, that figures."

"But let's get back on point. Understand this. Now that Diedra tipped-off somebody, the word about Beryl and Sally will have gotten back to him. We have to assume that.

"I want you to understand the situation. We don't know *when* he left Utah... or even *if* he left Utah, or what name he used when he purchased property. For all we know, he has had time to get to the Pacific. And he might have called ahead, ordering the marina to take his cabin cruiser out of dry dock and prepare it. Think about it. He's got eight women with him. He's not gonna stop in a motel for the night. That many women checking in at once would attract too much attention. He's driving, so it's likely that he's driving directly through to his destination which cannot be all that far.

"Since he wouldn't try to cross Death Valley, the nearest beach he could have gone to is in Southern California. But if he doesn't have any property there, where else could he go and have a boat in a marina and a beach house and get a controlled 'poolside' tan?"

George continued to think aloud about the possible destinations. "You know," he said, "it doesn't have to be an ocean. He could be headed for Lake Mead or Lake Havasu. There are plenty of places on the Colorado River in which he could have a beach house as well as a boat in a marina."

Liam came into the room, wanting to know what was going on. Akara briefly told him. George asked Liam to tell the others about the call that Diedra had made. Liam left to tell Nichols. "Oh, Jesus!" Nichols exclaimed. "I'll get on that right away and then get back to you."

Liam also called the sheriff and announced, "Last weekend, in Las Vegas, Diedra called a relative or friend of Avery Christian's named Eugenia Pulaski, in Knoxville, Tennessee. Everybody should be informed of that."

Akara continued to operate his equipment, using his iPad. "I'll check the possible places in other states on the Colorado River. He accessed the tax records for Clark County, Nevada, and immediately found the listing for a house owned by Jebel Kitchener in Boulder City. "Let's see it," he said. George came to the iPad. Akara yelped. "I've just googled an image of a house on Pasto Avenue that Kitchener owns in Boulder City, Nevada! And it's got a pool!"

Akara continued to search the marinas. He accessed marine records and found the registration for the cabin cruiser, Darien. "I'm searching the marinas nearest Kitchener's residence. Ok. Jebel Kitchener rents a slip... Number 24-D at the El Aqua Azul Marina. I'm googling the marina and accessing an actual photograph of the boat's specific slip area. Ok. The slip's empty. When this pic was taken the ship was either out on the water or in dry dock."

"The situation has just changed. I don't know what we should tell the authorities. I'll talk it over with Nichols and then call you back."

Sam Nichols considered a response. "I say that we don't tell anyone except on a 'need to know' basis. You know and I know half a dozen bureaucratic agencies are gonna shove us into the background and while they're arguing amongst themselves, something bad is gonna happen to Beryl and Sally. I've got an operative who lives in Boulder City. Let me get him on the line and we'll find out quick if they're there."

"Go for it," George said.

Sam Nichols called his operative who kept him on the line as he got into his car and drove a few blocks to the address on Pasto Avenue that Akara had given him. After an interminable five minute wait, he said, "The lights are on. The house is occupied. And there is a black Escalade parked in the garage."

Liam urged caution. "Nobody's got cause for a warrant and if we bust in and nothin's wrong, we'll get sued big time. If something is wrong, they can hold a knife to Sally's throat or Beryl's... and what are we gonna do about it? Get a lot of people killed, that's what. These people are not playing with a full deck. They're many degrees of insane."

The Novalis operative suddenly burst into the conversation. "Hey! If I'm not mistaken there's an unmarked sedan with a couple of suits in it. I think they're Metro cops from Vegas. This place is being surveilled."

Akara asked, "If different agencies are involved, who's gonna be in charge?"

"That's always the Number One problem," George replied. "The best one to lead the investigation is Novalis, since that's their home county. We can assume there will be the usual pissing contest between the local, state, and federal agencies. They will circle-jerk until something happens that forces them to act definitively... like a body floating in the water. Then the Health Department and the Environmental Protection Agency will get involved... and maybe Fish and Game. There ain't no end to bureaucratic cogs in the wheel of justice." He cleared his throat. "Listen, I shouldn't have jumped down your throat about Diedra's phone call."

"It's ok. I have a lot to learn. Like... when the hell can you depend on what someone promises you? Diedra had every reason to obey my simple directive. All good things were happening to her and I was the reason why they were happening. Well, Beryl and I. But still, the woman lied to me and broke her promise. I don't understand."

"Ah, the truth of false statements. You'll have to get Sensei to sit you down and instruct you. It takes a little time to explain. We'll talk about it later."

"I guess they didn't want us doing anything because they were already doing it. I sure as hell didn't give them any address in Boulder City. And now they're just gonna sit outside and watch and wait."

"Bullshit!" George said. "My partner is in there and I'm not waiting. We have to get them out of the house. Without a warrant nobody is gonna get inside. They can park the U.S. Army outside and nobody has to answer the goddamned door. Meanwhile, God knows what they're doing to the girls."

"Any ideas on how we can get 'em out?" Liam asked. "He could have driven right to the marina and put the girls in the boat and dumped them before they even went to the house. Have they been watching the marina?"

Nichols shrugged. "I don't know what they're doing. That Lake is deep. They could get those girls weighed down and out of sight so fast... Jesus! All I can think about is that when a body stays down there long enough, it turns to soap. I'm serious."

Akara asked George, "What good does watching the house do? We don't even know if Beryl and Sally are there or are on the boat or have already been disposed of."

George thought for a moment. "All right. Let's suppose that the people inside the house don't know that they're being surveilled. How do you get them out? The best thing to do is to get some of that smelly stuff they put in natural gas... thiophane or mercaptan... whatever it's called. Is Liam still there?"

"I'm here," Liam said. "What can I do?"

"Do you know anybody who works for the gas company? In a lot of those western towns, the gas lines will serve the urban population, but they may have an auxiliary outlet for propane users. Do you know anyone who handles methane gas and propane distribution here in Tonopah and can get you a small supply of the smelly stuff?"

Liam took out his iPhone. "Yes... yes... I know a guy who can get anything I need." He called a number. "Jack, I've got a strange and mysterious request to make of you. You know that smelly stuff that's put in natural gas... well... I need some."

Liam signaled a thumbs-up. "Yes. It's a matter of life and death and I'll be right over to meet you at the office."

George, with Sam Nichols still beside him, continued to talk to Liam. "We need a couple of uniforms that look like the kind the gas company uses. We need to rent a white van and use that washable paint to put the gas company's logo on the outside. It doesn't have to be museum quality. It won't be seen up close. Google the gas company and get a picture of their logo.

"One of us can first go around to the back of the house - I saw on the Google photo that it has a crawl space - and go under the house and release that thiophane gas while the other one knocks on the front door and says that the inhabitants have to vacate the premises temporarily because there's been a report of gas. They'll smell the stuff fast. The one who was under the house will join up with the one who knocked on the front door and the two will escort everybody out and then enter the house. If they've got Beryl and Sally inside, they will not bring them out. They'll probably dump them gagged and bound into a bedroom closet. We'll ask the folks to wait across the street while we fix the leak, and then we'll get the girls out the back door and if they can get through to the street behind, we'll just drive around and pick them up.

"I don't give a rat's ass about whether Avery and his Sisters are apprehended by the feds or the Ladies Auxiliary… or if they wait outside the whole night."

Luella MacDonald was standing in the doorway. "I can make those gas company patches on my sewing machine."

Akara said, "That's a good idea. Here's what they look like. And Liam will get that thiophane stuff."

"I can rent a white van down here!" Nichols said. "And I know a kid who's been fined numerous times for defacing public property… some mischief graffiti charge… he's great with paint and I don't care if it's spray paint and I have to pay to have the van professionally repainted or that he does happen to be my grandson. The kid has talent. I can check the gas company's colors. We can buy the paint when we buy the uniforms and rent the van. And we can pin the patches on down here. Ok?"

Liam got ready to go on the thiophane mission. He went into his dining room and came out with a Smith & Wesson revolver. *Have gun. Will travel.* Let's roll." He turned to Luella. "Caps and shirt pockets. We've got to look authentic."

Everyone agreed. Akara accessed the website of the gas company that served Boulder City and sent George a copy of their logo. He said to Luella. "George can get the paint… brown and tan and two shades of orange and two of blue… and some masking tape. Let me use your equipment and I'll print you some good color copies."

Liam received the thiophane in a sponge inside a plastic bladder. He brought it home. "We'll need something to pierce the plastic," he said; and Luella, who had just completed the patches on her "art capable" sewing machine, jury-rigged a sharp upholstery needle's point to the end of a long mop handle.

"That ought to do it!" Liam said. He called George who was shopping in the men's department of Wal-Mart. We're on our way and we'll meet you in the motel."

Liam and Akara, armed with the gas bladder and the piercing stick, got into the white Lincoln and started out for Las Vegas, two hundred miles away.

It was after midnight when they arrived. The white rented van was still being decorated with the phony logo.

FRIDAY, MAY 24, 2013

As soon as the artist finished copying the logo on both sides of the white van, he drove it to the motel and delivered it to Sam Nichols. A friend had followed him and gave him a ride back home.

It was close to 2 a.m. when they were ready to put the plan into action.

"Ok," Nichols said. "I'll ride with Liam in his car and George and Akara can pretend to be gas men."

As George got in the van with Akara, he said, "We've only got thirty miles or so to get to Boulder City. Don't get too comfortable."

"Do we have enough time for you to tell me about truthful lies or whatever you called it? Tell me why Diedra promised me she wouldn't call anyone and then just called... as if she hadn't given me her word. I really need to understand this."

George hesitated and sighed. "What the hell... I'll go over it briefly, and we can discuss it again later. If Sensei weren't beside himself with worry about Sonya, he'd have told you this stuff already. He should have.

"Whenever you encounter someone who has an unusually strong affect, or opinion, or attitude - or exhibits behavior that is odd or filled with unreasonable emotion - get suspicious. Diedra's belief that Avery Christian was a loving man was, considering the facts, bizarre.

"An ego defends itself against things that will diminish its value and provides itself with things that will enhance its value. It distorts reality to accomplish these objectives.

"The person is not aware that he's doing this. His ego has created the distortion, but the person believes that the distortion is accurate. Again, the person is unaware of the lies that his ego has created. He fervently believes them. We're outside of the 'blame-game' here... we can't accuse in the usual ways of assigning guilt.

"You thought she'd understand that she was living in misery until you came along and helped her. You thought she'd associate *you* with the new clothes and the medical care. She didn't. You were merely an instrument Avery used, a servant he used in the furtherance of his love for her. You were nothing. Her overarching desire was to tell the world how Avery had demonstrated his love for her. When you made her promise not to use the phone, you were trying to intrude on her sacred love. You were jealous or a liar, a silly man. And if you handed her a note written in Avery's own hand ordering her not to use the phone, she would have believed that he was simply being modest. He was so sweet and liked to praise others while taking no credit for himself.

"She was not and will never be grateful to you. You were not part of her self-deception. You see it with self-deluded nations and you see it with self-deluded people. You do something that you hope will be received with respect and maybe even a little gratitude. You get neither. You were just an instrument of God and how can you dare expect them to genuflect to you! You'll be lucky if you're not resented and despised outright. And you expect them to obey your rules? Never!

"There are seven basic strategies that egos use. An obvious lie is easy to spot. An unconscious strategy is not so easy. So don't look for the body language of a liar. None of that polygraph shit works with these strategies or mechanisms. They're powerful and subtle and reach into areas of behavior you can't begin to imagine.

"Whenever you encounter someone who has odd or unreasonable beliefs - suspect a strategy at work.

"There's no particular order, so I'll just give you the first one as *Displacement*. Someone hurts you physically or emotionally. You, for any number of reasons, cannot hurt him back. Your boss calls you a worthless idiot. You can't tell him off without losing your job. You're furious and your rage needs to be vented. You come home and kick your dog. Your ego allows you to substitute a target you *can* hit for one that you *can't* hit. You say that you were obliged to kick the dog because you've told it time and time again not to rub against your good pants, and it has to learn to obey.

"It can go the other way. A woman who has no child to love, or be loved by, gets a lapdog and lavishes love on it, dressing it like a human child, baby-talking to it. A man who has no friend he can trust gets a dog and forms a bond that rivals Damon and Pythias. Do you get this?"

Akara whistled. "Yeah. I understand this completely."

"Second is *Projection*. You've done or thought something that you know is wrong or sinful. Guilt is a terrible burden, but one that the ego is able to dump on someone else. You have the hots for the boss's wife. You see Joe X smile at the boss's wife. You suddenly find yourself insinuating to others that Joe X needs to get his libido under control... that the way he looks at the boss's wife is disgraceful. Suppose the boss finds out what Joe is thinking? He'd fire Joe... and Joe would deserve it, the horny son of a bitch."

"I get it. I get it. You know I used to bitch and moan about guys in school who cheated... like I never did? You have to write a stupid paper for an obligatory class in the humanities and you're all tied up in a project so some smart gal writes it for you. But you can't stand cheaters! Jesus. This is a real 'confessional.'"

"Third is *Regression*. You're 44 years old and worried about your prostate. You search your life for a time you didn't have such problems. When you were 20 you were Mr. Virility. So, you join a gym, buy a sports car, get a new wardrobe and some hair plugs, learn to dance and play tennis, go out and meet people. You're up against some primal fear of death and decay and what you're doing is re-living a safer existence. You'll see grandmothers gossiping like teenaged girls all day on the phone or internet. They will give you fifty reasons why they need to stay in touch with people who are total strangers. They're like cheerleaders. It's bullshit but they believe it."

"This is my father! The old man actually bought a Ferrari when he was fifty-seven years old! He said he always wanted one. I don't think he even knew how to drive a stick shift or even an automatic. He'd been driven around by chauffeurs his whole life! No wonder my mom left. He started to take dancing lessons and she had had a couple of fused spinal discs. Naturally, he had to hire a few pretty dancers 'for practice.'"

George laughed. "So you inherited your foxiness."

"Maybe so. But that's only three. I'm also persistent."

"Ok. Fourth is Repression. You bury a painful event in your mind so deep that you have no recollection of it at all. Oh... it will be there driving you to act in certain ways. You're a kid and nearly drown in the ocean and need to be rescued. You grow up and refuse to consider going on vacation at the beach because the sand is full of germs. When people who live by the water find their houses damaged by hurricanes, you oppose giving them loans to rebuild. Why should taxpayers have to fund their ridiculous need to look at the ocean? You think you're being fiscally reasonable. You might be stating a reasonable opinion, but your reason for having it has nothing to do with money."

"I'll have to remember a lot of shit I forgot. Whatever it was, it made me what I am today." He and George both laughed.

"The Fifth is *Rationalization*. You find a reason for not fulfilling a solemn promise. You borrow money from Joe and then don't pay it back. Why not? Well, you say, I did plenty of stuff for Joe and never got paid for it. To me, we're even. This can be tricky as when someone excuses his failure to pay by turning it around to shame the lender. 'My kid is sick. Is he so goddamned greedy that he expects me to deny my kid medical care just to pay him money that he doesn't even need?' You've probably have never given a rat's ass about the kid... but it's a great rationalization and it allows you to believe that you're a responsible father.

"Conversely, you try and fail to get someone or something. So your ego's strategy kicks in. You denigrate her or it. This is the fox and the grapes. When it couldn't succeed in getting the grapes, it pronounced them sour and not worth having. The gal you couldn't get is suddenly is a selfish, two-faced bitch.

193

"The Sixth is *Denial*. Not a day passes but that you drink two six-packs, but when asked if you have a drinking problem, you say, 'Me? No! Like anybody else I enjoy a beer while I'm watching a game. But I'm no drunk.' Well, you are but you don't believe you are. You honestly don't believe that you are addicted to alcohol or to any other substance or activity. But you are.

"The Seventh is the worst. Freud called it *Reaction Formation*. This is when you vehemently profess the opposite of what you really feel. You are a cruel person so you become an Animal Rights' Activist. You vigorously oppose the use of poor defenseless animals in medical experimentation. Maybe you pinch your own annoying baby when it won't stop crying. So you become an anti-abortionist. The problem is that many of these people are so by principle. But too many of them are acting out Reaction Formation. How can I be cruel if I try to save little animals? How can I be an abusive parent if I work so hard to prevent the murder of innocent babies?

"When you're up against one of these strategies, you can throw out the old sequence of Understanding, Feeling, and Acting. The strategy is formed at a much deeper area of the mind. A professional analyst can maybe plumb those depths and fix what's haywire. In Zen, you're required to do it yourself as part of the great 'Detachment' process. Self-delusions are dangerous. To one degree or another the self-deluded person is crazy. He cannot bring order to his thoughts and actions. He may be a gullible dupe, or an adult with a child's 'undeveloped frontal lobe' ethics, or he may be a closet sociopath.

"You should have been on guard when you saw how unrealistic Diedra's beliefs about Avery Christian were. By trusting a lunatic like her, you put a lot of people at risk."

"You have my word. I won't make that mistake again. Jeez. My education has been in math and science and Shakespeare. In the university they didn't teach us any of this psychological stuff."

"How can you study Shakespeare and not recognize these ego-generated strategies? His insights were merely wrapped in beautiful language. Go back and read him again, this time for what he was really conveying."

"Ok. I see now that the Sisters think it's right to take money from sinners who will only squander it on gambling and drugs. They don't think they're blackmailers. They're serving God. *Rationalization.* They consider themselves a loving Christian group and they decide that their victims are morally corrupt and this justifies their actions. In fact they are murderers, extortionists, whores, pimps, liars, sadists, and so on. *Projection.*"

"Right. And probably a few other things, too. But right now, we're coming into Boulder City."

At 3 a.m. Akara and George arrived at 311 Pasto Avenue, Boulder City, Nevada. The house was completely dark. An unmarked Ford sedan and a white Lincoln, each containing two men, were parked on the street.

George parked the van in the driveway. Akara got out, checked to see that the Escalade was still in the garage, and went to the rear of the house to see if there was easy access to the crawl space. He returned to the van.

He took the thiophane bladder and the mop handle with the upholstery needle fixed at the end. "Ok, George," he said, "I'm gonna do my crawling number. As soon as you see me come around from the rear of the house, you start pounding on their front door."

The plainclothes police in the Ford were not entirely sure of what the operation would entail; but Nichols had given them an acknowledging salute, and they were prepared to intervene.

The occupants of the house next door, roused by their barking dog, noticed the gas company vehicle parked in the driveway in the middle of the night. The husband came to George's window and knocked on it. "What's the problem here?" he asked.

"Sir," George said, rolling down the window, "I'll have to ask you to go back a safe distance. We've got the situation under control."

Akara looked back, saw the neighbor, and hurried to complete his assignment. Sam Nichols and Liam MacDonald jogged to the van. George again insisted, "We'd like to ask you gentlemen to maintain a safe distance from the premises. We're investigating a gas leak."

The neighbor, dissatisfied with George's response, called the gas company. The emergency clerk he spoke to assured him that no gas leak had been reported and that the company had dispatched no vehicle that address. They would immediately investigate.

Akara began to crawl under the house. He shimmied forward, pushing the bag until it was close to the center. He backed up until he could reach the bag by stretching and then he began to pierce it. He dropped the mop handle and shimmied backwards until he was no longer under the building. As he jogged to the front of the house he could smell the thiophane.

George, seeing Akara, got out of the van and began to pound on the front door. Akara quickly joined him.

Neighbors began to turn lights on and to come out of their houses to see what the commotion was all about. A police cruiser on a routine patrol saw the gas company and a few people standing on the street and came too see what was happening.

The front door opened. Sister Annie stood there with an incredulous look on her face as she saw the police car's flashing lights and gas company truck in front of the house. She immediately smelled gas.

Beryl, suspecting one of George's rescue ruses, shook Avery who, she could see, had obviously taken sedatives while she was asleep. He could hardly keep his eyes open. "Wake up!" she shouted. "There's a gas leak. We've been ordered to evacuate!" She was still wearing one of his shirts; but he was naked. She handed him a bath towel. "Here, put this around yourself!" He put the towel around himself and asked for his slippers. Beryl, barefooted herself, pulled on his arm as she tried to lead him to the front door. He refused to move without his slippers.

Annie turned back into the house to help Avery. She burst into the bedroom and confronted Beryl. "What do you think you're doing?"

"Oh, Come on!" Beryl shouted. "I'd love you to take another step in here." Instead of fighting, she jerked and then shoved Avery towards Annie who tried to guide him from the house. "Sisters!" Beryl shouted. "Get up and get out! There's a gas leak!"

As Annie reached the front door with Avery, she turned and hissed at one of the Sisters, "Put Sally in our bedroom closet! They won't look there to fix a gas leak." She shoved Avery out the door and helped him to cross the street.

Another Sister appeared in the doorway. "Madam," George said to the Sister, "we've had a report of a gas leak. Would you mind stepping out of the house and waiting across the street while we investigate? Are there other occupants or pets in the building?"

"Me and Four others." Two Sisters were rushing to the door and the last two were following them.

Beryl opened the drawer and got the zip tie lock reversing pick. She ran into the bedroom where Sally was kept. She unbuckled the ball gag and quickly released the lock on the zip tie. Akara appeared in the closet doorway. Sally was still naked. He grabbed a sheet to put around her. She tried to speak but the muscles in her mouth were in spasm from the ball gag. Nothing she tried to say was intelligible. Finally, she pushed Akara and Beryl together and gently shoved them out the bedroom door. She tried to explain why she wanted them to go, but they could not understand it.

Beryl went into Avery's bedroom to get her new suit from the closet. A shopping bag was on the dresser. She opened it and stuffed her suit, shoes, and underwear in it and ran back to see what Sally was doing.

Sally was carrying the shopping bag her clothing had been put into. No one could tell that at the bottom of the bag, the mysterious locked box was safely concealed.

A real gas company van pulled up to the curb. "What kind of dumb-ass impersonation is this?" the driver shouted. "What's goin' on here?" He called the local police department and almost immediately a police car came down the street.

Akara led the two women to the back door and then, as they stepped outside, he ran to the front and signaled George who backed out of the drive way and drove down the street and quickly turned the corner.

The gas company representatives, two burly men, could smell the thiophane and wanted to help, but they did not know what to do about the fleeing impostors. Liam and Nichols and the two police officers assured them that the situation was under control.

Liam approached the officers in the police car and asked to speak to their captain. He explained the convoluted circumstances and asked the captain to verify his story with the Sheriff of Nye County and to take the six Sisters into custody along with Avery Christian, a.k.a. Jebel Kitchener.

"The charges?" he was asked.

"Murder in Nye County, Nevada and kidnapping in Washington County, Utah. If you need to expedite the formal filing of these charges just let me know. If anybody wants to give anybody a hard time, call the Hotel Association guys and tell them we've rounded up a religious gang that's been extorting hotel guests for the last ten years. Detain the seven of them on any charges you can think of."

"So," asked the gas company employee, "is there a leak or not?"

EPILOGUE

Beryl and George, back again in Philadelphia, prepared for Beryl's gathering to watch the Indianapolis 500 in her upstairs apartment.

Groff Eckersley and Beryl's son Jack would be coming with two dates. Sensei came out of duty. He was still depressed with worry about Sonya Lee.

Akara had stayed with Sally Snyder overnight in her apartment. They had spent Saturday afternoon making statements regarding the events of the past days. Akara also had to attest to them in the name of the Wagner & Tilson agency. He arrived Sunday morning and specifically asked that Beryl pick him up at the airport.

George acted as host as Beryl drove to the airport.

"What's up?" Beryl asked as Akara got into her car.

"I don't know how to handle this... or if it's any concern of ours at all. Do you recall when we got Sally out of the closet and she pushed us out the door?"

"Yes. I went to get my new suit and she went to get hers."

"She got more than her clothing. There was a box... a locked box that Annie guarded."

"I know. I saw it."

"She had put that box at the bottom of the shopping bag. She couldn't talk until much later. I took her back to her apartment, because she was still a nervous wreck and she was scared.

"Sally asked me all about Martin's clients, Frank Goodrich and his wife Gwen, and that business about the switched diamond rings. Evidently when George and Nichols were together they discussed the case and how it dovetailed with Liam MacDonald's case with Niles

Portmann. She overheard some of the details. She asked me to go out
and get some cheeseburgers and fries and I went, and when I got back
she was on the phone and had that box in her lap. She wouldn't let me
see what was in the box and I didn't associate it with what went on in
Nevada. I couldn't understand why she was so scared; but I figured that
I was a P.I. too and that I ought to find out. I checked her phone when
she went to the bathroom - she took the box with her - and the call she
had made was to Gwen Goodrich."

"I saw that box. It belonged to them and since they guarded it, it must
have contained valuables... money and jewelry. If it does, then maybe the
reason she's scared is that she fears they know she has it and they need it
for defense attorneys. She'll fear that the Sisters and possibly Avery will
be out on bail and looking for her."

"Get Marty on the phone. I'll tell him I have a friend who may be
seeking her own justice."

Akara called Martin Mazzavini. He put the call on speaker. "Marty,"
Beryl explained, "I have a friend who was physically abused by a bunch
of criminals... extortionists... a murder or two. She was one of several
people who had been, let's say, physically abused by this group. When she
escaped from the group she stole a lockbox that contained, I'm assuming,
valuables... maybe jewelry and money. These extortionists are not in a
position to file charges against her... 'dirty hands' and all that. What
advice would you give her?"

"Are her initials BT?"

"No!"

"Gwen Goodrich left for Las Vegas, Nevada, this morning... and
Frank tells me she didn't take dressy clothes with her."

"Not a *gi?*"

"Yes... funny how you guessed that right off. You know I didn't plan
to charge Frank. And I was willing to pick up your tab, too; but Frank
acted like he intended to pay us. He asked me how much I would have
charged if I had charged him. I added in your business class air fare...
George's special trip... motel charges... food and other expenses... and
knowing what he's up against financially, I said it would come to more

than he figured. He insisted and I said, 'Ok, $50K for all of us, minus the dancing with my grandfather which we would give you a credit for.'"

"Bite your tongue. That man knows how to dance. Someday he and I are gonna meet in that big ballroom in the sky. Glen Miller will be playing."

"I'm gonna quote you."

"I hope you do. Now... what about the loot?"

"What loot?"

"Ok. Akara and I just thought we'd check. A few crooks we've heard of are gonna have to give a few public defenders some experience."

"Akara! This friend of Beryl's... Las Vegas might not be healthy for her. Think she might like to be a P.I. in Chicago? What does she look like?"

"Cute. And she's got these great nipple rings!"

"Call me back when *the Colonel's not watchin' the wall.*"

"All men are idiots," Beryl said before she disconnected the call.

-30-